ANAHID PLAYED SOORP

The Finding of Aran Pirian

BY MARK KADIAN

ISBN: 1477642218
ISBN-13: 9781477642214
Library of Congress Control Number: 2012910620
CreateSpace, North Charleston, SC

CHAPTER 1

Anahid lifted her violin to her chin and slowly pulled the bow against the violin's strings. The initial sound was discordant, as the bow scraped the strings as she prepared to play the first note. She then arched her elbow and flung the bow on a downward angle. At once her round brown eyes opened widely and turned sharply to her side, and a smile broke across her face, distracted by our father's attempt to carry her along with the long first note as he sang, "Soo—————rp," the primary lyric in the music's first verse.

"Beautiful, beautiful, Anahid," our father bellowed, as Anahid pushed the bow back through the strings and up again, her face now stern. Our father continued, "Soo—————rp... Soo————rp..." his light hazel eyes glowing against his dark complexion, as he pushed his eyebrows up, encouraging Anahid to hit the music's high initial notes. He then stood from his chair, and as he did he became silent and transfixed as he watched Anahid.

While Anahid played, the light in the room dimmed and brightened with each stroke of her bow, the effect given that the only source of light into the room was from the small window in front of which Anahid played her violin. As the light came and went, the rich woven rug on which Anahid stood, with its red, white, and green threads, revealed itself, then became concealed again. Across the room, our mother sat in a chair placed in the opposite corner. Our mother was a diminutive and strikingly beautiful Armenian woman with dark brown, shoulder-length hair that framed her protruding cheekbones and lovely round brown eyes, all features that Anahid inherited. As Anahid played, our mother smiled gently and listened quietly, not at all prone to the outward displays of emotion shown by our father.

Our mother was a musician, a cellist by training. Her professional life was short, having played in a few quartets after her formal training ended. She primarily loved the Baroques. She ensured that our home was always filled with music, and I believe she thought it would be best ensured by having Anahid learn to play the violin. I don't believe, however, that our mother insisted that Anahid play the violin. Instead, she allowed Anahid to take to it on her own accord, perhaps understanding that the ability to play the violin, or any other instrument for that matter, is not acquired through the rote memorization of notes or a base proficiency in the mechanics of making the instrument produce sound. Rather, the music must be felt from within, no differently than the process by which the mind formulates a thought first before the thought is voiced.

Anahid continued to play, her arm now pitching the violin lower, while she pushed the bow more arduously. Anahid played through the music's long and beautiful middle strains, and as she did her face relaxed, her eyes closed, and the music that poured from her was now seamless and melodic. Anahid was only ten years old, but she had played the violin from as early as I could remember and, although by no means a virtuoso, she had become accomplished enough by that age that she could play a substantial repertoire of music competently and without the need for sheet music. The song "Soorp, Soorp," which was simply referred to as "Soorp" by Anahid, was one that Anahid played the most proficiently. It was an Armenian piece of music, which she first heard in church, and Anahid seemed to love it the first time she heard it. "Soorp" was a piece written for the liturgy, but that purpose had no bearing on the effect that Anahid's playing it had on me, nor, do I believe, did it contribute in any manner to the effect that it had on Anahid.

I first remember Anahid humming the song with our mother, perhaps as early as the age of four years old or so, before she learned to play it on the violin. I also remember the first time she played "Soorp" on the violin in its entire length. Chords dropped off abruptly and discordantly then resumed again, until the song's ending, and Anahid fought the instrument the entire way through. Now Anahid played as if the violin were a part of her, and she made it clear to me then that although "Soorp" may never have been intended for the violin, it was intended for Anahid.

The strains of the music were building to their end, and the deep and moving tone of the piece carved its way through the room. Anahid's hand pushed the bow through, and she opened her eyes and turned them sharply to her side, as she watched the bow pass its way over the strings as the final chords played.

She lowered her violin and placed it in a small, black leather case, which leaned against the wall just below the window. As she did, our father, as he always did when Anahid completed a piece, applauded. He then said, "It was beautiful playing, Anahid. You make your mother and father very proud. It will not be long now before I shall hear you play in the great music halls of Europe. It is a great thing to hope for, Anahid, and someday you must know that it will come true. But you must love it, Anahid. You must decide first that you love it and that it brings you joy. Does it, Anahid? Does it bring you joy?" Anahid, who was quiet like our mother, nodded and laughed self-consciously at the attention that our father was giving her. Our father looked to our mother, who was still seated across the room and said, "Isn't it true, Marem, that we will hear Anahid play one day in Paris or Brussels?" As our father spoke, he had a tone of lighthearted teasing, but I do think he recognized that Anahid's playing the violin was an integral part of her, not to be necessarily reduced to the practicalities of a vocation, but rather as something essential to her, the very part of who she was and who she would be. Our mother looked at our father and simply waved her hand at him in a dismissive manner, and as she did, he lowered himself back into his chair and sat quietly, pretending to be hurt from not being taken seriously. It was their way. It was at these times that our mother and father distilled to its essence the ethic that they wished Anahid and me to live by: an appreciation for beauty, and an enduring sense of hope, joy, and faith. It was a simple formula for living, really, but not easily grasped and even more difficult to keep.

After a few moments, our father shifted his attention and looked at me and said, "Come, Aran. Sit by your father, so that we may plan what we shall do today." I walked to him and leaned against the arm of his chair and asked, "Father, can we walk to the Hippodrome today?"

The Hippodrome was toward the center of Constantinople, a few kilometers from our residence, and I loved to visit it to see the monuments there. Our father would colorfully and dramatically describe the scenes of gods and emperors as we viewed the monuments, and it excited me. He paused for a moment then said, "Yes, I believe it should be fine to visit the Hippodrome today." He looked to Anahid, who had completed placing her violin in the case, and said, "Anahid, please come, too. Your violin needs some rest."

Reaching the Hippodrome from our house required about thirty minutes of travel time by carriage. The travel this day took longer, given the increasing number of Ottoman soldiers and militia in the streets, who appeared to be holding up travel. Upon leaving the carriage, our father, Anahid, and I walked around the periphery of the Hippodrome; then we walked to the Obelisk of Thutmosis III, a giant obelisk-shaped monument at one end of the approximate central portion of the Hippodrome. Upon reaching it, we looked back across the length of the Hippodrome to the Great Walled Obelisk that was directly opposite from where we stood. Our father, instead of describing the lives of the gods and emperors as I had learned to expect, began speaking in a somewhat more disconsolate tone. "Anahid and Aran, you should realize that this Hippodrome is known for as much as what was here, than what is here now," he said, now looking toward us, while pointing in the distance. "Did you know that there were great statues here? They were taken or destroyed through the ages by one army or the other who came to sack Constantinople. Even worse, some were destroyed by the people of Constantinople themselves, not realizing what a treasure they had; rather mistaking their treasure instead for a curse." He looked at Anahid and me, then pointed to the area surrounding the Great Walled Obelisk and said, "There was once here a statue of the great Greek goddess Athena. The people of Constantinople smashed the statue because they thought Athena was calling the Western armies to invade Constantinople. So do you see, Anahid and Aran?" Our father paused, as if waiting for an answer, but then finished his thought. "The worst destruction to the Hippodrome wasn't done by invading armies, but by the people of Constantinople themselves who thought that they were saving the city from destruction. They destroyed themselves, Anahid and Aran. They simply destroyed themselves. If only they knew what they had." Anahid and I nodded as he spoke, more, I think, as a polite gesture, than one intended to acknowledge any particular understanding.

We walked for another twenty minutes or so, and our father was mostly silent. He then pulled the watch from his pocket, opened its face, then clicked it shut and said, "It is time for us to go back home, Aran and Anahid. This may be the last time that we can come to the Hippodrome for a while. The city is starting to grow too tense because of the war, and it is best that we stay out of the center of the city until matters become calmer." This was the first time that our father really spoke about the war, and, I believe, it was the first time that I sensed that the war would impact our lives. He placed his arm around me and Anahid, and as we walked back to the carriage, he said, "But you don't need to worry, Aran and Anahid. The Ottoman Empire has a large and strong military. It will keep out any army trying to march down the road to Constantinople to destroy the city. I just hope that the people of Constantinople have enough sense not to destroy the city themselves."

I sensed that our father was saying more to me. Not so much in what he said, but in what he left unsaid and unexplained. It couldn't have been that plain, could it? I didn't have the faculties to discern it then, but I did believe there was something more to what he was telling me, something more complicated. Perhaps I knew inherently that his words meant something more existential. I didn't know enough to ask him. What did it all mean? It would have been a simple enough question to ask him. What did it all mean?

CHAPTER 2

Approximately one month had passed since our visit to the Hippodrome. It was becoming clear that the impact of the war on Constantinople was not to be limited to the center of Constantinople. The Ottoman Empire had joined World War I on the side of the Central Powers less than a year prior and had been since engaged in the conscription and mobilization of forces in a feverish effort to increase the military from its peace-time strength. The rebuilding of the Ottoman military was now almost complete.

The section of Constantinople where my family lived was primarily populated with Armenians. We lived in intimate quarters where modest homes made of local stone and century-old timber hugged close to dirt roads that were barely wide enough to accommodate a single horse-drawn cart. Our section, like the other residential sections of Constantinople, flanked the city center, and although somewhat separate physically from the ancient buildings there, the clear view of the entire city from our residential section provided a sense of complete immersion in the life of Constantinople. Our lives and our culture were inseparable from the city, and it was that way since the earliest times.

The Armenians were among the ancients of Constantinople, and we were raised to sense our primordial beginnings in the city, so much so that we saw ourselves cast in its stone. Our ancestors' blood and dust were part of the stone's constituents, and their images were carved in the stone of building friezes. We were, in that way, born from Constantinople and felt an essential part of it. We were made to understand, though, that inasmuch as we may have been among the ancients of Constantinople, we were never to feel comfortable that our lives would remain there, or any place. We were aware of the realities of our history. The Persians and Byzantines took their turns at us, driving us out of one place or another, and then others had their turns in later times. I saw our history in the stone of the building friezes. I imagine that the Armenians were the ones in front of the chariots driving from behind, and the ones strewn on the frieze's outer edges, forced off the building, just as we were forced off of the earth. Even our language accommodated our history and our place. Among each other we spoke Armenian and Turkish in a manner that produced a hybrid dialect, part Armenian and part Turkish. It was enough Armenian to recognize our identity as Armenians, but also enough Turkish to realize our place.

Although all strata of the Armenian population lived in our section, it was heavily concentrated with Armenian clergy, academicians, and businessmen. The only authority that was ever present in our section were clergymen from the church who lived among us. The government had never paid us any attention and largely left us to govern ourselves. Now the presence of Ottoman militia and soldiers was seemingly everywhere, including on the streets that surrounded our section. Their presence was increasing over the past month, and I sensed that the war was building around us, and we were inevitably becoming a part of it.

Our mother and father preferred to tell Anahid and me very little, but we knew that affairs were growing serious. Our father's disposition was becoming stern. The Armenian men in our section of town gathered at night to speak about matters among themselves, and they met at our house on a few of those nights. Our father didn't share with us any of the particulars, but I heard the whispers as the men spoke while I pretended to sleep. It was the same manner in which they spoke about the church and the clergy when they didn't want anyone to hear. The clergy were among the visitors, though, so I knew they weren't speaking about the clergy or the church. I heard one of the men ask one night, "How can we leave?" but he was quickly hushed, and I could not gather enough context to make any sense of it.

The onset of World War I, and the Ottoman Empire's engagement in it, seemed to focus the government's energies on fighting the war against the Allies, but that focus appeared to be changing somewhat, and I was beginning to sense that Armenians were becoming a target of some sort. I heard our father speak about a man named Talaat Bey, and how he wished to lead the Turkish people and reclaim their history. This man didn't speak about the Ottoman Empire. He spoke about being Turkish, and I sensed that we should be even more leery of the government. It was an awareness without any real understanding, and I believe my parents wanted to leave it that way, at least until we were older and better able to grasp matters. Perhaps it was a luxury to be young, protected as we were from the truth, and my parents seemed to want to preserve as much of that luxury as they could.

It was a Saturday in April of 1915, and we had just finished eating supper. Our father was looking out of the window in our home, and I walked to him. Two soldiers were standing in the street approximately ten meters from our home. The soldiers wore long, dark brown wool coats that formed a tight collar at the highest point in the neck and extended just past their waists, with a slight flair at the point of ending. Their pants were the same brown color, bunched at the thigh and neatly tucked at the knee into long boots made of dark brown leather. Each soldier appeared tall and elegant, with long tufts of black hair and bold features. Other soldiers were in the street as well, but they stood at a substantially greater distance. One of the two soldiers standing near our home began to approach, and as he did, our father placed his hands firmly on my shoulders and turned me away from the window and pushed me toward the back bedroom, which opened directly into the living room.

"Marem," our father called urgently to our mother, who was in the back bedroom with Anahid, "come take Aran!" Our mother came quickly. "What is it, Hovan?" our mother asked. "It is a soldier. He is coming toward the house," our father replied. Our mother grabbed me by the forearm without saying a further word and rushed me into the bedroom. Our mother placed Anahid and me on the bed. The cover on the bed felt like ice. The door of the bedroom remained almost always closed to conserve the sources of heat in the living room. Consequently, the bedroom remained chilly in the colder months. The thick cover placed on the bed was meant to compensate for the lack of heat, but I was atop the cover not beneath it.

Our mother walked toward the bedroom door, and as she did, she tersely instructed, "Aran and Anahid, lie quietly until your father and I come to get you." Our mother then closed the door behind her, and there was almost total darkness, except for the limited amount of light that shone through the space between the bottom of the door and the floor. I felt Anahid's breath against my chin, as she was now curled up next to me. We were both trembling, from cold mostly but also from fear.

"Aran, what is happening?" Anahid whispered softly to me.

"I don't know, Anahid, but I saw a soldier coming toward our house," I replied.

There were then two loud knocks on the front door of our house. I heard the voice of a man but couldn't hear the substance of what he said. Our father's voice was audible, though, as he replied, "I am the only male. I will go with you, but what offense have I committed?"

Having entered the house, the man's voice was now audible, as he pressed, "Do you have a son? The list says that you have a son." Our father replied, "I have a son, but he is only a boy. He is only twelve years old." After a moment or two of silence, footsteps entered further into the house. I heard the hard clacking sound of bootheels against the wood floor, then the muffled sounds of the heels as they hit the rug, then hard again as they hit the wood floor now just immediately outside the bedroom. The door flung open, and light streamed in, enough that I could see the soldier as he entered. Our mother approached quickly and grabbed me from the bed, and as she did, I stared directly into the soldier's face. At this distance he did not appear elegant at all, as he had appeared through the window. His face was worn, and his skin was sallow. His eyes were sunken and vacant, and he had a nervous manner about him as he twitched his eyes open and shut repeatedly. He then pressed, "This is your son?" Our mother quickly swung around and walked to the corner of the room and pulled me along with her. As the soldier began to walk forward, our father pleaded with the soldier, "Take me, but leave him. He is not old enough to be conscripted!"

It was the first time that I heard the word conscripted. What did it mean to be conscripted? I thought. Did they want to kill me? Is that what it meant? I was scared that I was apparently the subject of what the soldier wanted and why he forced his way in. It seemed incomprehensible to me. Why would they want me? I could feel our mother weeping, her tears wetting my cheeks as she pressed her face firmly against mine. I looked out of the corner of my eye at the soldier, and he began to approach me. He stopped and looked at me for a moment. His eyes were wide, and he seemed to be more scared than I was. He took another step toward me then he abruptly turned and grabbed our father by the arm and led him out of the room. The front door of the house then slammed shut.

CHAPTER 3

Anahid and I remained in the bedroom after our father was taken. She was still in the bed, and I was in the corner cowering in a ball and shaking in fear, now almost uncontrollably so. Anahid was weeping. The room was too dark, though, to see her completely, and hearing her, even though weeping, provided me some bearings as I tried to collect myself. "Are you alright, Anahid?" I asked.

"I don't suppose I know just yet, Aran. Is father gone? Did the soldier take him?" Anahid asked haltingly, attempting to regain control of her breath.

"Yes, Anahid, I think he is gone. I heard the door slam, and I don't hear Father anymore."

"Is Mother still there, Aran? I can't hear Mother!" Before I could answer, Anahid called for our mother urgently, "Mother! Mother! Are you still there?"

"Yes, Anahid, I am here," our mother answered from the main room. Our mother's voice was quivering, and she seemed to be trying to collect herself. I heard our mother walking toward the bedroom, then she opened the door, and the light came back in. As it did, I stood and walked from the corner of the room.

Our mother grabbed me and took me to the bed, where she also grabbed Anahid. Our mother sat between us and pulled us close so that my head and Anahid's head touched.

"We must try not to be too worried," our mother said. "If we are too worried, we will be paralyzed, and we have much to do." Our mother was wiping tears from her eyes, and her voice became calm and composed as she continued. "We must leave here quickly. You must help me pack our belongings. We will be leaving tonight. We cannot pack everything, mind you, just your clothes and perhaps an item or two that can fit in the trunk, and we must do it with haste." Our mother held Anahid's face in her hands, and with her thumbs she wiped away Anahid's tears.

There was so much about which Anahid and I were unaware, and we simply sat, confused. I felt steadied, though, by our mother's certainty in her response to what had just transpired and our mother's seeming awareness of where we were going. Our mother, it appeared, had already charted our course.

Our mother's demeanor was constant. She seemed always at ease, as if the course of her life were predestined. In that way, she appeared to live effortlessly, accepting difficulties as they came, as if their appearance were expected, even tardy in their arrival. She was not, however, pessimistic or fatalistic, as such a profile would suggest. She simply lived her life with awareness and without any pretense, traits that made her plain and genuine.

Our mother returned to the main room with Anahid, while I remained in the bedroom. I sat for several minutes, unable to move. Our mother reentered the room and saw me still sitting on the bed. "Aran, we haven't much time. You must pack a few of your things, and we must go. There will be plenty of time for thinking later."

I stood from the bed and began looking for an item or two to bring with me to wherever our mother was taking us. I leafed through books that I had received for one occasion or another, and my sketch tablets that contained my drawings. I am uncertain of my early predilection for drawing, but I believe a part of it was the ability to allow me an escape under the temporary cover of an acceptable pretense to fantasize without consequence. The process of drawing would take me there, to a place where I could imagine anything, and convince my mind that it was real.

I had many books, too. These books were stacked in the corner of the room near my bed on a small table that had a leather top bordered by an inlay of wood and chips of quartz. One book, in particular, was a survey of ancient architecture and included many of the buildings of Constantinople. It had abundant pictures of architectural ruins of temples, the sculptures of Greek gods, emperors, and warriors, and ornate sculptures of mythical creatures. The pictures were in black and white and appeared to have been drawn in their original form by an artist in a fine-penciled manner, perhaps to be later reproduced by lithograph or a similar technique. I was particularly intrigued by this book, as it had all of the elements a boy of my age would be drawn to, and which I loved to live among, including fanciful monsters, scenes of warriors, the lives of emperors, and the omnipotence of pagan gods. The pictures depicted my life, or the one I wished to live, carved in stone. It was from this book that I developed an interest in drawing and a bit of skill. I studied each stroke of the drawings in it. I started by copying one stroke at a time, until I was able to copy an entire picture. Using this technique, I became somewhat adept at copying almost any picture. This was originally our father's book, and I grabbed it from the stack with a fresh sketch tablet and a pencil to place within the trunk. I walked to the trunk, which our mother had placed on the table in the main room, and worried as I did that the trunk would not provide adequate room for even my few items. It was a small trunk, not more than three feet in length and two feet in both width and depth. It was a plain piece. The case and lid were made solely of burgundy tanned leather. The lid was shaped in a half round and gave the trunk the appearance of an unimportant child's sarcophagus. Our father had fashioned straps of mismatched leather that he took from an old riding saddle and affixed the straps to the trunk to permit the trunk to be strapped to the back. As I approached the trunk, Anahid, who stood beside the trunk, looked closely at me and the items in my hands and appeared to be taking account.

"Mother, can I take these?" I said, holding up the book and sketch tablet so that our mother, who now stood at the threshold of the bedroom door, could see the items.

"Yes, Aran, but that is all," she replied.

The lid of the trunk was open, and our mother had already begun placing items in it. The trunk had a particular odor, as if it were a crucible used to melt every part of my childhood within it, including the food we ate, the clothes we wore, our father's pipe tobacco, our mother's perfume, and the odors of everything else that permeated our home. The trunk was used not only for travel but also as the means to carry everyday items, like grains, meats, and cheeses from the market. Its use encoded it with our lives. I found an empty corner in the trunk and stuffed my items in it.

After I placed my items in the trunk, Anahid went to the bedroom while our mother folded white linens in the main room.

"Mother, where did they take Father?" I asked. Our mother looked at me, then she looked toward the bedroom to ensure that Anahid was not close enough to overhear us.

"Aran, you mustn't tell Anahid anything. She is only a little child, and I don't wish her to know what I tell you. You only need to know that the government wants your father because he is a professor, and he will return when they are done with him."

"Are they making him be a soldier to fight in the war, Mother?"

"No, he is not going to be made a soldier, Aran. They want him for other reasons."

"What other reasons?" I asked.

"Reasons that involve your father being a professor. They took him with other professors to a special place to ask him questions. There is nothing more that you need to know. He will return when the government is done with him," she replied.

"When will they be done with him, Mother?"

"Nobody knows that yet," she replied. Our mother placed the linens that she was folding in the trunk, then scurried about the living room collecting more items. When she walked back to the trunk, I asked, "Why did the soldier want me, too, Mother?" She kept her head down as she arranged the items in the trunk, and she didn't respond, so I pressed.

"Did they want me to be a soldier?" She looked at me, took a few steps closer to me, and whispered, "No, they were mistaken. They only want to take men, not twelve-year-old little boys. It became obvious to the soldier when he saw you that he was mistaken. You are just a little boy. Little boys are not meant to be soldiers. Now we can't waste any more time speaking about it. We must pack our things."

Anahid and I sat nervously on our beds the rest of the night, unable to sleep and with unsettled stomachs. As we sat, Anahid asked, "Do you think that the soldiers will come and take everything in our house, Aran?"

"I am not certain, Anahid. I hope not. I hope that we are only leaving for a short time, and everything will be here just as it is now," I replied.

"I don't know how that could be, Aran. They will know that we left and will probably come in as soon as we leave and take everything," Anahid replied.

It did strike me that there was so much that must be left behind, and I wondered whether our mother intended that we would leave forever and later send for the items or whether we were simply leaving for a short time and would return with the items placed where we left them. It seemed more plausible that anything left would be taken or plundered, if not by the soldiers, then by common thieves. It seemed an unimportant matter, though, and we didn't speak about it any further.

It was almost entirely dark when we left. Although I am uncertain of the exact time of our departure, I estimate that it must have approached approximately 3:00 am. Our mother called from the living room, "Anahid and Aran, you must wear your thick-soled boots. We must walk. Your father's horse and carriage were taken by the soldiers." Our father's horse was kept with the carriage in a small stable building, which was adjacent to our house. The exact time the soldiers took the carriage was unknown, but they must have ensured it was gone before we could use it, if for no other reason than to make matters more difficult for us. I thought it was of no consequence, but Anahid's fears about the soldiers stealing from us were apparently well founded, however inconsequential their stealing was to me at the time.

Travel by foot would be difficult. The dirt streets near our house were of uneven grade, although the center of the streets remained somewhat level from the constant pounding of pulling horses. As we walked from the house, our mother grabbed firm to Anahid's hand. Anahid in turn grabbed my hand tightly.

At this time of night, the streets were almost entirely vacant, and I was relieved not to see any soldiers. Their particular operations of the prior day were apparently suspended for the night, and when they would resume, or if they would at all, I was unaware. The only other people in the streets were a few merchants transporting their wares. Whether they were coming or going to the market area in the commercial center, I could not determine, the only sign of their occupation being the familiar, small, two-wheeled carts the merchants pushed and upon which were stacked goods of one sort or the other.

It is a commonly known matter, although nevertheless curious, that when one sense or the other is deprived, another fills the void. As we walked, my sight was limited by the depth of the darkness, but the familiar curves and straights of the road began to provide some degree of sense of place. After some distance, the grade of the streets became more level, a sign that we were outside of the more residential areas of the city and nearer the commercial center, where the streets were better tended.

"Where are we going, Mother?" Anahid asked. Our mother paused, as if to consider the amount of information that she wished to offer us, and then whispered, "We are going to the university. We are going to see Professor Daigneau."

I knew Professor Daigneau somewhat, as he was a colleague of our father. He was a science professor at the university, just as our father was, and our visits to the university in the past often led to our seeing Professor Daigneau. He was an extremely friendly man who had the peculiar affectation of speaking in the manner of a thespian delivering the lines of a monologue. He was Turkish. When we saw him, our mother and father spoke to him in Turkish. It was, after all, a matter of knowing one's place. Although Armenian was only spoken among Armenian people, and even then with some degree of self-consciousness, Professor

Daigneau did not treat the protocol with any rigidness, as he also spoke fluent Armenian and used it on the occasions that I saw him. Our father had referred to Professor Daigneau in the past as a good friend, but I knew little of whether it was a mere salutation or if our father really meant it. I do know that our father spoke often of him in a fond manner, and it was apparent now that Professor Daigneau had some importance that I was to this point unaware.

We walked for over two hours, and we were nearing the university. As we approached, the glow that precedes daylight illuminated the buildings just enough that I could recognize the building in which our father had his office. We walked to the steps that led to the front doors of this building. Our mother walked to the top of the steps and pulled the handle of the door. As she did, the locked bolt of the door rattled against the doorframe. We then walked to a side entrance, where the steps led to a basement level. She tested that door, and that door was also locked. Our mother, after peeking through the glass window of the door, turned and, while pointing to the steps instructed, "Sit down. We will wait until the doors are unlocked, then we will go see Professor Daigneau."

"Mother, will Father be able to come back?" Anahid asked as she sat.

"Yes, he will be able to return at some time, but not now. We must be patient. I am certain that your father will do everything possible to come back as soon as he can," our mother replied. Of course, our mother said what would be soothing to Anahid. Whether her response was truthful did not require any further inquiry at that point, and Anahid didn't press.

"Are you cold, Anahid?" our mother asked. Anahid nodded in reply, her teeth chattering a bit, while our mother tightened the collar of Anahid's coat. Anahid then asked, "Mother, when will Professor Daigneau be here?"

"He should be here within the hour. All the professors arrive at about 7:00 am. Classes begin soon after that," our mother replied as she came to sit between Anahid and me.

"Will they take you, too, Mother?" Anahid asked, as she pushed closer to our mother and placed her head in our mother's lap. Anahid's question distilled our fears most succinctly. Now that our father was taken, we could perhaps entertain in our minds the prospect of his return and keep it there in the abstract. The loss of our mother, though, struck to the most fundamental fear of any child.

"You must not worry about that, Anahid. I won't leave you," our mother replied.

After approximately one hour of sitting on the side entry steps, we saw some light through the glass window of the basement door. "The front doors may be unlocked!" our mother said with some tone of relief. We walked up the basement steps and onto a path that led to the front steps of the building. As we reached the top of the front steps, our mother grabbed the door and swung it open.

The entry foyer of the building was quite large. The ceiling of the foyer reached a height of approximately three stories. The edges of the ceiling, where the ceiling met the walls, had an ornate cornice that formed the boundaries of the ceiling. Each floor was visible from the entry foyer. The floors were each supported by fluted columns, which gave the foyer the appearance of a museum gallery. To each side of the foyer were wide staircases that led to each of the floors. I remembered from prior visits that our father's office was on the second floor. Our mother turned toward the staircase that was to our right, and we quickly climbed the stairs. At the top of the steps was a wide corridor that wrapped around the entire floor. Our father's office was to the immediate right at the end of a narrower hallway that led from this main corridor. As we walked, there was not a single person in any of the corridor areas. Our mother hurried Anahid and me past our father's empty office. A few steps away was the office of Professor Daigneau. As we approached, our mother stopped short of the closed door of Professor Daigneau's office. She raised her hand to the door, and quietly, with just a few gentle raps, knocked on it. I heard the creak of a chair and a scraping sound as the feet of the chair dragged along the floor.

The door opened, and there stood Professor Daigneau. His eyes opened widely and fixed on our mother, as if taken by some degree of surprise. His face was almost unrecognizable in its sullenness. In the times prior that I saw Professor Daigneau, his face had displayed a lightheartedness. Professor Daigneau was a rather tall and large man with thick black hair, which he wore slightly long to the point of curling at the nape of his neck. He had a well-groomed mustache that extended beyond the corners of his mouth, so that when he smiled, his mustache would lift and exaggerate his expression. When he laughed, his entire middle section would shake, his shoulders would lift, and he would throw his head back while letting go of a burst of laughter. Now his back was hunched and his eyes darted nervously. "Najat," our mother said, addressing Professor Daigneau by his first name, "they took Hovan." Professor Daigneau nodded his head in response, seeming to have known what had happened without our mother having to tell him. Professor Daigneau took our mother by the shoulder and led her into his office. Anahid and I followed.

Professor Daigneau looked at Anahid and me, and then again at our mother. He placed his hand on my head and the other on Anahid's cheek then quietly said to our mother, "This is an impossible situation, Meram. Although it was spoken about in some form or the other, nobody thought that it would occur now, not like this, anyway."

Our mother nodded as Professor Daigneau spoke, then replied, "I came to you first, Najat, just like Hovan told me, but I don't want to cause you any difficulty."

"I am happy that you came, but it is not safe here," Professor Daigneau said. "I will take you to another location in the building, and I will make immediate arrangements for you to move to a safer place. Stay here for a moment. When I reach the end of the corridor, I wish for you to follow me. We must be overly cautious," Professor Daigneau instructed. Our mother, Anahid, and I waited at the threshold of Professor Daigneau's office then began to walk, upon Professor Daigneau having reached the end of the corridor.

We descended the broad staircase to the lowest level of the building, where Professor Daigneau led us to a small room filled with books. The room had a musty odor, apparently caused by the countless books absorbing the basement's dampness. We stood in the middle of the room for a moment. Professor Daigneau then said, "Marem, I want you to stay here, until I have someone call for you. It may be a few hours, so don't be alarmed if some-one doesn't appear for a time."

Our mother smiled at Professor Daigneau. "Thank you, Najat," she said.

"There is no need to thank me," Professor Daigneau responded. "I consider you part of my family, Marem. You are like a sister to me. You must not worry, either, Marem. Hovan and I spoke often recently about what may happen, and if it did, what we would do. So Hovan and I made plans. These things have been thought about. Nobody could have ever foreseen the abruptness of it, though."

Professor Daigneau turned and walked toward the door. Professor Daigneau looked back, and as a smile came to his face, he said, "Aran, I thought this room would be a perfect place for you to rest, as your father tells me that you have many books. I must confess, however, my inability to prevent a small trag-edy. These books are destined for the fire, and all of the words in them will not amount to anything more than just a pile of ashes. They have been deemed not useful any longer by some, too impractical they say, but I disagree, so I have taken a few of the better ones without anyone finding me out and have saved one to give to you when I see you again." He then turned back toward the door, opened it quickly, slid himself out, and pushed the door shut behind him.

CHAPTER 4

"**M**arem?" a woman's voice called from the hallway just outside the room in which Professor Daigneau had left us. She spoke in a whisper, loud enough for her to be heard inside the room, though not loud enough to alarm us or to be heard by anyone except us. "My name is Evren," she said, still whispering. "I have been sent by Professor Daigneau to take you to someplace safe. You can open the door."

We remained in the room for approximately three hours. We were extremely weary, and the prospect of leaving was obviously welcome. Our mother approached the door and opened it slowly. The woman walked in and closed the door behind her. She was a tall, exquisite woman, with very light brown hair and large brown eyes. She wore a long dress that extended to her ankles and was made of a fine fabric woven with intricate, colorful, square patterns. She wore a dark black cloak over her dress, which appeared to be made of a silk lace, as it shimmered as she moved. She had a kind demeanor and smiled as she looked at us. "You are Anahid and Aran. Am I right?" she asked. Anahid and I almost simultaneously nodded in acknowledgment. She then turned to our mother and said, "I have a carriage waiting for you outside. I am going to take you to my home, where you will stay until circumstances improve."

She led us from the room and down a narrow hallway that led to the exterior side steps where we had waited earlier that morning to see Professor Daigneau. We walked up the steps, and just a few meters away was a carriage with an enclosed coach. The carriage was of an expensive quality. It had finely carved spokes that comprised the wheel hubs, and an impeccable coat of black lacquer on the sides of the coach. The driver jumped down from a seat placed in front of the carriage's coach to assist in lifting the trunk that our mother had since unstrapped from her back. He placed the trunk on a platform at the rear of the carriage. Evren took Anahid's hand and lifted her onto the carriage's outer step, from which Anahid was able to enter the coach. Our mother then guided me likewise, and I climbed aboard. Our mother and Evren followed.

As we began to travel, Evren kept a steady, serious expression on her face, looking forward throughout the first half hour or so of the ride, only breaking her expression on a few occasions to whisper a few words to our mother, but nothing that I could decipher. She sat next to our mother in the carriage seat facing forward. Anahid and I sat in the seat facing the rear of the carriage. My gaze switched from our mother and Evren to the scenes on the streets, the buildings we passed, and then back again. Perhaps sensing that Anahid and I were beginning to grow a bit uneasy, Evren began to speak.

"Aran and Anahid, we are all going to my home, where you and your mother will stay with me for a time. It will take another hour or so until we arrive, but I think you will like it there." Anahid and I looked at her but did not say anything in response, while our mother nodded. Evren continued, "Do you know, Anahid and Aran, that I am a mother? My children, however, are much older than you, and they no longer live in my home. I have a son, Aran, and you remind me of him when he was your age."

Evren was trying to invite me into some conversation, but I was unable to utter a word. Evren, I think, sensed my inability to speak and turned to Anahid. "Is it true, Anahid, that you play the violin?"

Anahid looked at our mother, as if wondering how Evren knew this about her, and then turned back to Evren and replied, "Yes, I do."

Evren now seemed somewhat relieved that at least one of us could engage her in conversation, and she continued, "Anahid, what is your favorite music to play?"

"I love to play all types of music. My favorite song is 'Soorp'. My mother taught me to play it," Anahid replied.

Evren looked at Anahid as she spoke, nodded her head several times quickly, and replied, "I believe that the violin is the most beautiful instrument, and it seems to me perfectly obvious that such a beautiful girl would play the violin." As she finished speaking, Evren became distracted by what she apparently observed happening on the streets. Evren leaned forward and lifted herself enough to reach her head outside of an open window of the coach. "Is the road open ahead?" she asked, tapping on the top of the coach roof to attract the attention of the driver.

"I don't know for certain, madam. I believe it could be but can't be sure until we draw closer," the driver said.

"Can we take another street, instead?" Evren asked. "I would prefer a less traveled road." The driver, in response, pulled the carriage hard to the left. As the carriage turned, the reason for Evren's concern became apparent. Several groups of men were situated along the edge of the traveled portion of the street. They did not look official in any capacity, and seemed disparate, but were clearly beginning to organize in some form or the other, as a line of men was more clearly formed further up the street. As this line became visible, Evren craned her neck a bit for a better view, then shook her head and whispered with a tone of disgust, "Conscripts!"

As the carriage made its way further down the road, I saw the full length of the road. The road was fronted by several large Byzantine domed buildings, and on the opposite side of the street where the line of men was forming, and along the open curve of the street, were several military carriages. To each carriage was hitched a wheeled artillery piece. On board each of the carriages were eight to ten men. The freshness of their Ottoman military uniforms suggested that they were new soldiers being readied to mobilize. Evren was studying the soldiers closely. Evren then looked at our mother, and instead of whispering, she sharpened her brow and snapped, "I think I would rather like to see the Allied armies in the streets of Constantinople!"

CHAPTER 5

E vren's estimate of the length of travel from the university to her home was correct. We traveled for nearly two hours. We were delayed somewhat by the Ottoman military on some of the city streets and the need to take alternative routes that ensured a relatively uneventful passage out of the center of the city. We were in the outskirts of Constantinople. I was unfamiliar with the area and could not accurately estimate the distance of travel nor an approximate relative location, other than a sense that the city center was a substantial distance away.

The carriage turned to the right from a more traveled road onto what appeared to be a strictly residential street, similar to the one that led to our house, although the homes here were not at all like my house. These homes were much larger in size, and the properties that surrounded them were significantly more expansive. Each property had a rather long road that led from the public, residential street. The homes were situated at some distance from the street, which lent a sense of stateliness. The people who lived in these homes were of apparently substantial means and social position.

The carriage continued down the road approximately fifty meters or so and stopped. The driver leaned over and bent his shoulders so that he could place his head below the coach roof and into the window near Evren's seat and asked, "Shall I take the carriage to the back entrance, madam?"

Evren stood slightly from her seat to place her ear closer to the driver and replied, "Yes, please do. I don't wish any attention drawn to us as we unload."

The driver straightened himself, and with a quick yank of the horses' reins, the carriage turned to the right and down the long, narrow road leading to a particularly beautiful home. It had a simple facade made of light gray granular limestone blocks, which were set so closely together that only a thin, almost imperceptible mortar joint was left between each block. The front elevation of the home had a large, dark wooden door with rectangular raised panels. The door was placed within a smoothly arched portico, flanked by two plain limestone columns with Doric capitals. In front of the entry portico, the road forked in two directions. The carriage took the fork to the left, and the road curved to the back of the residence. The driver took the carriage to the end of this road and placed the carriage directly in front of the back entry door. The entry here was much simpler in design than the front entry and consisted of a wooden door made of vertical planks, hinged flush against the stone facade.

We entered into a long corridor that led to a large parlor having dimensions of approximately twenty meters in both length and width. The parlor's walls were the interior exposed surface of the granular limestone blocks that constituted the exterior facade. The room had a dark coffered wooden ceiling that reached a height of two stories. The coffers that formed the ceiling were each made of two distinct boxed patterns with a substantially smaller box within the outer box. In the middle of the ceiling in the center coffer was a finely carved head of a Gorgon. The ceiling was wrapped at its edges with an intricately carved white plaster cornice having a serpentine motif. The floor was made of a light, earthen-colored travertine with deep fissures, which in the deepest crevices of the fissures was encrusted with a translucent white crystallite. This type of travertine was fairly ubiquitous in the buildings of Constantinople, and I suspected that this stone may have been extracted from the same ancient quarry somewhere in the heart of the Ottoman Empire. It was a soft and easily carved stone, a perfect medium to tell a story.

The furnishings in the room included four large embroidered cloth armchairs in the far end of the room. There were no other furnishings or decor in the parlor, except for six large kerosene lamps, made of a matte-finished black metal and clear glass. These lamps were affixed to the stone walls of the parlor and flanked each side of three large windows. In the far corner of the parlor, on the wall situated opposite the windows, was a staircase faced with the same stone of the parlor's walls. The staircase had approximately eight steps with treads made of the travertine that comprised the parlor's floor. This staircase led to a balcony situated midway up the parlor's wall. The steps and the balcony were wrapped their entire length with a black wrought iron railing having a grapevine motif, which was so intricately detailed that the thin veins on the underside of the grape leaves were depicted with delicate threads of metal.

Evren pointed to these stairs and, as she approached them, said, "Follow me, Meram. I will show you and the children to your room." We reached the top of the staircase and the balcony, which led directly into an interior bedroom. "This is where you will be staying," Evren said, pointing to a largely empty room, except for the placement of four bed frames with bare mattresses. The beds were placed two apiece against the opposite walls of the bedroom.

The room was cold and dark and had the feeling of a place that could serve no good purpose other than hiding. It appeared a secure place. Nobody would suspect to find a few Armenians here, nor would it be a sensible place to fight a war. No invading army would march down the streets here.

Anahid and I shuffled about in the room from one end to the other, trying to find an appropriate place to put ourselves, and Evren looked at us as we did. She apparently sensed that we felt displaced, and as she looked at us, she said, "Don't fret, children. I will do my best to make you comfortable here. I will come back with the linens so that we can prepare the beds. At least then you can rest. You will feel better after you rest."

CHAPTER 6

Our mother left with Evren to help bring the linens for the beds. While she did, Anahid and I looked around the bedroom to take some measure of our surroundings and circumstances.

"Why are we here, Aran?" Anahid asked as she sat down on the bed situated approximately a meter from the bed on which I was seated. I could not answer Anahid's question, as I had no particular information. I was, though, aware of the situation more generally and had made some deductions. There was a war being waged, and the war could be fought in the streets of Constantinople. The fact that soldiers were in the residential areas of the city may have suggested that a fighting war could break out around us and that we wouldn't be safe if we did not move further from the city center. These were obvious deductions to my mind, and after some brief moments, I replied, "We are further away from the city here, Anahid, so we are safer here in case they start fighting the war."

Anahid nodded her head then asked, "Do you believe we will be staying here for a long time, Aran?"

"I don't know, Anahid. I hope it will be short, and we will be able to return home," I replied.

"I am very frightened about Father, Aran. Do you think Father will be home when we return?" Anahid asked.

"I think he will, yes, Anahid. I think he will be home," I replied.

"Where did he go, Aran? They won't make Father go fight in the war, will they?"

Anahid's expression was anxious and burdened as she spoke.

I felt constrained by our mother's instruction not to share any information about our father with Anahid. Anahid, however, had already touched upon what our mother told me, so there seemed no use in not telling Anahid what I knew.

"Mother told me that he is not being put into the army to fight in the war like other men. Father was taken to a special place with other professors so that the government can ask him about some matters that the government wants to know about, and after that Father and the other men will be allowed to go home."

My explanation to Anahid did not appear to alleviate any of her worry, as the strained expression on her face remained. I then offered more, which wasn't information provided by our mother, but was, rather, my deduction. "The government is probably just trying to make decisions on how to fight the war," I said. "Father knows many things that may help the government, and the government, I am sure, needs Father's help. Don't worry, Anahid."

I imagined our father's seizure by the Ottoman authorities to be a type of de facto military draft, and as a boy, I had formulated in my mind an almost romanticized version of the notion. Our father was an academician. The government simply seized him to convert his knowledge to the government's uses. I imagined him seated at a table in a large and secure government palace with important military and government leaders, providing them with his knowledge on one subject or the other, a sort of captive and prized government resource. What government he would serve, and why he would serve it, was unknown to me. I had some understanding that as Armenians we were different, and there was some distrust of the government, and some distrust of the Armenians by the government. My parents spoke of it on occasion, but typically only in the context of church matters and only to the extent necessary that we understand the government's sensitivity to our outward displays of our culture and identity. We should be reserved, my parents instructed us, and nobody will pay us any attention. It was enough to form an understanding and keep matters as they were, and as they should be.

Anahid's sensibilities were consistent with a young girl who had her father taken from her, was scared for him, and missed him terribly. Separation from our father, even for a short time, was unnatural to us. He made certain throughout our childhood that Anahid and I felt his deep affection. We were made to feel essential to him and, in turn, we felt that he was as indespensible to our lives as we were to his. Anahid was tremendously perceptive, and the lack of information about our father's whereabouts caused her a substantial amount of additional anguish. After my responses to her questions, she withdrew into herself and lay silent, and I sensed then that her mind was rummaging through all the past bits of information she may have acquired and cataloged in search of some direction to his possible whereabouts. In this way, Anahid and I were made of different cloth. I was given to transforming events. My mind wove an intricate tapestry, with threads of different colors woven thread upon thread into themselves, until the constituent materials were unrecognizable and the meaning told by the final weaving, not the constituent parts. Anahid was made of plain cloth.

I heard our mother walking up the steps, her conversation with Evren now apparently concluded. She approached the top step, carrying a tray of food. The tray was filled with a plate having soft round bread and another plate having various pickled vegetables. Our mother placed the tray on the floor, opened two pieces of bread with her hands, and placed the vegetables in it. As she handed the food to us and we began to eat, our mother said, "I spoke to Evren. We must stay here for some time, at least until matters settle down. We will need to stay in this room for the most part. We will not be able to go outside until it is safer."

"Mother, will it be possible to go outside for just a little while?" Anahid asked. Our mother stood up, and while attempting to straighten the wrinkles in her dress, replied, "Perhaps we will be able to at some time, Anahid, but Evren thinks it best now that we stay inside, so as not to draw too much attention to ourselves. We need to be private about the fact that we are staying here."

Anahid stood, walked over to our mother, and buried her head into our mother's stomach. Our mother reached her arm around Anahid's shoulders and stroked the back of her head with her other hand.

"I hope our lives will be normal again soon, Anahid and Aran," our mother continued, "but we will try to make do until then."

CHAPTER 7

However unable Anahid and I were to fully understand what was transpiring around us, we were fully absorbing the reality of our confinement. Looking around the room in Evren's house, it seemed impossible to imagine that we were not readily able to move about as we wished, and that condition was imposed by others who we did not know and for purposes Anahid and I were unable to fully comprehend.

One would think that the predominate emotion after some time of confinement would be boredom, or at least some dulling of the senses, if for no other reason than the mind's way of lessening awareness of the slow and, at times, imperceptible movement of time. I found soon that, at least in my experience, the mind is not given to such charity and, instead, seems to sharpen the senses the longer the confinement lasts.

It was the third Sunday since our arrival at Evren's house. Since our arrival, we spent most of the time in the bedroom upstairs. We would on a few occasions walk down to the parlor, and then only to accompany our mother when she and Evren would engage in some conversation or the other, which conversation was always of a rather superficial nature when Anahid and

I were present. I could only assume that our mother and Evren spoke of more substantive matters when we weren't present, as Evren and our mother, I think, made great efforts to protect Anahid and me from subjects that would have caused us additional anxiety.

We began to look forward to seeing Evren, if only for a brief time. She was an extremely pleasant woman who always gave me a feeling of being welcome. I didn't know anything about her, except that she was Turkish. She was the only person we saw in the house to that point and seemed to have lived in the house entirely alone for some period of time.

Our mother was awake for most of the prior night. She walked downstairs a few times during the night, and I heard her speaking to Evren. I had been falling in and out of sleep, and at some time early in the morning I must have fallen into my deepest state of sleep and stayed there until I woke at approximately 10:00 am. Our mother was downstairs, which was usual by this time, as she and Evren would often start the day with some conversation over a cup of Turkish coffee while Anahid and I slept.

I sat up in my bed and looked at Anahid lying in her bed, which was situated parallel to my bed and on the same wall against which mine was placed. Anahid, whose eyes were open, looked at me with an annoyed expression as I pointed toward the balcony and the staircase leading to the parlor, trying to direct Anahid's attention downstairs.

"What is it, Aran? Are you eavesdropping again?" Anahid asked.

"Listen, Anahid. Can you hear that?" I asked.

"Hear what?" Anahid tersely replied.

"Do you hear a man's voice coming from downstairs?" I asked, causing Anahid to immediately pop up in a seated position. Anahid and I sat silently, while we both strained to hear the man's voice.

"Yes, Aran, I do hear a man's voice," Anahid replied, "and I hear Mother's voice, and Evren's, too. Do you think Mother and Evren would be upset if we came to see who it is?"

"We mustn't go down yet, Anahid. Let's try to wait for Mother to come up. It may be someone that Evren and Mother don't wish for us to see, or to be seen by," I said.

"Can you hear what they are talking about?" Anahid asked.

I again paused, trying to hear something of what was being said, and then replied, "I can't be sure."

Anahid and I sat silently for several minutes, trying to decipher a word or two of what was being said. I could hear our mother and Evren in conversation with the man. I determined that they were not anywhere in the parlor, as any sound in the parlor readily traveled into our bedroom. They were most certainly further into the house.

"Aran, do you think that they are talking about Father?" Anahid asked, her voice in a whisper, not wanting her voice to carry beyond my ears, given my previous admonition. I did not immediately reply to Anahid, as I was still attempting to decipher what was being said.

Anahid asked again, now a bit louder, "Aran, did you hear me? Do you think that they are talking about Father?"

"Perhaps they are, Anahid," I replied.

We sat several minutes more then heard footsteps walking closer to the staircase leading down to the parlor.

"Anahid and Aran, please come down. There is someone here that wishes to see you," our mother called.

Anahid and I jumped from our beds. As we reached the top of the stairs, we saw our mother standing alone at the bottom of the staircase.

"Come, Anahid and Aran, and follow me," our mother said as she pointed toward the corridor that led from the parlor into the inner portion of Evren's residence.

Leaving the parlor to enter this corridor was strange. To this point, the only room that Anahid and I had been permitted to enter on the first floor was the parlor. The corridor that led out of the parlor was dark, as the substantial length of it allowed only a small amount of light from the parlor to transmit through to its innermost portions. At the end of the corridor was a room.

It was a small room, which seemed to serve as a tearoom, with floor-to-ceiling shelves on the far end. These shelves were filled with various teacups made of a fine, richly colored porcelain, with matching dishes. The other walls of the room were paneled with a dark, tightly grained wood, which, although beautiful, gave the room no benefit of any reflection from the limited sources of light. Our mother pointed to the man sitting at the large table in the far corner, on which sat a kerosene lamp having a white, etched glass shade, which threw a ball of glowing white light onto his face. As Anahid and I focused, we instantly recognized him. It was Professor Daigneau.

CHAPTER 8

"Hello, Anahid and Aran," Professor Daigneau said, as we stopped in the middle of the room. "I came to see you, to make sure that you are fine." Professor Daigneau looked at Anahid and me with a serious expression. He then continued, "I am sure that it is not easy to be confined to this house, but hopefully you are making the best of it." Professor Daigneau paused while awaiting a response, although neither Anahid nor I offered anything.

Professor Daigneau smiled then looked at me directly and asked, "Are you and Anahid getting along fine, Aran?"

"Oh, yes sir, we are fine. Thank you, sir," I replied nervously.

Professor Daigneau continued to sit at the table, and as he did, he pulled a tightly wrapped cigar from a wooden box, which sat on the corner of the table almost flush with the table's edge. He left the box open for a moment, revealing a small but intricate carving of an acanthus leaf on the top of the box's lid. He placed the cigar in his mouth and chomped at the tip, then raised a match to light it, his eyes squinting slightly as he did, all the while looking at Anahid and me, clearly still having more to say, but at the present being unable given his momentary preoccupation. Professor Daigneau drew the cigar away from his mouth and began to speak again. "Did you know, Anahid and Aran, that Evren is my sister?" Professor Daigneau asked. While Professor Daigneau spoke, he exhaled a puff of smoke from his cigar, and I could smell the sweet scent of his cigar's tobacco as it made its way through the room. "Yes, it is true, Anahid and Aran. I am Evren's little brother," he said with an amused tone as he flashed a quick gaze at Evren, who was sitting in a chair next to the table at which Professor Daigneau was sitting. "Did you also know, Aran and Anahid, that when I was a child, I lived in this house?" Anahid and I listened carefully as Professor Daigneau spoke, his strong and colorful personality at once intimidating and mesmerizing us. Anahid and I both smiled and nodded in response to Professor Daigneau, not wishing Professor Daigneau to think us inattentive or impolite. "And, Anahid, you are so quiet. Please tell me how have you gotten along since your arrival here?" Professor Daigneau asked.

Anahid seemed unable to say anything at first, but then she replied softly, "I have been fine, sir, thank you."

Professor Daigneau sat for a moment and looked at the tip of his cigar. The ashes of his cigar began to appear as if they would begin spilling off, but they remained hanging, suspended by some invisible bond, and simply glowed. Professor Daigneau placed the burning cigar in a dish to his side without tapping off the ashes. He then looked again at Anahid and said, "Anahid, I have a very large favor I wish to ask of you, and I hope you will not say no, as I would be so disappointed." Anahid had a puzzled expression on her face as she looked at Professor Daigneau. "Anahid, would you play your violin for me?" Professor Daigneau asked. His question was asked almost apologetically as if sorry that she wasn't asked sooner or, probably more accurately, sorry that the circumstances to that point had not permitted the question at all. Indeed, our circumstances required more than just our confinement. It required our suspension to ensure that we were not heard, not seen, and not found.

Anahid looked to our mother, appearing to seek her approval. Our mother simply looked back at Anahid and opened her eyes widely, prompting Anahid to respond. Anahid shifted her eyes back to Professor Daigneau then replied softly, "Yes, I would like to very much, sir."

Our mother then turned to me and instructed, "Aran, take Anahid upstairs and help her with her violin."

Professor Daigneau broke into a broad smile, and as he stood from his chair, he said playfully, "Excellent, Aran and Anahid, we will wait for you, then, in the parlor, and please hurry. I have been waiting to hear Anahid play her violin for quite some time."

Anahid and I turned and walked out of the tearoom and back down the corridor that led to the parlor. As we walked up the staircase and into the bedroom, Anahid said nothing. I walked with Anahid toward the trunk, which to this point was only accessed by our mother to take from it what we needed. I grabbed the latch on the front of the top of the trunk and lifted it high, balancing the top at the point of adequate opening to access the violin, which was packed in its case in a corner of the trunk. Anahid reached in and grabbed the handle of the case and pulled it out. Anahid carried the violin case to her bed, placed it on the mattress, and stood for a moment and just gazed at it.

Other than her clothing, the only item that Anahid packed in the trunk before we left our home was her violin. Although perhaps to many, bringing a violin under the circumstances would seem frivolous, to Anahid, bringing it was a necessity, and it was among the first items placed in the trunk. Our mother packed it carefully and tucked it securely away to ensure its safekeeping. Since arriving at Evren's house, Anahid had not asked our mother for permission to remove the violin from the trunk. I think Anahid was simply satisfied with the knowledge that she knew where the violin was and that so long as she did, nobody could take it from her.

Anahid opened the violin case and carefully grasped the neck of the violin with one hand and the bottom of the violin with the other and lifted it from the case. It was a beautiful violin, the body of which was made of a matte-finished walnut, which Anahid kept in immaculate condition. The only sign of use was the wearing on the black chin rest, where Anahid's chin rubbed against it as she played, exposing an area of raw wood, and at the neck of the violin near the finger piece, where the oils of Anahid's hand created a dark patina. Anahid placed the violin back into the case on the bed and walked to the trunk. As she lifted the lid of the trunk and looked inside, she said calmly, "Aran, I believe I left all of my sheet music at home. I don't know why I forgot to put the music in the trunk, but I did."

"Don't worry, Anahid," I replied. "You can play without looking at the notes. Can't you?"

"Yes, I suppose I can," Anahid replied. She closed the lid of the trunk, walked back to her bed, and lifted her violin from its case.

With the base of her violin tucked neatly under her arm, Anahid looked at me and asked, "What do you think I should play for Professor Daigneau?"

"I am not sure, Anahid," I replied. "Maybe you should first ask him what he would like for you to play. I am sure he will like anything."

As we walked from the bedroom, Anahid said, "I am nervous, Aran. What if I can't remember all of the notes of the music that he asks me to play?"

"If you are worried, then just play 'Soorp,' Anahid. You will never forget 'Soorp'."

Anahid and I then walked down the stairs. Our mother, Evren, and Professor Daigneau were sitting in the large armchairs in the far end of the parlor. Professor Daigneau sat extremely upright with his back stiffened against the back of his chair. He was dressed impeccably, as he always was, with a dark outer vest and trousers, and a tight bow around his stiff, white-collared shirt. Professor Daigneau's dress and posture added formality to the moment as Anahid approached to play her violin. Anahid stopped in the middle of the room, unsure of where she should place herself. Professor Daigneau motioned with his hand for Anahid to walk closer to him, and the sound of the hard leather heels of her shoes echoed as she walked across the travertine. I sat next to our mother on the floor beside her chair. Anahid stood directly in front of Professor Daigneau, approximately three meters or so away.

"What do you wish for me to play?" Anahid asked, her eyes dancing from her violin to Professor Daigneau as she spoke.

"Play your favorite music, Anahid. I want to hear you play your favorite music," Professor Daigneau responded.

Anahid lifted her violin to her chin then lifted the bow to the strings. She slowly moved the bow upward, and Anahid began to play "Soorp." The sound streamed from her violin and filled the room. Anahid's face was aglow, as it always was when she played. Anahid was breathing life again into the violin, and the violin was breathing life into Anahid.

She was now approaching the middle chords of the music, where typically Anahid would begin to tire and, almost on a musical cue, whenever our father would listen, he would carry Anahid through, exhorting her to carry the long notes that comprise most of the music's middle chords, chords that when played on the violin make the strings of the violin sound like a human voice.

Anahid pushed the bow strongly through the middle and final notes, and as she finished, she placed her violin and bow down by her side. Anahid's round eyes looked up to Professor Daigneau, and she was happy, her smile now wide on her face.

"Anahid, it is no wonder that you were so quiet," Professor Daigneau exclaimed. "Your voice was trapped inside that violin!"

CHAPTER 9

Professor Daigneau left later that night. Upon his departure, he told us that he would return the following Sunday, and we looked forward to his return. The Monday morning immediately after Professor Daigneau visited was a particularly bright day, and the morning sun was illuminating the parlor from the room's three large windows. These windows were approximately three meters in height and reached from approximately waist height to just below the cornice of the ceiling. Despite the windows' sizable dimensions, the only views to the outside were of leafy trees and a bushy hedgerow.

"It looks like a beautiful day for a walk. Shall we take one?" Evren asked my mother, who was looking out of one of the windows.

Our mother seemed surprised by Evren's suggestion. Since arriving at Evren's house, we had remained inside the entire time. I felt no danger in the prospect of a little fresh air, maybe more due to my craving for it than any particular deliberation over our apparently precarious circumstances. Our mother paused while she continued to look outside.

"I suppose it would be fine, Evren, provided that we stay on your property and don't venture onto the public road," our mother replied.

"Certainly, Meram, we will take our walk in the back garden. Nobody will pay us any bother there," Evren said.

Anahid and I went upstairs and hurriedly prepared for our walk with Evren. When we returned to the parlor, Evren stood waiting for us in the threshold of the corridor that led to the back entry door. Evren had covered her formal dress with a gardening apron made of a coarse, buff-colored sailcloth.

My senses upon first stepping outside were quite strange. Although one might imagine that the sense most stimulated at the moment of stepping outside for the first time in several weeks to be sight, with the sunlight direct and unfiltered, the aromas seemed to most pervade me at that moment. It was the middle of spring, and the strong scent of the fertile earth and the blooming vegetation was overwhelming. This scent was perhaps made more prominent due to the humidity that filled the air. The aroma was heavy and sweet all at the same time, so much so that it was as much a sensation of taste as it was of smell. We crossed the narrow private drive. Directly ahead was a stone wall that was approximately a meter in height and twenty meters or so in width and made of irregularly shaped field stones set in a light gray mortar. In the center of this wall was a colonnade made of four plain stone columns supporting a wooden arbor. In the center of the middle columns of the colonnade was a wooden gate made of weathered gray wood assembled in a picket fashion.

Evren approached the gate and swung it open and held it there as our mother, Anahid, and I entered. "This is my garden," Evren said, pointing ahead to the vast expanse.

The garden was in the shape of a large rectangle. In the center was verdant grass, the most lush grass I had ever seen. The grass was cut very short and seemed to be of an exotic species, more fitting, it would seem, for more temperate areas. Bordering the outer edge of the grass along the garden's full length and width were narrow paths made of pulverized gravel. On the outer edge of these paths were colorful flower gardens, which constituted the outermost portions of the garden's full length and width. The flowers alternated in colors of white, yellow, and red. The most prevalent type of flowers in the garden were red tulips, and this variety formed the band of the innermost flowers facing the gravel stone paths, and were, therefore, the most accessible.

"Come, Anahid. Let's pick some tulips," Evren said as she grabbed Anahid's hand and led her to a patch. "In a week or so we will be losing all of the tulips until next spring, when they will all come back in even greater numbers than are here now, so we can take as many as you would like," Evren continued, as she pulled a pair of gardening shears from the pocket of her apron. Anahid seemed to be delighting in the garden and in Evren's invitation. Anahid ran quickly to Evren. "Here, Anahid, I will bend the stem, and you cut the tulip where I bend it," Evren instructed as she handed the shears to Anahid. As Anahid cut tulip after tulip, Evren began to bundle a bouquet of tulips in her opposite hand.

"Now, Anahid, take this bouquet and give it to your mother. We will then cut more just for you," Evren said as she handed the large bouquet to Anahid. Anahid took the tulips in her hand, pressed them to her nose, and deeply inhaled. She then walked to our mother, who was standing beside me, and as she handed the bouquet to our mother, Anahid said, "Here, Mother, Evren and I cut these tulips for you. Don't worry, though, Mother. Evren says that many more will grow next spring."

Anahid spent a large part of the remainder of that day with Evren and our mother, preoccupied with the tulips cut from Evren's garden. They took a good many of the tulips and placed them in large vases dispersed around the periphery of the parlor floor.

Anahid seemed most preoccupied by trying to press the tulips, a craft that Evren taught her earlier in the day. Evren had given Anahid a small flower press to use, and because it was only about the size of a book, Anahid was permitted to bring it upstairs. Evren also gave her a box of red tulips, and Anahid sat on the floor of the bedroom with the flower press, hard at work trying to press the tulips, while I attempted to pass the time with one activity or the other. Anahid had already pressed a few of the tulips onto white parchment, and she did not appear happy with the results, as the red tulips, when pressed, bled onto the paper around it. Anahid's efforts to rub off the red pigment were to no avail.

"I wonder how Evren keeps the color from running all over the paper," Anahid said, with the frustration caused by her failed efforts to preserve whatever the tulip once had evident in her voice. I had no knowledge that could help Anahid on the matter but tried anyway.

"Perhaps the flowers are too fresh, Anahid. Perhaps you should wait a few days before you press them, so that they have some time to dry," I said.

Anahid looked at me with an expression of exasperation and snapped, "No, Aran, if you let the flower dry, it becomes brittle, and if you try to press it then, it will crush the flower into pieces. A fresh flower can be pressed, and it bounces back without breaking, see?" As she spoke, Anahid took a petal from one of the tulips, placed it between her index finger and her thumb, and pressed her fingers around the petal along its length, then opened her fingers again to show the petal returning to its prior form. Anahid shook her head and took another flower from the box, placed it in the press, and tightened the screws that held the two parts of the press together. Several minutes later, she loosened the screws of the press and looked at the results. "The color ran again," Anahid said with a tone of resignation. "Perhaps you are right, Aran," Anahid continued, "I will let the tulips dry for a few days, then I will try to press them."

CHAPTER 10

The following Sunday came, and we eagerly awaited Professor Daigneau's arrival as he had promised. Almost the entire Sunday had passed, and there was no sign of him. As evening approached, Anahid and I sat in the bedroom, despondent in the belief that Professor Daigneau would not be coming. It was about then that I heard Professor Daigneau's voice call from the parlor.

"Anahid and Aran, your distinguished guest has arrived, and, yet, I have no welcoming party. Please come and greet me," Professor Daigneau's voice bellowed in a tone of feigned indignity. "And, Anahid, please bring your violin," he added.

Anahid and I raced to our feet. Anahid grabbed her violin, and she and I ran down the stairs, our mood instantly elevated by the sound of Professor Daigneau's voice.

Professor Daigneau stood in the middle of the parlor with Evren, and our mother stood behind him. "Come, Anahid and Aran," Professor Daigneau called, his arms outstretched. Professor Daigneau placed his arms around Anahid and me, and as he did, he said, "I am so sorry that I am late. I was delayed coming here. The roads are getting more difficult to pass, so it took me longer than I had planned. But I am here now and cannot wait any longer to hear Anahid play her violin."

Professor Daigneau walked to the armchair, the same one that he sat in the prior Sunday. Evren and our mother sat in the flanking chairs. "Will you play 'Soorp' for me, Anahid?" Professor Daigneau asked.

Anahid nodded her head and walked to a spot on the floor in front of Professor Daigneau. She lifted her violin to her chin, and Anahid played "Soorp."

When she finished, Professor Daigneau smiled and said in an uncharacteristically soft voice, "Thank you, Anahid. I shall look forward to next Sunday, when I hope you will play for me again." Anahid placed her violin back in her case, and the room was silent.

Professor Daigneau then began sifting through a bag that he placed beside his chair, and he pulled a book from it and said, "Aran, as I promised when I saw you at the university, I have a book that I wish to give to you. It is a book of Turkish poetry." Professor Daigneau opened the book to a page that he had already marked with a small fold in the page's upper right corner. "I will read a poem to you. When I see you next Sunday, you can tell me what the poem means, after you study it a bit over the week." Professor Daigneau pointed to the floor in front of where he was seated and said, "Come, Aran and Anahid. Sit here, and I shall read it to you." As Anahid and I sat, Professor Daigneau began to read the poem aloud.

Come, let's grant the joy to this heart of ours that founders in distress:
Let's go to the pleasure gardens, come, my sauntering cypress...
Look, at the quay, a six-oared boat is waiting in readiness—
Let's go to the pleasure gardens, come, my sauntering cypress...

Let's laugh and play, let's enjoy the world to the hilt while we may,
Drink nectar at the fountain which was unveiled the other day,
And watch the gargoyle sputter the elixir of life away—
Let's go to the pleasure gardens, come, my sauntering cypress.

First, for a while, let's take a stroll around the pond at leisure,
And gaze in marvel at that palace of heavenly pleasure;
Now and then, let's sing songs or recite poems for good measure—
Let's go to the pleasure gardens, come, my sauntering cypress.

Get your mother's leave, say it's for holy prayers this Friday:
Out of time's tormenting clutches let us both steal a day
And slinking through the secret roads and alleys down to the quay,
Let's go to the pleasure gardens, come, my sauntering cypress. *

As he completed reading the poem, Professor Daigneau stood from his chair and repressed the bend in the upper right corner of the open page, then closed the book and handed it to me. "Aran, did you understand what I read to you?"

I wished to be polite to Professor Daigneau but truthfully did not comprehend the poem, and I replied, "I am uncertain, but I think I might after I spend some time reading it."

Professor Daigneau nodded and said, "Reading poetry is like searching for hidden treasure. The poet will make you find the clues first, and they are not easily found, so you must be prepared for a difficult journey. Beware, though, Aran. The poet can play tricks on you, and what may seem obvious is just a little game that the poet plays to make you walk in the wrong direction. It is just his way to better hide matters. In that way, poetry is much like life. Almost everything that you wish to discover is hidden beneath one thing or the other, and a great amount of time often is spent simply looking." Professor Daigneau then turned and disappeared into the inner corridor that led to the tearoom.

Anahid and I left the parlor and returned to the bedroom. I spent a good part of the remainder of the evening thinking about what Professor Daigneau said and attempting to read the poem in the book that Professor Daigneau gave me. I had difficulty deciphering even a single word.

CHAPTER 11

It was the Wednesday immediately following Professor Daigneau's prior visit. We had just finished lunch. Anahid and I sat in our room upstairs, while our mother remained downstairs with Evren. Anahid continued to fuss with the flower press but quit the activity after a short time upon growing increasingly frustrated at the propensity of the red tulips to bleed their color and make a mess of the white parchment. I cast aside Professor Daigneau's book of poems, as it frustrated me, perhaps as much as Anahid had been frustrated by the flower press. Professor Daigneau's book had no purpose other than to preoccupy me, and I easily discerned the transparent purpose of it. I did not resent Professor Daigneau for trying, however. I did feel that he was earnest in not wishing me to fall victim to boredom, and the book of poems and a useless exercise in puzzle solving probably seemed to him better than being idle.

I decided to draw a picture of the garden described in the poem. I had imagined it to look much like Evren's garden, with tulips and grass. I drew it in that manner, like a beautiful garden should be drawn, with flowers and grass. Because I only had a lead pencil, I could only draw the garden in black and white.

The grass was easily drawn with small strokes, and the flowers and trees were simply larger strokes with some leafy extensions. It was enough to imagine that the garden could be real. It was the images of the people that caused me difficulty. I couldn't conceive of the people in the poem, so I left them out of the drawing. I couldn't draw what I couldn't see. It was as simple as that.

"I shall practice another piece to play for Professor Daigneau," Anahid said to me, as she stood from the place on the floor where she was trying to press tulips. "I don't want Professor Daigneau to think that I can only play one piece." Anahid lifted her violin to her chin and bounced her bow on the strings of her violin while she thought for moment. "I shall practice the Bach pastoral piece. Do you think that he will like that, Aran?" Anahid asked.

"What piece is that one?" I replied.

"Aran, you know which one it is. It is this one," Anahid replied as she began playing a few notes on her violin.

"Oh, yes, Anahid," I said, now recognizing the music, "I think that Professor Daigneau will like that very much."

Anahid began to play. She halted frequently, searching to recall the next note as she went, then she stopped completely and placed her violin and bow to her side and said angrily, "I cannot remember the notes, Aran. I have lost the notes in my mind, and I left all of my sheet music in our house. The soldiers probably took it and destroyed it by now." Anahid sat on her bed and placed her hands over her eyes and began to cry softly.

"Anahid, when Mother comes up, she will hum the notes to you, and you will remember them. Mother will help you," I said. Anahid sat for a few moments longer with her hands still over her face. She then removed her hands from her face, and while still crying, a slight smile came across her face, and she nodded slightly, but she said nothing.

Our mother came up the steps several minutes later, stood in the middle of the room, and looked at Anahid, her eyes still wet and red from crying. "Anahid, have you been crying?" our mother asked.

Anahid said nothing, so I intervened. "Mother, Anahid is trying to play a piece of music, and she lost the notes in her head.

I thought that maybe if you could hum them to her, she might remember them."

"Certainly, Anahid," our mother responded, as she walked over to Anahid and sat beside her on the bed. "What piece is it, Anahid?" our mother asked.

"It is the pastoral piece by Bach, and I lost all but a few notes of it," Anahid replied.

"You didn't lose the notes, Anahid," our mother said. "They are still all in your mind. Once you play a piece of music, it always stays with you. Now lift up your violin, and let's try to find the notes." As our mother spoke, Anahid stood from her bed, lifted her violin to her chin, and began to play the first few notes. As she did, our mother began to hum the notes while Anahid played. Anahid waited for our mother's cues at first, then began to push her bow more certainly. Our mother stopped humming, and Anahid played the music the entire rest of the way through.

As she finished, Anahid looked at our mother and said, "Do you think that Professor Daigneau will like it, Mother?"

"Oh yes," our mother replied to Anahid. "I believe that Professor Daigneau will like it very much. I also think that Professor Daigneau will like it even more if you tell him that you had difficulty remembering the notes at first, but that they were in your mind all along and you found them so that you could play the music just for him."

Anahid remained sitting on her bed the rest of the evening holding her violin, seemingly satisfied that she had with her everything that she needed. She didn't play a single note for the remainder of the day.

CHAPTER 12

Sunday arrived, and as he had promised, Professor Daigneau came to visit. He arrived in the middle of the afternoon with his customary apology for his tardiness, but we had no particular expectation of a time of arrival; Anahid and I were just extremely excited to see him, so no apology seemed at all necessary. Professor Daigneau took up his now-customary seat in the armchair in the parlor, and Anahid and I sat on the floor in front of him.

"Well, Anahid and Aran, where did we leave off last Sunday?" Professor Daigneau asked, as if already knowing the answer. "Oh yes, I recall," Professor Daigneau continued. "We were reading a poem. Aran, did you study the poem that I read to you?" he asked.

"Yes, sir, but it was very difficult to understand. It made my head hurt, so I put it down. I do know that they are in a garden, like the one outside," I replied.

Professor Daigneau looked at me and gave out a hearty laugh. "Aran, you are beginning to realize that the treasure is not easily found."

I thought for a moment, then asked Professor Daigneau what I believed to be the obvious question in hopes of simply learning the answer, without wasting any more time reading the confounding poem. "Professor Daigneau, how do you know when you have found the treasure?"

Professor Daigneau looked at me pensively for a moment then replied, "You will tell yourself when you have found it, Aran. You may not even realize that you found what you were searching for at first. You will realize it one day, nevertheless, perhaps while just walking down a street. When you find it, please take a moment to rest and think of your friend, Professor Daigneau, won't you?"

Professor Daigneau paused for some moments while he looked at me, and perhaps sensing that I was perplexed by the entire exercise, said, "Aran, you are owed a clue. You may be surprised that what you are searching for may have been within your reach all along, but sometimes that makes the searching for it much more difficult, because when something is too close, it can be more difficult to find."

Professor Diagneau did not await any reply from me, nor did I have one, and he immediately looked toward Anahid and said, "I see that you have your violin with you. Are you ready to play for me?"

"Yes, I am," Anahid replied.

"And what do you wish to play for me today, Anahid?" Professor Daigneau asked.

"I am going to play a piece by Bach for you," Anahid replied.

"Oh, excellent, Anahid, Bach is one of my most favorite of all. Play on, Anahid."

Anahid stood and lifted her violin to her chin and began to play. Anahid's first few notes were soft and tentative, and I could not ascertain if Anahid was simply nervous or whether the initial chords of the piece gave this effect as intended. The tempo of the piece soon quickened, and as it did, the expression on Anahid's face grew increasingly serious and determined. Bach's pastoral pieces suited Anahid well, as the notes when played by Anahid sounded pure, organic, and uncomplicated. I don't, however, believe that I perceived this fact at the time and have tried to determine since whether this conclusion came later to me, or whether I knew it then, but did not have any particular understanding of the effect. Nevertheless, I do know that I never mentioned this fact to Anahid at the time in even the most unrefined way.

Anahid played the piece the whole rest of the way through with each note flowing into the next, just as it was written and as she had practiced. As she finished, Professor Daigneau rose from his chair and clapped enthusiastically, and as he did, he said, "That, I am sure, is a very difficult piece to play, and you played it beautifully. Thank you, Anahid."

Anahid didn't respond at first, but then said, "Professor Daigneau, my mother wanted me to tell you that I couldn't remember the notes to that music at first, when I tried to practice it a few days ago, but then I remembered the notes, so that I could play the music for you. They were in my head all along."

"A good memory is a very special gift, Anahid. It allows you to keep what you wish without having to carry anything in your hands. That way nobody can take anything from you," Professor Daigneau replied.

Professor Daigneau left within the hour, and Anahid and I wished that we did not have to wait another week for Professor Daigneau's return. Almost immediately after Professor's Diagneau's departure, Anahid and I returned to the bedroom, and Anahid began practicing her violin for Professor Daigneau's next visit. She seemed intent on proving to herself that all the music that she had learned to play was still stored safely in her mind and on proving right what Professor Daigneau had told her, that nobody could take it from her.

She played the violin incessantly in our bedroom each day of that week, starting one piece or another, playing several notes, then rapidly moving on to the next, as if to test her memory of the music in her repertoire. The effect resulting from her manner of practicing in this way was at first simply discordant and caused me, admittedly, some nervous aggravation that I did not initially mention to Anahid. By later in the week, though, her practicing in this way built to an effect of an almost unbearable cacophony that I could no longer withstand.

It was later in an evening of that week when I succumbed to it. "Anahid, will you please stop! Playing in that way is going to send me into madness," I yelled. Anahid almost immediately stopped playing and looked straight down at the floor. She was, it was clear, extremely hurt by my outburst and said nothing. She then walked to her bed and sat on its opposite edge, so that her back was turned to me. She stayed there silently for several minutes. I began to feel increasingly guilt-ridden at having snapped at her and was moved to apologize.

"I am sorry, Anahid. I shouldn't have yelled at you. I was completely wrong for doing that," I said. Anahid remained silent, and I continued, "Anahid, I do love to hear you play the violin. It makes me very happy. Please begin playing again."

This was the first time, I think, that I ever told Anahid how much I loved to hear her play. I never expressed myself in that manner to her. Her playing the violin was a part of my life, as much as it was a part of hers, and I was realizing how much hearing her playing meant to me. At the age of twelve, I was unable to fully articulate this to her. What I said to her then was completely inadequate to have communicated the importance of her playing to me. Anahid still remained completely silent, and I began to plead with her.

"Please, Anahid, please play again. Play a song just for me," I begged, but Anahid didn't respond. She sat silently until dark and went to sleep not having uttered a single word to me for the rest of that night, and I feared that I lost something that I could never get back.

CHAPTER 13

Anahid and I waited for Professor Daigneau's return the immediately following Sunday, but he didn't come. Anahid remained mostly silent and distant from me the entire week, still upset that I shouted at her. Anahid was punishing me. She knew it, and she appeared to have no intention of providing me any relief from it. She remained cold and inanimate, not moved in the least to accept any of my apologies.

It was now the second Sunday since Professor Daigneau last visited, and it was late in the afternoon. We were sitting in the bedroom, resigned to the prospect that Professor Daigneau would miss another Sunday visit. At about that time, we heard our mother call from the parlor, "Anahid and Aran, Professor Daigneau is coming in through the back corridor. Come and greet him."

Anahid grabbed her violin, and I grabbed Professor Daigneau's book of poems, and we rushed downstairs to greet Professor Daigneau. Anahid and I waited in the parlor with our mother, while Evren opened the back door for Professor Daigneau.

We heard Professor Daigneau's footsteps through the long corridor that led from the back entry into the parlor. As he appeared through the corridor, the expression on his face was unexpectedly somber. He stopped as he entered the parlor and looked at Anahid and me and said, "I am coming too much into the habit of saying apologies, but I am so sorry to have missed my visit with you the last Sunday. Come with me. I have something very important that I must tell you."

As Professor Daigneau walked, Evren and our mother followed and spoke to each other in whispers. I sensed that our mother already knew what Professor Daigneau would be telling us. We walked through the dark and narrow corridor toward the tearoom and entered it. Professor Daigneau walked to the table in the far corner of the room and lowered himself into the chair. He lit a cigar and sat silently and pensively, alternately placing his cigar in his mouth, then removing it and staring at it as the tip of it burned away. Professor Daigneau then began to speak. "Evren has told me how much she has enjoyed having you here." Professor Daigneau's expression was now very serious, and his eyes were fixed down on the desktop. "Evren does not wish for you to leave, but it is necessary to make new arrangements. The war is coming too close for you to be safe here any longer." Evren's head was down, her chin almost tucked completely into her throat. Our mother placed her hand on my back and placed her other hand on Anahid's cheek and nestled Anahid's face close against her waist. He rose from his chair and snuffed out his cigar in a dish that was filled with ashes almost to the point of overflowing. Professor Daigneau approached Anahid and me and said, "I so much wanted to have you here longer, but the war is much too close now."

I didn't know what Professor Daigneau meant about the war being too close, and the direct impact on us at the moment was unknown. Were the armies preparing to march down the road that fronted Evren's house? Who were we to take cover from now, the Ottoman army or the Allied armies? Were we becoming a danger to Evren and Professor Daigneau by having inadvertently attracted some unwanted attention? The only matter that was clear was that we were to leave Evren's house, and I felt as though we were being cast out into the depths. I wanted to know more, but I was too afraid to ask, so I just stayed silent.

Professor Daigneau walked toward us and kissed Anahid and me on the very top of our heads. Professor Daigneau then said, "Anahid and Aran, please return upstairs. I wish to speak to your mother."

Anahid and I returned to the bedroom. Anahid sat on the edge of her bed with the tips of her shoes barely reaching the floor, and I sat on the edge of my bed and faced her. The room was very dimly lit, as the only source of light was from the kerosene lamps that were burning in the parlor. Due to the lack of light, and despite my close proximity to her, Anahid appeared to me mostly in silhouette. Anahid picked up her violin, then looked at me and asked, "Would you like me to play something, Aran?"

"Yes, Anahid," I replied, "play 'Soorp.'" And Anahid played "Soorp," and she played it softly, so that only Anahid and I could hear it.

CHAPTER 14

We would leave early the next morning when the sky had reached total darkness. Although I did not have complete awareness of it at the time, circumstances were, in fact, growing increasingly serious, and rapidly. So rapidly, in fact, that there was little time to react to the noose that was tightening around the Armenians living in and around Constantinople. Ottoman soldiers and militia were placed on roads leading out of Constantinople and were quickly closing in on all Armenians living in the city and its immediate environs. Although our mother did not completely explain the full extent of it, I did understand that we were caught in the throes of a policy instituted by Ottoman Turkish nationalists to deport all Armenians from the Empire. Armenians were simply not wanted in the Empire any longer. Why we were no longer permitted to stay was not explained to me. Our mother did explain that no matter how certain the policy of expulsion was, the means of our expulsion were unknown. It was feared that Armenians might not be permitted free passage out. Ensuring an escape without notice by any of the authorities was the primary objective, the details of which I presumed were the matter of extensive discussions between our mother, Evren, and Professor Daigneau. The immediate destination was not known to either me or Anahid, but I believed the intent was to travel out of Constantinople a substantial distance and into a less conspicuous area where we would not be found by the Ottoman authorities.

After speaking with Professor Daigneau, our mother returned to the bedroom. Our mother's face was serious, and her eyes were wet with tears. She was composed and resolute, though, and gave Anahid and me strict instructions.

"Our features will give us away, so we will hide under a blanket on the floor of the carriage. Evren will be placing linens and other items on top of the blanket so that it will appear that she is simply traveling alone with her personal items. We must remain extremely quiet, particularly if the carriage is stopped by the soldiers."

This was the first time that our mother spoke with Anahid and me with such austerity. I believe to that point she strained to sterilize the reality of matters, but there was no sense in it now.

"Mother, what should we do if the soldiers find us? Should we try to run away?" Anahid asked. Our mother was folding some clothing while Anahid spoke and did not look up.

"If that happens, you will grab my hand and not let go, and we will do what we are told," our mother said emphatically. There were a few moments of silence, and our mother was still occupied with folding the various items of clothing. Our mother then looked up and directly at both Anahid and me, and completed her sentence, "...except, if they try to separate us, then I will fight them."

Anahid nodded, seemingly comforted by our mother's honesty. I believe this honesty was also an essential constituent of Anahid, but I was unsure whether I was made from it, too, and I think I envied Anahid for having it. I believed I had a weakness that Anahid did not have. I deluded myself to salve my fears and insecurities. Anahid faced matters straight on and had no use for any contrivances, while I grabbed for them to support all of my weight.

"I will fight them, too, Mother," I said, trying to summon a warrior's tone of defiance. As the words left my mouth, I felt no authenticity in them, and I could not shake the fear of the possibility as we prepared for our departure.

CHAPTER 15

It was past midnight, and Evren and our mother led me and Anahid out through the back corridor of Evren's residence to the waiting carriage, which was ready for our departure, the driver already holding the horses' reins.

"I will help you step into the carriage," Evren said to Anahid and me as she took each of our hands and held them as we steadied ourselves onto the carriage's outer step. "Take a seat first, then we will prepare where you shall lie once we are all aboard." Once in, Anahid and I sat on one of the carriage seats together as we were instructed. Our mother followed and sat beside me. Evren then stepped into the coach and sat on the seat facing us. The door of the coach closed shut.

"Lie here," Evren said, pointing to the floor of the coach. Our mother lay down on the floor first, and then Anahid and I lay down on opposite sides of our mother across the width of the coach floor.

"I am sorry that it is so uncomfortable, but hopefully we will find an area of road without any soldiers on it, so that you may come out for a time and stretch," Evren said. I was consumed by thoughts of what would become of us if we were found. It was the first time in earnest that I considered possible outcomes. Capture seemed the most possible, but death did not seem plausible. Being young would prevent that possibility, I thought. Nobody would kill a child, not intentionally, anyway.

The coach rocked and tilted to one side as someone was apparently climbing onto the carriage's outer step. The door opened, and we looked up. It was Professor Daigneau. I assumed that he'd left the prior night and that we wouldn't see him again. His eyes were wide, and he smiled. I felt calmed immediately upon seeing him. It was assurance of some sort that we would be protected no matter what circumstances we were about to encounter. He seemed always in control, and I thought that he knew events before they occurred. He seemed supernatural to me in that way, and I felt comforted by it.

As Professor Daigneau climbed into the coach, he looked at Anahid and me and said, "It would be my great honor, Anahid and Aran, if you would allow me to take this journey with you. Your mother and Evren have already granted me the permission, so I hope that you will say yes, too." Anahid and I nodded our heads in reply, and as we did, Professor Daigneau slid into the seat next to Evren without saying a further word. Evren unfolded a soft, velvet-textured blanket and spread it over us. She then placed a number of items over us, and everything turned completely dark. The items placed upon the blanket were items of a soft and light nature, but given their abundance, nevertheless, they created the sensation of being buried alive.

I felt the pull of the horses as the carriage began to move forward then accelerate. The carriage wheels made grinding and popping sounds as they turned over the dirt street, and the horses' hooves made low clopping sounds as they pounded the road. Nothing could alleviate the extreme discomfort of our position, as there was no brace against the shaking and jarring of the carriage as it moved across the bumpy road. As we traveled, Evren whispered small narratives to us, providing some orientation of place and distance, while Professor Daigneau remained entirely quiet.

We had traveled for approximately one hour. The carriage began to slow, and as it did, Evren whispered, "Be still; there may be some soldiers ahead." As the carriage slowed to a complete stop, I could hear Evren. Her voice was now slightly more distant, because, I surmised, she placed her head outside of the coach's door to speak.

"Hello, sir," Evren said in the most impeccable Turkish.

"Hello, madam," a man faintly replied, the man apparently located at a distance from the carriage. "What is your name?" he asked.

"My name is Evren, and this is my brother, Najat," she replied.

"Where are you headed, madam?" the man asked.

"We are traveling to visit friends," Evren replied.

"Very well," the man replied. "Beware, though, that the traveling may be slow. You will find that the road will be filled with Armenians being deported, but soon we hope to be rid of all of them."

"Very well, sir," Evren replied. After the coach accelerated, Evren said to Professor Daigneau, "It was difficult for me not to tell the imbecile that it is they who should be expelled from the Empire, not the Armenians."

"Don't let them be the wiser. We must maintain the ruse," Professor Daigneau replied.

To this point, I had believed that our circumstances may have been a limited experience, perhaps limited to Constantinople, and perhaps only to families like ours, and I believed that the primary peril that we sought to avoid was being held in confinement in the Ottoman Empire, not driven from it. I felt an odd sense of relief in the counterintuitiveness of it, that we were not escaping from potential imprisonment but were seemingly being allowed to leave, and forced to leave, in fact, and en masse with other Armenians. After we traveled for several more minutes without incident, I whispered, "Mother, why are we hiding?"

"Please don't say anything, Aran," our mother replied. I fell asleep a short time later without saying a further word.

CHAPTER 16

"Empty this carriage! Empty this carriage immediately!" I was jolted awake from a light sleep of an indeterminate amount of time by the man's orders.

"How can we help you, sir?" Professor Daigneau calmly said. "My name is Najat Daigneau, and this is my sister, Evren. We are Turkish. We are simply trying to make our way to visit friends. Will you allow us to go on our way, please?"

There was no immediate response from the man. I heard at least two more men approaching from a distance. The men were speaking in Turkish with a regional accent of which I was unfamiliar. "Sir and madam, you must empty this carriage," another man said, in a starkly more subdued, even polite, manner. Evren and Professor Daigneau must have initially frozen, because I felt no movement in the carriage.

Professor Daigneau then began to speak. "Sir, if you will, please. I am a professor in Constantinople, and I am as Turkish as you are. It would seem unnecessary for you to require me and my sister to leave our carriage. I would again ask, sir, that you permit us to be on our way. It is very late, and we wish to reach our friends by some reasonable time in the morning."

There was some momentary silence, then the man replied to Professor Daigneau, now in an insistent tone and with a clarity and volume that placed the man directly aside the carriage. "I have orders that we must stop everyone leaving Constantinople. I am under specific orders to ensure that no Armenians are permitted passage out. Now step off the carriage," the man demanded. The coach of the carriage rocked as Professor Daigneau and Evren stepped down, and as they did, I was paralyzed with fear. Our mother clenched her arms around Anahid and me in an awkward manner as the blanket that covered us was tugged and pulled from around us. Our mother, Anahid, and I were exposed. I looked up and saw the face of a man, a very short and thin man, with a long sharp nose and attired in a drab olive-colored military uniform. He looked directly at us and exclaimed, "Get out!"

Anahid, our mother, and I were pulled out of the carriage by the soldier. The soldier pushed us to the side of the street. It was a beautiful residential street lined with fine houses and beautiful gardens, not far at all from the outer limits of Constantinople, as the glow of white stone buildings in the city was visible in the distance. We had not traveled far from Evren's house. Our planned escape had been thwarted before we even left the city, it had seemed.

Professor Daigneau and Evren stood by the carriage and watched us as we tried to gather ourselves. Professor Daigneau and Evren were initially silent, their eyes wet and their faces filled with fear as they stared at us. Professor Daigneau then straightened his back and, while pointing to us, said to the soldier in a stern, yet respectful manner, "Sir, these are just small children with their mother. Let them come with me, and we will go on our way and not mention anything of the encounter. I will assure you, sir, that I will not mention a single word of it."

The soldier looked at Evren and Professor Daigneau and then toward Anahid, our mother, and me, and he appeared to be considering Professor Daigneau's request. After several moments, the soldier replied, "I am under specific and absolute orders to round up all Armenians. They will be found sooner or later." He then looked at Evren and Professor Daigneau and continued,

"Because you are Turkish, and distinguished, I will permit you to leave and return to your home, but these Armenians are coming with me." Professor Daigneau looked at Evren and whispered something to her that I could not decipher.

Professor Daigneau then stared at the soldier for a few moments and said defiantly, "If you will not let them go with me, then my sister and I wish to be treated just like you treat them, as Armenians."

The soldier looked back at Professor Daigneau with a somewhat surprised expression, then after collecting himself a bit, sneered coldly, "'Very well, we will treat you as Armenians, too." The soldier directed Professor Daigneau and Evren to stand by the side of the coach. The soldier motioned ahead to the other approaching soldiers and pointed to Evren and Professor Daigneau and yelled in a mocking tone, "These are Turks who wish now to be Armenians." Professor Daigneau and Evren were then taken by the other soldiers and walked back in the direction from which we traveled with the point of one of the soldier's rifles at their backs. Anahid, our mother, and I were abruptly turned and marched approximately fifty meters ahead to join a line of Armenians that was formed in the middle of the street, and as we did, I lost sight of Professor Daigneau and Evren.

We assumed our place in the back of the line. I stood on one side of Anahid, and our mother stood on the other. Anahid pushed up against my side, and as we began to walk with the line, she leaned close to my ear and mouthed almost inaudibly, "Aran, do you know where they may be taking us?" I looked behind me to see where the soldiers were to ensure their adequate distance before I responded to Anahid. There were two soldiers to our rear, keeping a distance of approximately ten meters, enough that I felt able to respond to Anahid.

"I don't know, Anahid, but I think we are leaving Constantinople." As I responded, our mother turned her head to me, and I expected her to order me quiet, but she turned her head back and looked forward.

"Do you think that they are taking us to the same place that they took Father?" Anahid asked.

"That is a possibility, Anahid. Maybe we are all being taken to the same place," I whispered in reply.

Anahid was quiet for a few moments then said. "I will be so much less afraid if Father is there." Anahid and I looked ahead, and all that we could see was the long line of people in front of us, which stretched around a long curve in the road and faded out of sight in the distance. I think it struck Anahid, as it did me, that this line could include almost every Armenian that lived in Constantinople. Anahid turned to me again a few moments later and said in a soft whisper, "Father could even be in this line ahead of us. Do you think that we can look for him in the morning?"

"Yes, Anahid," I replied. "We will look for him in the morning."

We had walked only about one hundred meters or so when we heard the echo of two short shotgun blasts from a distance behind us, in the area that the soldiers took Professor Daigneau and Evren. The sound of the blasts made Anahid and me recoil. We looked quickly behind us without being permitted to pause in our stride and were overwhelmed with the fear that we would not see Professor Daigneau or Evren again.

CHAPTER 17

We walked the entire night. Among the soldiers were a number of gendarmes. The gendarmes were more authoritative and seemed to view themselves as higher in rank than any of the soldiers, perhaps because the soldiers were just general conscripts having no particular skill or vocation. One gendarme, in particular, walked close to us the entire night. He was a fat man who walked on his toes with a quick gate. His uniform was sloppy and oversized, and the heels of his boots were worn to the leather at their outer edges, the apparent result of his off-balance gait. The standard-issue uniforms of the gendarmes were neat and plain, with straight brown trousers and a tight-fitting coat that was waist length, and without any of the frills of the Ottoman military uniforms. The fat gendarme, though, perhaps wanting to appear more important and regal, dressed his uniform up with a colorful red kerchief, which he tied around his neck and tufted outward. That addition to his uniform, together with his short, fat legs and his extremely large waist and buttocks, made him look like a circus clown. He was unaware of this effect, though, as he pranced like a show stallion. He was particularly petulant. He shouted at us, like you would speak to an animal, and he seemed to have pleasure in it. He shouted orders in rapid succession and looked around as he did to gauge the effect. He seemed intoxicated by the exercise. He wanted to humiliate, and he did. He shouted vulgarities at the women, including our mother, and when he did, he chose Armenian slang in an apparent attempt to deepen the effect. His treatment of us made it clear that we were nothing more than unwanted cattle in his mind, and he wanted to make us feel it.

The line of deportees was almost completely silent. All that I could hear were the shouts of the fat gendarme and the sounds of hundreds of feet dragging along the dirt road. The entire line had been driven all night. Some were added during the night. When people were added, the line would stop. The gendarmes seemed to have lists, which they reviewed when they approached a house, and they would pound on the doors and order the people out.

Unless elderly, the gendarmes separated the men from the families as they walked out of their houses. They separated the men at the point of a rifle and in front of their children. They wouldn't show anyone any mercy, not even long enough to let the children say appropriate good-byes to their fathers. We came to a house where a family of a mother and father, perhaps in their early thirties or so, were ordered out of their house with three little girls, the oldest child being no more than eight years of age or so. The oldest child grabbed at her father as he was being led away by a gendarme, and the gendarme hit her with the stock of his rifle in the side of her head. She fell to the ground. Her screaming mother knelt to pick her up to carry her while her other two children clutched each other as they were pushed into the line. The child appeared to be unconscious in her mother's arms, and the other gendarmes just laughed and sneered at them, with one gendarme shouting to the mother, "I would have rather put a bullet in her head."

We were made to parade when we entered a village. We were taken down the middle of the main village street. People looked out the windows of their houses at us. We were a spectacle created for their amusement. Many times in the night when we were stopped, people shouted obscenities and insults at us from their homes. When they did, the fat gendarme laughed. "Look at those dirty Armenians!" a woman shouted from her front door as we walked down the road of a village.

The fat gendarme replied to her, "At least you only need to look at them. I am forced to have to smell them, and worse, I am forced to look close at their ugly faces while I do." It was this way the entire night.

As daybreak came, I could better grasp our circumstances. We were in a line of approximately five hundred Armenians, mostly women and children. There were a good many men, but most appeared older, substantially older than the age of general conscription. Anahid and I studied the makeup of the line closely, as we began to do at daybreak what we had resolved to do the night prior. We were looking for our father. We were made to stay within the confines of the line, so our efforts were limited to looking ahead in the distance and behind us. I strained to look at every male in the line around us. My looking for him, although futile, occupied a good bit of the early morning and at least took my focus off of the inane orders of the fat gendarme.

By the middle of the morning, we arrived in a small village at some distance outside of the center of Constantinople and stopped there. It was one of countless nondescript villages. These villages were all the same to me, with most structures built of cream-colored stone rubble and thatched roofs. The roads were narrow and untended, and the landscape was barren and colorless. A particularly narrow road led to a large stone-walled building placed within the boundaries of high, rubble-stone revetments. We were marched beyond the revetment walls and into an area that formed the interior grounds of the building.

The gendarmes ordered the line into two groups. The men were made to stay outside on the grounds. Women and children were ordered inside the building. As we were marched in, the soldiers shouted repeatedly, "You are entering a deportation center. You will be prepared here for expulsion." Each soldier repeated the same statement as they walked up our line. It was apparent that what they said was rehearsed and government issued. They said it without emotion, and I don't think that they even believed it. This was a prison with iron bars in every window opening. The room that we entered was a large space with dirt floors and caged areas that appeared to be separate holding cells off of a main corridor. The stench was so foul that I gagged when entering the room and did all that I could to avoid vomiting. Anahid, our mother, and I, along with about twenty others, were placed in one of the large caged areas, which had dimensions of approximately ten meters in length and width. There were already ten or so people occupying this cell area. They were all women. Some had small children, a few no more than two or three years old. Their faces were dirty with earth. They were all very thin and appeared to have been here for quite some time. Most looked down to the ground as we entered and those that didn't had gazes so empty that they appeared to have been resigned to their circumstances, so much so that I sensed that they may not have been aware of our presence.

We sat in the corner of the cell. Anahid and I sat on each side of our mother. The trunk that our mother managed to pull from the coach when the soldier ordered us out was placed in front of us. We were ordered not to speak, and after all were placed inside, an iron-barred door was closed behind us. The gendarmes who had driven us all night entered the large corridor outside of our cell. Among them was the fat gendarme. He approached our cell, turned his back, and assumed a guard position across the corridor several meters from our cell door.

After about an hour or so, the fat gendarme left his guard position. He then left the building through two large doors that opened directly off the middle of the large corridor. The doors remained opened, and I heard him shouting to the men who remained outside, "You dirty Armenian dogs. Get in the wagon, and leave your belongings on the ground. You won't need anything for the trip you will be taking. Place everything in a heap, so that we can burn it all in one big pile." A few minutes later, I could smell a heavy, musty smoke, the same type of smoke that comes from burning damp wood, and it made my eyes burn. The fat gendarme returned to his guard post, and as he walked back, he saw that we were rubbing our eyes due to the effects of the smoke that was now clearly visible within the building. "Are you crying because your men are leaving for a trip?" he asked sarcastically, and then continued, "Save your tears. Those men are not worth crying for. They are just dogs. You can always find a new dog." The fat gendarme's words stung, but no one said a word in response. We just sat submissively, and our submissiveness seemed to embolden the fat gendarme even more. "They are old mangy dogs," he said in Turkish, biting off his words. As he spoke, he peered at us, and his face grew serious and angry, then he spat in a tone of disgust, "We don't like your mangy dogs."

We spent the entire rest of the day huddled there. The fat gendarme did not allow us to move. We had no relief until he left at dark.

Each day of the next several were identical. We were made to remain sitting on the damp dirt floor of our cell. We were told not to talk. We were permitted to leave the cell once a day, late in the morning. We were taken to a yard each day to relieve ourselves in a large, public, mass latrine that consisted of nothing more than a hole in the ground. It was better to relieve ourselves in private than to be subject to the humiliation, so mostly we were made to live in our own filth, and the filth of others with no accommodation given to wash. They would give us food in the same yard as the latrine, a few crumbs of bread and some foul water, with this meant to provide for us the entire day. The food and bread could have served no good purpose given the scant portions and its foulness. It was either intended to hasten death or prolong it just long enough to permit us to know that we were dying.

We were not deportees waiting for passage out. We were prisoners, and as each day passed, we were made to give away bits of ourselves. The first few bits, our freedom and our dignity, were relinquished consciously, if unwillingly, and they were taken in the open where everyone could see it. The other bits were lost more imperceptibly, and I struggled each day to keep an account of what I still had. They intended it this way, I think. It is often much easier to take from someone when they don't realize what's being taken from them, until all of the pieces are gone.

CHAPTER 18

Our mother first started showing signs of illness within one week of our imprisonment. She began coughing lightly and intermittently, and it seemed nothing more than the initial symptoms of the common cold. Within a week of the initial symptoms, her coughing became heavy and incessant, and I began to fear for her. Within this time, our mother, Anahid, and I were moved to a small separate cell in the same corridor with the large cell in which we were originally placed, but several meters further and apart from any other cell or occupants in the prison. We were the only occupants in the new cell, and I was relieved when they moved us into it. I believed when they moved us that they determined that our mother was sick and the move was made to better her care. I made this presumption, in part, because the large cell in which we were originally placed was so crowded and filthy that surely they knew that a person who was sick needed a better accommodation to get well. Within a week of our move, I began to sense that our mother was being left to die. The little food and water that was given to us came in even smaller quantities, and what was given seemed now even more stale and putrid. The only luxury given from the move was the ability to speak more freely now, if only in soft whispers, without any repercussion.

We had been in the prison for approximately three weeks. It was late in the afternoon, and Anahid had fallen asleep on the floor of our cell. I sat leaned against the wall, while our mother lay supine, her back flat against the dirt floor. She lifted her head slightly and propped her head on some linens. Our mother was becoming extremely thin, and her face was almost now unrecognizable. When she spoke to me as a child, I remember her eyes, which would dance excitedly when she looked at me. Now her eyes were sunken, inanimate, hollow, and stationary. She turned her head to me slightly and began to speak hurriedly and urgently, but softly so as not to wake Anahid, "Aran, I have things to say to you that I have needed to tell you for some time. I hope you will forgive me for not speaking to you about these matters sooner." I was somewhat alarmed by the way in which our mother was speaking, and the tone of her voice, at once anguished and resigned, provided some brace for what I presumed she was about to tell me. "Aran, your father..." As she began to speak, she halted and repositioned her head on the stack of linens to more squarely face me, then continued. "Aran, you must understand that we are in the middle of a war."

Our mother stopped speaking. She seemed to have no more energy to say anything further. I was scared about what our mother was about to tell me and wanted her to get it over with as quickly as possible.

"Yes, Mother, I know about the war," I said, urging our mother to get on with it and tell me what she knew, and to affirm what I had already surmised. I had believed that our father was forced to work for the Ottoman government in some way because they needed him. I sensed that our mother probably knew more than what she told me before, so my mind filled in the empty parts. I wanted our mother to continue and to tell me what became of our father. I drew close to her and pressed my face against her cheek to enable me to whisper directly into her ear, so that Anahid could not overhear me. "Is Father a soldier, Mother? Is he being made to fight in the war? Will they not let him leave until the war is over?" Our mother's eyes remained closed, and I could feel my cheek become wet. "Please, Mother, tell me," I begged.

Our mother responded in a soft, strained tone, "Your father is dead."

My body numbed, and my head and ears burned. "Why did he die, Mother?" I asked. Our mother remained silent at first, and it didn't appear that she was willing or able to tell me anything further. "Please, Mother, tell me why he died," I pleaded.

"Professor Daigneau told me that the government killed your father the night that they took him. They killed him because we are Armenians," our mother replied. I sat, still numb, and tried to force myself to cry, but I couldn't.

"Professor Daigneau and your father knew what was being planned. Professor Daigneau knew that when your father was taken, he would be killed. Your father knew it, too. They thought there would be more time to arrange an escape," our mother continued.

"When did you learn that Father was killed, Mother?"

"The night before we left Evren's house," she replied.

"Why didn't you tell me before, Mother?" I asked.

"You and Anahid needed hope. I didn't want to have you know the truth until we escaped and were safe. There was too much to explain about what it all meant. I didn't want to explain to you about all the killing and all the people dying. You are too young to know about dying. Your father had already made plans with Professor Daigneau, in the event he was taken. He asked Professor Daigneau to help explain matters so that you could comprehend it a little at a time and so that you would eventually understand everything that you needed to know," our mother replied.

"Everything about what, Mother? About people dying?" I asked.

Our mother was exhausted. She sighed and closed her eyes. I thought that she would leave it there, but after a few moments of silence, she gathered enough energy to open her eyes slightly and replied, "Not about dying. About everything you need to know about living: information that you need to make use of to live."

Our mother closed her eyes; she was unable to offer anything more, and I did not press for any further answers. There was no sense in questioning the merits of our mother's decision not to immediately inform us about what happened to our father, and any thoughts that her decision amounted to deceit would have been a needless preoccupation. I believe I knew that our mother felt that preserving our hope may have been one matter that neither the gendarmes nor anyone else had authority over, and I believe she wished to preserve as much of it as she could.

We had reached the point—our circumstances now demanded immediate measure of the practicalities of our survival—and our mother had made some determinations. How does one preserve hope, when at the same time the harshness of our conditions demanded some sobering assessment of the enemy and the means by which we were each separately being targeted for extermination? Perhaps it was necessary to construct a false reality, for oneself or for others, at least in some selective way, to survive, and that to preserve our minds and our bodies, the truth would have to be the chosen casualty from time to time. Our mother opened her eyes and looked at me. I wondered about what Anahid should know and whether I should be the one to tell her.

"Should I tell Anahid about what happened to Father?" I asked.

"No, you can't let Anahid know anything about this," our mother replied. "She needs to believe that he is still alive." Our mother's expression was stern and unyielding as she spoke. "You will need to protect Anahid. Protect her from all of the harms. Don't let anybody separate her from you." I nodded my head and could feel our mother beginning to let go of me as she did.

CHAPTER 19

The numbers in our prison were becoming smaller. Each day for the past week or so, at least a person or two died. I knew someone died when the two large doors in the middle of the large main corridor opened. Through the doors I could see from our cell the field where they put the dead people. A few times I saw the gendarmes carry a body out, but on those occasions they were always at some distance. The first time I saw the gendarmes carry a body, I thought that they were carrying a bundle of tangled limbs from a tree. I asked our mother then why the gendarmes were collecting wood for a fire. She told me that it was a dead person, not sticks for a fire. I watched the gendarmes carry the dead bodies to the threshold of the door and could see directly out to a heap of corpses just beyond the door.

My mistaking the first dead body I saw for wood was understandable, I suppose. The bodies were so emaciated upon death that there was nothing much left of the natural human form, and the manner in which the gendarmes would grab the corpse by the ends of its four limbs would cause the unsupported head of the corpse to drag beneath the torso, so that all that could be seen had the appearance of a twisted trunk with gnarled limbs.

It was particularly disgusting to see the treatment of the corpses by the fat gendarme, who seemed to delight in the exercise of tossing the bodies on the heap of corpses. He would swing the corpse to harness the force captured by the momentum and fling it wildly, and laugh all the while, as the corpse bounced off the heap and rolled down the pile. The fat gendarme seemed to scan the prison for corpses like a buzzard, circling for a corpse to pick at. With his fat body, which was disproportionate to the relatively small size of his head and neck, he seemed to fit the part.

About four days had passed since our mother told me that our father had died. I was tormented with thoughts of our father and his death. My torment, I believe, could be traced to a single source. It was this simple fact, I believed, and this was the essential element: I was never able to say good-bye to our father. I felt estranged from him because of it, as though, because my final moments with him were not marked with any particular words of affection as one might express, or even any awareness of the fact of it, made him distant and lost to me forever. He was simply made to disappear, and my mind would not permit me so much as a clear image of his face or the recollection of the sound of his voice. The only trace of him that my memory would permit was my recollection of him standing at a distance watching as Anahid and I played one game or another in a vast field near our home. At these times he was purposeful in letting us know that he was there, close enough to hear our call for him to provide salve for a skinned knee with a kiss or a cradle in his arms, but also at enough distance to allow Anahid and me some time to develop our relationship with some degree of independence. Now we needed his embrace, and he was gone, and no amount of calling out for him would bring him back. I had avoided any discussion of our father with Anahid to this point. It was in the middle of the night, and I was awoken by Anahid.

"Please, Aran, please wake up. I am frightened." I opened my eyes but saw nothing. There was absolute pitch darkness in the cell. Anahid was pressed close to me, and she spoke directly into my ear in a soft, but piercing, tone. "I can't see Mother, Aran. Is she here with us? I can't see if Mother is with us."

When I fell asleep, our mother was just a meter or so from me, and as Anahid spoke, I extended my arm to reach for our mother. As I reached for her, I became afraid. Our mother had grown very weak. She slept for a good bit of time. Our mother was dying, and I was beginning to fear that if she died at night, the fat gendarme would circle and take her from us while we were sleeping and throw her on the heap of corpses. I did not speak to Anahid about our mother's condition and thought perhaps that Anahid believed our mother's illness was only temporary. I touched our mother's hair, then her shoulder, and as I did, I replied, "Yes, Anahid, Mother's here. She is right next to us. Don't be afraid."

Anahid was quiet for several moments. I thought she had begun to fall back to sleep. As my senses began to dull again, Anahid, again whispering directly into my ear, asked, "Aran, what do you believe ever became of Father?" Of course, it was inevitable that Anahid would ask the question, but I feared her asking me, nonetheless, because I didn't trust myself to keep the secret.

"I don't know, Anahid," I replied softly.

"We will find him, though, won't we, Aran?" Anahid asked.

"Yes, Anahid, we will find him," I assured Anahid. She exhaled deeply, and for a few moments she was quiet.

Anahid then nestled up very close to me and almost imperceptibly whispered, "What will we do, Aran, when Mother dies?" Anahid's question stung me, not only for the clarity in which she expressed her awareness of our mother's condition, but also for the circumstances that to this point I don't believe I permitted myself to fully accept. Anahid and I would be alone, and I was frozen with fear of the eventuality. Both Anahid and I then permitted each other to cry quietly without saying any further words to each other that night.

CHAPTER 20

The fat gendarme had remained in charge of our cell area since our imprisonment. After some time of hearing his rants, though, they became nothing more than an indecipherable din.

The fat gendarme patrolled with a soldier who appeared very young, perhaps no more than eighteen years old or so. The fat gendarme had treated him as nothing more than a lackey. He did just as he was ordered by the fat gendarme and remained entirely silent, avoiding any interaction with us, even so much as eye contact. He was, it appeared, as much a prisoner as we were. His primary duty was at night, when he was one of the sole remaining soldiers left by the gendarmes to patrol the prison camp. During the last couple of nights, he'd sat on the small stool outside our cell, with his back turned to us. When it became dark, he pushed his stool toward the wall outside our cell and leaned his back against it.

I had just fallen asleep when I heard a voice ask in a very soft whisper, "Would you and your sister like a fig?" I sat up and focused my eyes. It was the young soldier. I saw his face, which was lit by a small lantern that the soldier began hanging outside of our cell at night, and the light from it the last few nights provided some comfort to Anahid and me. As the soldier awaited my response, he looked nervously around him, apparently to ensure that there were no other soldiers in the area who could hear him speak to us. He looked directly into my eyes, and he had an impatient expression on his face. "Do you?" he repeated. "Do you and your sister want a fig?" He reached out his closed hand toward me as he spoke and dropped two small figs in my hand. I nudged Anahid to wake her, and as she opened her eyes, I handed Anahid one of the figs. The young soldier turned quickly around and sat rigidly on his stool. While Anahid and I ate the fruit, the soldier, with his back remaining turned to us, whispered, "My name is Bahir. I know you are Anahid and Aran from your papers. I am from Constantinople, just as you are." Neither Anahid nor I responded, as speaking at all in the prison to anyone but ourselves was strictly forbidden. "Don't worry. I am alone. Officer Demir is not here. He left before night." It was the first I heard of the fat gendarme called by a name, and it struck me that he was aware of our fear of him. Despite having a name, I resolved that in my mind he would always remain known to me as the fat gendarme. As Bahir spoke, Anahid and I nodded to acknowledge him but did not say a word. "I see that your mother is quite sick," he said, looking at our mother who lay in the corner of the cell where she had remained all day, unable to do much more than open her eyes from time to time. We were aware now that our mother only had a little more time before she would pass, and we had resigned ourselves to it, but I did not want anyone to know it for fear that the gendarmes would take her and throw her on the heap of corpses. The fear was enough to move me to speak.

"She is not too sick. She is getting better," I replied.

Bahir looked at our mother, and then to me, and I sensed that he knew I was fabricating matters. He, nevertheless, obliged me and replied in a compassionate tone, "Yes, I will try to smuggle in some fresh water so that you can properly take care of her so that she does." He then turned upon his stool so that he faced outward with his back to us, and after a few moments continued to speak in a very soft tone. "I had many Armenian friends. You mustn't be scared of me. I am an unwilling participant. I am a conscript." He then turned back toward us and looked at me directly in the eye. "Please don't think me as one of them." As he spoke, his face looked pathetic and scared, and Anahid and I could say nothing to assuage him.

CHAPTER 21

The young soldier, Bahir, brought figs each night for the next few nights. He also brought fresh water on each night. Our mother was now to a point of debilitation that made her unable to swallow the water, and we could only place a few drops on her lips. Bahir was fully aware of our mother's grave condition and her inability to drink, yet he brought the water each night. On the third night, just as during the nights prior, Bahir approached us when there was almost complete darkness, except for the small light that he carried, and no one within range of our cell. As he handed me the figs and the water, I said to him, "You needn't bring any more water for my mother. She has not been able to drink much of what you brought her the night before, and it is wasting." Bahir had a pained expression on his face. He turned and sat on his stool, and said nothing in reply.

Anahid was in the corner of the cell placing the water on our mother's lips. I wished to tell Anahid to stop. That it was simply a waste. That placing the water on our mother's lips was just spoiling good water, and that Mother was going to die anyway. I continued to look at Anahid as she remained hunched over our mother.

Anahid poured the water in her hands, then placed it on our mother's lips, and repeated this several times until the water was almost gone from the cup and what she had placed on our mother's lips was now spilled on the floor of our cell. Anahid cried as she poured the last bit of water into her hands and onto our mother's lips. I walked to Anahid and knelt beside her. Between her sobs, Anahid said, "I still can't get Mother to drink."

I looked at our mother, her face wet with the water, then replied to Anahid. "Bahir will bring some water for Mother again tomorrow. Perhaps she will feel better tomorrow and be able to drink a little bit." I continued to kneel beside Anahid for several moments longer.

As she continued to collect herself, she said, "Perhaps tomorrow when Bahir brings the water, you can help me lift Mother's head up so she has a better chance of swallowing."

"Yes, Anahid," I replied. "We will lift Mother's head up tomorrow. She may be able to drink the water then." Anahid then lay down by our mother. I walked to the front of the cell. Bahir was still sitting on his stool. I pressed my face against the bars of the cell and whispered, "Bahir, I was wrong. Our mother was able to drink the water." Bahir turned and, with a slight smile on his face, replied, "I will try to bring an extra amount tomorrow."

It was silent for over an hour, and Anahid had fallen asleep. The predominate fear that I had continued to be not of our mother dying but of what would become of her body. Bahir had just returned to the stool by our cell. I was apprehensive about raising the matter with Bahir but felt that I could trust him enough that perhaps I could enlist his assistance. "Bahir, can I ask you a question?"

"What is it?" Bahir replied.

"If our mother dies, can you make sure that they do not take her body and throw it on the heap outside?" I whispered.

Bahir looked straight ahead as I spoke, and the length of silence made me uneasy. As the seconds passed and my unease began to grow to regret that I had even spoken to him about the matter, Bahir stood from his stool, approached me, and in a faint whisper replied, "Yes, I will help. I will see to it."

CHAPTER 22

Early the next morning, the fat gendarme shouted obscenities as he walked past the cells. Bahir walked to the side
and just behind the fat gendarme. Bahir was expressionless, and as he walked past our cell he gave no hint or gesture of
familiarity. It was reasonable to assume that Bahir had to play the
part he was given, and no sense of familiarity was expected.

"Come here," our mother whispered to me with her eyes
just slightly opened and fixed upon me. Her eyes were glazed,
and her face remained expressionless as she began to speak. It
was the first our mother spoke in some time, and I quickly rose
and walked toward her. "Can you tell me why we are here?" our
mother asked. I was confused by our mother's question, because
I wasn't prepared for what it meant.

I searched for something to say and replied, "We were taken
here to this camp...this prison camp, after they found us." She
continued to look at me with an empty gaze. I then asked, "Do you
remember that, Mother? Do you remember that they brought us
here, after we were found in Evren's carriage?"

She closed her eyes briefly, then reopened them as she
appeared to be summoning some energy, then replied faintly,

"No, I can't. I can't remember anything." She then closed her eyes. I feared that they would not open again, and I did not want to let her go without saying something to her.

Reflexively, I asked, "Do you remember me...me, Aran?" I waited for some response from her. After a bit of time I repeated, "Do you remember me, Mother?" As I spoke, the words seemed strange and unnatural. Her eyes remained closed, and she said nothing. She appeared to remain awake just long enough to make it clear that we had been pulled apart, severed from each other, and that there was no hope of any reconstitution. I sat for several moments staring at her and realizing that she was utterly transformed from the person that I knew. Her face was unfamiliar, with deep hollows where her cheeks had been and empty black circles by her eyes. Our mother, I believed, finally let go of me then, and I felt empty and abandoned.

She died late that afternoon. I knew that she was dead because I began to train myself to watch the rise and fall of her chest as she attempted to draw a breath in and struggle to exhale it. Her chest was still and her mouth and eyes were open, which made me think that she died trying to force another breath in. I hid the fact of our mother's death from Anahid until night by placing all of the blankets that we had on our mother and telling Anahid that our mother was cold and asked that I place blankets on her to keep her warm. I struggled with what to tell Anahid and when to tell her. I determined to tell her that evening, so that we could make plans to tell Bahir and take care of our mother's body before the fat gendarme learned of it.

Just prior to dark, I sat next to Anahid, who was partially asleep, and said to her, "Anahid, Mother has died." Anahid lifted her head and, without saying a word, began to weep. I then continued, "When Bahir comes, I will ask him to take Mother away. Bahir promised that he would take Mother so that she is not thrown on the heap." Anahid then crawled to our mother and curled up beside her until Bahir came.

At his usual time, Bahir came and sat on the stool outside of our cell. I stood and walked toward the cell door and said as quietly as I could, "Bahir, are you alone?"

"Yes, I am," he replied.

"There is something that I need to tell you."

"What is it?" he replied.

"Our mother is dead," I said.

Bahir turned to me and nodded his head. He reached toward the lantern that hung outside of our cell door, removed it from its hook, then walked down the corridor. He returned approximately fifteen minutes later with a cart and a blanket. He set the cart down, and as he did, both Anahid and I stood by the cell door. "I will take your mother."

"Where will you take her?" Anahid asked.

"There is a hillside only a few kilometers away from here. I have already located a place to bury her. It is a safe place that nobody will find. I have it all arranged." Bahir then looked around him as he unlocked the cell door and walked in. He knelt down where our mother was and picked her up. He picked her up awkwardly, and her head fell back over Bahir's arm. Bahir stopped and repositioned her head on his forearm and carried her to his cart. He placed her in the cart, and I was struck at how gently Bahir lowered her into it and covered her with a blanket. He then closed the cell door behind him and wheeled our mother away. Anahid retreated to the corner of our cell, where she wept for several minutes.

I sat beside her in the dark and offered what conversation I could in an attempt to console her. "Anahid, do you know that Mother woke earlier today to tell me something?"

"What did she say?" Anahid asked.

"She said that she was feeling very sleepy but was not in any discomfort and that she had just woken from a dream," I replied.

"Did she tell you what she was dreaming of?" Anahid asked.

I paused for some time to collect some thoughts then I replied, "She said that she was dreaming that you were playing your violin and that it made her very happy."

"Did she say what music I was playing in her dreams, Aran?" Anahid asked. I stared at the floor for a time, trying to arrive at a proper answer, and as I did, Anahid pressed, "Did she, Aran? Did she say what music I was playing?"

"No, Anahid, she didn't say, but it makes no difference, does it?"

"I suppose not, Aran," Anahid replied, "but I wish she would have told you anyway."

CHAPTER 23

Anahid and I fell asleep while we waited for Bahir to return. I awoke from the light of his lamp. "Bahir, did you bury my mother?" I whispered to Bahir, who was sitting on his stool.

"Yes," Bahir replied.

It occurred to me that there would be no practical way to find where our mother was buried, and I decided not to ask Bahir any particular details about the location. It was enough that she was buried, and in a place that nobody could find. I did, though, wish to know where we were, if for no other reason than to know that she was somewhere with a name.

Bahir remained sitting on the stool and silent, with his head looking straight at the ground.

"Bahir, where are we?" I asked.

"What do you mean?" Bahir replied.

"I mean, what town are we in? I was never told."

"We are still in Constantinople, Aran. We are in a village on the outskirts, but we are still within the city," Bahir replied.

I had hoped we had left the city and perhaps arrived at some town with another name and another history, but we hadn't.

When we first arrived at the prison, I still believed that we had a chance to return home and our lives would return to the way it was before. It made no difference now. It was all being smashed to bits anyway, and there would be no means of recognizing anything.

"What will happen?" I asked. Bahir didn't respond at first, and I repeated myself, but this time with more specificity. "What will they do with us, now that our mother has died?"

"You can't stay here. Everyone here is meant to die, whether here or someplace else. Children like you who have mothers and fathers that are dead are taken away. If a child is young enough and doesn't remember anything, an orphanage is usually the place. But you and Anahid are too old, and you have memories. Having a memory is dangerous," Bahir replied. I thought it odd that Bahir was speaking with a broad assumption, that our father was dead, without ever hearing it from me or from anyone else to my knowledge, and it prompted me to inquire.

"Bahir, who says that anything became of my father? He might just be alive for all anyone knows."

Bahir looked at me with a pained expression on his face, and after a short pause replied, "I know what happened, Aran. It is in your papers." I felt embarrassed that I tried to lie to Bahir, and Bahir knew it. As Bahir finished speaking, I became alarmed. Bahir didn't know that Anahid was unaware that my father was killed, and I didn't want Anahid to find out, at least not now, and not from Bahir.

"Bahir, Anahid doesn't know. Anahid thinks that my father is still alive. My mother told me not to tell her. Please don't let Anahid find out."

Bahir sensed my alarm and replied, "I won't say anything, Aran. You have my word."

I was scared at what was to become of us and needed for Bahir to tell me more. "What will they do to us?" I asked. Bahir turned and walked toward his stool and seemed at first not willing to provide any further details. "Bahir, please tell me. What will they do to us?"

Perhaps he knew that not knowing would be more torment to me. Bahir turned and looked at Anahid, who was still sleeping. He then motioned for me to draw nearer to the cell bars, and in a faint whisper continued, "Older boys, depending on age, are conscripted in many cases, and sent to the front or put in camps. Everyone is slaughtered at the front, and the camps are made for dying." Bahir stopped speaking and looked down the corridor to ensure that nobody was overhearing him, no matter how soft he was whispering. Bahir then continued, "They planned it this way. That is what they told us when I was conscripted. That we are to do our part to kill the Armenians. That the Armenians are the enemy and that we are to kill them and show them no mercy. You must understand that they intend to try to kill you one way or the other, particularly if they find that you have secrets to tell. Because of that, nobody must know about what became of your parents. You must pretend that nothing happened to them. It will give you a better chance."

I couldn't let the conversation end there. "Where will they try to take Anahid?" I asked. Bahir sat back on his stool and placed his hands across his face.

"Bahir, tell me. What will they do to Anahid?" Bahir removed his hands from his face and looked at me, and his expression grew more strained and troubled.

"It is unspeakable. There is no need to talk about it now. I am trying to arrange a way for you to get to the desert," Bahir replied.

As a child, I had very little understanding about the desert. It was, I knew, a place that bordered the Ottoman Empire, but it was not a place that anyone traveled to, or for that matter, traveled from, not even for trade purposes. It was simply a barren place, where the Empire ended and nothingness began. The thought of being sent into the desert scared me. The feeling of oblivion, the simple state of nothingness, scared me the most. It was what I imagined death to be: an empty place with no beginning and no end, a state of suspension where one is forced to exist without actually being. It was the thing of nightmares, where one is shaken awake in freefall into nothingness. The fall would last forever in a place like that, unless one could shake himself awake and gather his senses, before oblivion envelops him and doesn't let him out. Bahir was beginning to walk away from the cell, and I caught him before he left.

"Why would we want to go to the desert?" I asked.

"There is a caravan of Armenians there that can be joined for passage out of the Empire. It is extremely dangerous there, but it is your best chance to survive, provided you understand what you must do. I have been trying to make arrangements. I will tell you more tomorrow. In the meantime, keep some blankets in a bundle to make it appear that your mother is still here and that she is sleeping."

Bahir didn't offer anything more, and I don't believe I was capable of completely understanding the breadth of our circumstances, so I let the conversation end there.

It was premature to discuss with Anahid what was to become of us, and I had determined to tell her nothing of what Bahir told me. Anahid and I both observed over the past several weeks spent in the prison camp that children were being sent off daily. They all appeared to have in common the absence of any parents. Some simply circulated through, already apparently alone. Others, like us, who arrived with a parent, were placed in cells then later sent off when their parent disappeared or died. Most would file past us on their way out, and they seemed too gaunt to survive a passage of any distance. I believe that I began to sense at some level that we would eventually be killed in one manner or the other, but, I think, Bahir telling me of the extreme and apparently imminent danger that we were in was the first moment that I formally faced the issue of my own survival and Anahid's. We were both in poor condition, and any objective assessment would lead to the obvious conclusion that we were in threat of dying. As a child, though, to this point I had an innate sense of immortality and a sense that the certainty of our survival was predetermined. This sense was beginning to erode, but I determined that nothing could be said to Anahid that would take from anything that she still had. I would not betray our mother.

I bundled some blankets before dawn to make it appear as though our mother were sleeping beneath them, just as Bahir instructed. The gendarmes came and went past our cell in the morning and looked past us, without any apparent knowledge of our mother's death. There were more Armenians brought to the prison that day. They were still clean and well fed, probably taken from their homes the prior night. A long line of them was marched past our cell by the fat gendarme. Many of them looked at me. I sensed that they were scared at what they saw. I felt like an animal in a cage. I tried to look beyond them, and I must have looked hollow and detached. I worried that the fat gendarme might put some of them in our cell, but he didn't. They were just marched past us. I think maybe the fat gendarme wanted to show them what was to become of them, too. Perhaps they thought that I was too far gone to have noticed them, but I saw each one of them.

There was still the matter of what to tell Anahid. We talked very little during the night, and to this point in the morning she remained curled up in the corner of the cell. I decided not to tell Anahid anything about the desert and hoped that Bahir could explain more later. Anahid would only ask questions to which I had no answers, and I was too exhausted to be able to give her any comfort.

There was very little to do but wait. I placed some damp dirt from the floor in my hand and rubbed it until it pulverized to a paste, and I thought it interesting that the dirt had more to drink than the humans left to rot upon it. This was the plan. Reduce us all to less than dirt. Pulverize us, so that we become unrecognizable. This was something that I should have known but couldn't yet fully grasp.

Bahir paced in front of our cell intermittently throughout the entire day and seemed nervous. His eyes shifted quickly to our cell, then forward again, and I sensed that he was worried that the gendarmes would find us out and send us off before he could intercede. Night came slowly, but it came. The corridor emptied of all of the gendarmes, and Bahir resumed his position outside our cell. Anahid remained where she had been the entire day, alternating between resting against the back wall of the cell and lying supine pressed against it, as she was now. Bahir waited approximately a half hour to begin any conversation, and he looked about in the same nervous manner as he did earlier in the day. When it appeared that the corridor was fully clear, Bahir motioned to me to come nearer to him.

"You will need to leave here tonight," Bahir began in a whisper. "I have a friend who works in the detail responsible for deportations. Your best chance is to escape beyond the borderlands with the caravan of Armenians there. You will be placed on a train tonight. Don't ask any questions. Tell Anahid, and gather your things."

I did not expect the abruptness of our departure. I was only prepared for Bahir to give me more information about the plans for our escape, and I expected to have a chance to speak to Anahid and prepare our minds for it. My legs began to tremble, and I didn't have any confidence that I could even make my way to the back of the cell to speak to Anahid, any more than I could walk with a caravan across the desert.

I walked to the back of the cell where Anahid was sleeping and sat beside her. I pushed against her shoulder with the tips of my fingers to nudge her awake, and as I did, she turned to me and opened her eyes. "What is it, Aran?" Anahid asked.

"Bahir has told me that he has arranged for us to leave here tonight," I replied.

"Tonight?" Anahid replied as she sat up. "Where are they taking us?"

"We are going on a train. There is a caravan in the desert that we will join that will take us out of the country, where we will be safe."

"What about Father?" Anahid asked. "How are we to find Father?"

As soon as Anahid's words hit me, I felt panic. I did not anticipate that she would immediately raise the subject, and I now struggled for a response that would satisfy Anahid but would not betray our mother. Anahid's face had an alarmed expression. My anxiety was heightening, and I hoped that I would not reflexively spill the truth to her. "We can perhaps find him when we reach the caravan," I said. As I heard the words leave me, I felt the dishonesty in them, but was, nevertheless, relieved that my response was plausible under the circumstances.

"Could we, Aran? Do you think that we may find him there?" Anahid replied.

"Yes, Anahid, we will find Father."

Bahir motioned to me to approach him, and I stood and walked to him.

"He will be here shortly," Bahir said. "Quickly collect your items, so that you are ready when he comes."

Anahid and I collected our items and placed them in the trunk. We dressed in the same clothes that we had on when we left our home in Constantinople. We then waited to be taken.

CHAPTER 24

Bahir's conscript friend arrived. He was a very tall man. His face was boyish. He looked tentative and anxious. His boots were shiny, and his uniform looked like it had just been pressed. He spoke in whispers with Bahir for a few moments. Bahir opened our cell door and walked inside, while his friend remained outside the cell. Bahir knelt on the floor of our cell and took from his coat pockets two leather flasks and some bread. "Place these with your items. Only take small sips a few times a day with a few crumbs. Food and water will be hard to find. My friend will tell you everything that you need to know. Listen to what he tells you and do what he says." Bahir spoke to us firmly, and as he spoke, he looked into our eyes. When he finished speaking, he remained staring in our eyes, waiting, I think, for some assurance that we heard what he said. Anahid and I nodded our heads, and when we did, Bahir stood. With his head down and no longer making eye contact with us, he said, "Please forgive me. This is the only way. I have been told that this is the only way." Bahir spoke in a tone that made me feel condemned. I was taught that forgiveness is only asked when the soul demands it, and it is not to be requested lightly or asked on behalf of others. It is, rather, to be considered the last resort to avoid a self-imposed damnation for those with a conscience. This wasn't a matter between the wrongdoer and God. It was between the wrongdoer and his conscience, but Bahir did nothing wrong. He had no reason to ask for forgiveness. I didn't think to question Bahir. My trust in him was not a blind faith, nor do I believe I was naive. My trust was warranted by what he offered on his own accord, and at substantial personal risk.

Bahir stood with his head down for several moments, and I thought to thank him and to tell him not to ask for forgiveness, but I remained silent. We walked with Bahir's friend out of the door of the prison at the far end of the corridor. Bahir remained inside to resume his watch.

There was a foul, acrid smell outside the prison. I suspected the odor was the dead bodies decomposing on the heap in the back of the prison, but the sources were, I am sure, of multiple origins. Where we walked was a narrow alleyway. This alleyway was flanked on one side by the stone wall of the prison and on the other by a brick revetment that formed the outer boundary of a secured yard of some sort. The ground we walked upon was mud, and my boots stuck to it. On the brick revetment were several rusty oil lamps that smelled of their burnt fuel and provided a smoky light, enough to make out the end of the alley.

"My name is Jemal," the conscript said while looking down at Anahid and me as we walked immediately in front of him. "You do not need to fear me. Bahir is my friend, and I will make certain that you are placed upon the train and that no one will bother you," he continued in a soft voice.

We reached the end of the alley, where a large iron gate hung on the revetment wall and latched to the facing prison wall. Jemal took a set of keys from his pocket, which were hooked through a round black leather strap. He plucked from the set a rather long key. It was comprised of a simple long shaft with only a small knob at its end, and it struck me as so simple in design as to not even constitute a key. There was no complexity in it, and, thus, no mystery in the inner workings of the lock that it was fashioned to open. Jemal placed the key in the lock and slightly rattled the key as he turned it. The lock clicked open, and Jemal swung the gate outward. He motioned with his hand for Anahid and me to walk through. The area here was a square yard. It appeared to be a place of heavy foot travel, as what little grass remained was sparse and scarred. There was nobody in the yard, except for a couple of conscripts standing at its edge where the yard met a road. The oil lamps on the revetment provided only a little indirect light in this area, and the yard was otherwise unlit, with visibility of only approximately ten meters or so.

"We will wait for a few minutes. A wagon will be by to take us to the train," Jemal said. Anahid and I stood silently beside Jemal. I held Anahid's hand as we waited. Her hands had become so thin that it felt that I was holding brittle sticks. Her hand was shaking in my hand, and I attempted to think of something to whisper to her to calm her, but couldn't. I simply squeezed her hand tightly so that she knew that I wouldn't let her get away.

I heard the horses pulling a wagon from about fifty meters. "We must walk toward the road," Jemal said. We stood in the road, and as the wagon came nearer, Jemal raised his hand toward the wagon and the horses began to slow, then stop in the street in front of the prison yard. There were several children in the wagon. Each sat with their legs crossed and stared at Anahid and me as we were placed in the wagon. Jemal boarded, and the wagon began to move.

It was approximately two hours of travel to the train. When we arrived, we were left to stand upon the wooden platform aside an enormous cargo car. It was dark with little artificial light, and all I could see was the train car to our side and mildew-stained wood beneath my feet. The platform was crowded with children. The children were of various ages. Everyone appeared substantially better nourished than Anahid and me. Most appeared as we did when we were found in Evren's carriage and marched to the prison. Some children were laughing and playing as if they were preparing to depart on a holiday trip. Lines were beginning to form in several rows along the full length and width of the platform. Anahid and I stood in a small cleared space. We appeared to be among the last to arrive. Jemal stood next to

Anahid and me. Anahid and I were among the oldest children here. Some were infants being held by an older brother or sister. Most appeared no older than six to seven years old. Several soldiers walked among us and made their way to the end of the platform. "Form a line," a soldier ordered. As he did, the other soldiers motioned, and the mass shaped itself so that all within it faced the soldiers. We stood somewhat in the middle of the mass. "Stay silent and do as I tell you," Jemal said to Anahid and me. "I will handle matters with the soldiers." We left matters to Jemal and said nothing as we moved near the front of the line. All were asked the same question.

"Do you remember your mother or your father? Do you, boy? Do you remember?" a soldier barked in Turkish to a young boy of probably no more than three years old, as the boy took his turn in the front of the line. The boy didn't respond. Another soldier took the boy swiftly by the arm and led him to a group being readied to board the train. Succeeding children approached the front of the line. Each was asked the same question and was, depending on the answer, placed in separate groups on the platform. It became the turn of a boy of approximately eight years old, who held in his arms a girl of no more than two years. I assumed that she was his sister. The soldier looked at the young girl and asked, "Do you remember your mother or father?" The girl said nothing in response and was taken from the boy's arms and placed in the group boarding the train. The soldier then looked at the boy. "Do you remember your mother and father?" The boy had a bewildered expression on his face and replied, "Yes, sir." The soldier looked down at some papers, then motioned to another soldier who walked forward, grabbed the boy, and walked him several meters away and placed him in a large group, which was kept at that distance and not permitted to board the train. I thought then can a memory, or a lack of one, determine one's fate that simply and quickly? There were two lots cast for the children on the platform: those with memories and those without. The latter were to be given a place on the train and an apparent chance to wander in the desert in search of salvation. Jemal's papers apparently were meant to disguise our lot. Despite Jemal's assurances, I shook with nerves.

We were now in the front of the line. Jemal stood immediately in front of us. His back blocked us almost entirely from the soldier. Jemal began speaking to the soldier, and as he did, Jemal handed him papers. "I am on the deportation detail and was asked to bring these children. I am ordered to place them on the train for transfer." The soldier looked at Jemal, then he peered around Jemal and looked at me and Anahid. I began to panic that he was about to ask us if we remembered our parents, just as he asked the other children, and that we would share the fate of those with memories. The soldier looked again at the papers, then handed them to Jemal and pointed his finger toward the open door of the cargo car. There was nothing more to it than that. Jemal walked us to the train, and as he helped us board, he whispered instructions. "When they let you off the train, there will be a large camp nearby. Don't walk to the camp, or any camp. If you go, you will die there. If you find yourself at the camp, you must escape. You must reach the caravan, and once you reach it, stay within it. The caravan will eventually lead you out. Just walk toward the sun each morning. Keep to this path. It will take you east and deeper into the desert, but away from the camps, and in the path of the caravans leading out. You will eventually find the caravan. The caravan will be your best chance. Do you understand?" Anahid and I nodded our heads. Jemal left without saying anything more and disappeared into the dark beyond the far side of the platform.

The train was crowded and had no source of light. Anahid and I sat pressed closely together against the steel wall of the car. The train remained mostly silent, except for the sound of footsteps hitting the steel floor of the car as people boarded, and the occasional cries of a child, following by the hushes of others trying to quiet them.

As the train began to move, the loud grinding sound of the wheels against the tracks filled the car, and the steel walls of the car vibrated against our backs. Anahid grabbed my hand and asked, "Aran, do you know where we are going?"

"Yes, Anahid," I replied. "We are going to the desert."

"I know we are going to the desert, Aran, but that's not what I am asking you."

"Then what are you asking, Anahid?"

"I suppose I don't know. I just wondered if the place we are going to has a name," Anahid replied.

CHAPTER 25

The train stopped after nearly a full day and a half of travel. It was in the morning when the train stopped. Anahid and I, among others, were ordered to leave the train. Only the youngest on the train were not ordered out. We were placed upon a large wagon, among several wagons, each of which had ten or so children aboard. We were driven for several kilometers into the desert. We stepped off the wagon there and into the burning sand. The wagons all left but one, which remained with a soldier aboard. There was a large tent less than a kilometer in the distance. Except for the tent, it was almost an entirely barren desert landscape for as far as I could see, with nothing more than sandy hillsides and sparse vegetation.

The others that were let off the wagon with us at first huddled among a patch of fruitless sumac trees. Some began to walk toward the camp. The soldier climbed down from the remaining wagon. "Walk to the camp," he yelled in the general direction of those huddled by the tree. "To the camp." Those who were standing by the sumac trees began to walk toward the camp, as ordered. Anahid and I didn't move.

"Is he speaking to us?" Anahid asked.

"I'm not sure. Let's just remain here. Perhaps he will leave us," I replied. I hoped the soldier wouldn't pay us any attention, but he continued to approach, now at a distance of no more than twenty meters.

He looked at Anahid and me directly and yelled, "Walk to the camp. You must walk to the camp."

"He's speaking to us, isn't he?" Anahid asked.

"Yes, I think he is," I replied.

"But we are not supposed to go to the camp. Jemal told us not to go to the camp," Anahid said.

"Yes, I know, but we may have no choice," I replied

The soldier continued to approach, and he appeared agitated. "Did you not hear me?" the soldier yelled. The others were making their way toward the camp, and Anahid and I were now completely isolated. I felt entirely vulnerable to anything the soldier might do, and it struck me that it would have seemed perhaps easier for him to have just shot us.

I grabbed Anahid's hand. "He is angry, Anahid. We must do as he says. He may try to do something to us if we don't." Anahid and I began to walk quickly toward the camp, fearful that if we didn't do as the soldier said, we would be shot right there. The soldier curled behind us and marched us to the camp. We were given no choice in the matter, and we did what we were told.

The first sight upon entering the tent was children who were approximately my age, looking like the dead people that the fat gendarme threw upon the heap. There were some adults among them. They were all still alive, though barely. They sat on the sand with their legs crossed and their elbows resting on their knees. They appeared at first to be holding sticks in their hands, but the sticks were their limbs. We stood at the edge of the entry into the tent. The soldier that marched us to the tent walked back to the wagon and left. A couple of other soldiers roamed around the periphery of the inner part of the tent. They appeared not to notice that we had arrived, until one of them walked nearer to us and pointed to the ground and yelled, "Sit!" That is all that he said before he turned his back and walked back toward the far end of the tent.

Anahid and I sat in the sand. We sat apart from those who had apparently been at the camp for some time. I knew from the prison that it would not be long before they would be dead. I assumed that there was a heap behind the tent that they would probably be thrown on.

The soldiers remained a substantial distance from us and intermittently walked in and out of the tent through the slices in the tent's canvas walls. The appearance of the tent was strangely antiseptic. The tent was nearly the same shade as the sand. This did not have the feel of a prison, but I had no idea of what it was or why we were placed here. I did know that this was not in the plan that Bahir and Jemal prescribed. We were to find the caravan and not go to any camp. I did not blame Bahir, as he would have no way of accounting for the stubborn soldier. If it weren't for the soldier, Anahid and I would have been free and on our way to join the caravan.

"We shouldn't be here," Anahid whispered to me.

"I know, Anahid," I replied.

"What shall we do?" Anahid asked.

"I haven't any idea at the moment, Anahid," I whispered. "But I know we must find a way to leave."

We sat silently for a couple of hours with nothing given to us to eat or drink. I counted only three soldiers in the camp. Whether there were more outside the camp who had not entered the tent, I could not determine, but it only appeared that there were three in total. The soldiers said nothing for the first couple of hours. Evening was approaching. A soldier walked to the front of the tent where we had entered. He was not more than twenty years old. His uniform was tattered and soaked in sweat.

"You are in a deportation camp. Soon you will be taken from here. You will not be permitted to leave until then. You will be told when you are to be taken," he instructed in an emotionless, rote manner. I did not believe a word he said because of what Jemal told me and because there were people just meters from me that were rotting to death with apparently nothing to eat or drink for many days. The soldier turned and walked out of the tent with the other soldiers.

Darkness came. Anahid and I found an area at the edge of the tent where we could rest some distance away from the others. We nestled closely to each other. It remained quiet. There was no conversation among anyone, except a few indecipherable whispers that we heard from time to time.

"I am hungry and thirsty," Anahid whispered.

"Take a few sips and a few crumbs from what Bahir gave us," I whispered. I reached a flask and gave it to Anahid and heard her softly sip the water.

"Only take a little, Anahid. We will need it for later," I said. Anahid was very frail, and she needed to eat and drink, but we had nothing to sustain us beyond the amount Bahir gave us, so we were forced to conserve if we were to make our escape and reach the caravan.

"How are we to leave here?" Anahid whispered.

"There may be no soldiers. Perhaps we will be able to just walk out. We will wait until morning to see," I said. The soldiers had not returned to the tent, and I wondered if they had left for good. It was too dark to determine now.

"How will we find the caravan, even if we are able to escape from here?" Anahid whispered.

"We will just walk toward the sun as Jemal told us," I replied.

"How do we know that Jemal was telling us the truth?" Anahid asked.

"Because he is Bahir's friend, and Bahir wouldn't have his friend lie to us," I replied.

"How do you know that?" Anahid asked.

"I suppose I don't, Anahid, but we have no choice. We can't stay here. Do you want to be left to die, like the people in this tent?"

Anahid and I then closed our eyes and tried to sleep.

I stayed awake for a time, despite trying to force myself to sleep. I was preoccupied with the thought of Anahid dying. I had no specific fear that her death was imminent. My fear was that her death was inevitable. She was beginning to labor to breathe, and her chest sounded congested with fluid. My last thought before I finally fell asleep was that I might die, too. I began to think that it might be a way to a place better than here and perhaps a place that we should seek to find.

CHAPTER 26

I was in the middle of sleep when Anahid tapped me on the shoulder. I was glad that she did, because the sleep was of no use. It was such a light state of sleep that it was not enough to give me any rest, while subjecting me to an assortment of nightmares, none of any particular form, just a dull sense of fear and imminent assault. These feelings were indistinguishable from my waking state, other than their acuteness and the sense that they could not be controlled.

"Why did they kill Professor Daigneau and Evren?" Anahid asked. Anahid was pressed up against my back, and when she spoke, her words were muffled but just audible enough to hear. Since that night, Anahid and I hadn't spoken a word about what happened to Evren and Professor Daigneau, but we were both certain of what became of them, and it consumed me from time to time.

"I don't know why, but I think it was because they tried to help us," I replied.

"That shouldn't have been a reason, Aran. I feel guilty because of it."

"You mustn't feel guilty. It was no fault of ours," I replied.

"Perhaps it was, though, Aran. We could have tried to escape alone. There was no reason for them to come with us."

"That wasn't the reason they were killed, Anahid."

"Then what was it, Aran? What was the reason?"

"Because they didn't do what the officer said," I replied.

"Why is that a reason, Aran?"

"It's not a reason, I suppose."

"I am afraid that if they catch us trying to escape, they will kill us, too. Mother told us to do what the officers tell us. They told us that we couldn't leave here," Anahid said.

"I think that she would tell us now to try to escape, if she could."

"Well, she can't tell us anything now, Aran. She told us to do what the officers tell us to do, unless they try to separate us. They haven't tried to separate us. They have kept us together the entire time, Aran."

I wished to tell Anahid that I feared that we were about to be separated, that she was about to be sent off away from me. I imagined it to be a place with no beginning and no end, and once there, she could never return. I wondered if she knew it, too, that we were about to be separated, perhaps not tomorrow, but soon and inevitably. I turned over and faced Anahid. She was not more than six inches from me, but I could not so much as see the outline of her face. The darkness shrouded everything.

"We just need to find the caravan. That is what we were told we needed to do. Nothing else matters now than that, Anahid."

"But what if they catch us?" Anahid replied.

"Then I will fight them, just like I promised Mother," I replied.

Anahid was losing her breath, and she didn't say anything more. The tent flapped all night. The wind seemed to catch it from the roof first and pressed upon it until the roof crushed to the edges of its cloth gables, then popped up to regain its original shape. This action repeated itself countless times throughout the night. Each time the action caused a sound, which upon repetition linked the notes into a measure. It taunted me and served to induce a particular nightmare during which my body felt the pressure of being crushed. The nightmare built on itself the entire night, as if a single stone were dropped upon my back, then one by one additional stones were piled, so that I could feel the crushing sensation as each stone fell. I woke the following morning with the sensation.

Anahid and I spent the entire next day huddled where we slept. I watched in an attempt to ascertain a pattern followed by the soldiers. A few arrived in the middle of the morning, then left and didn't return. The soldiers that came stepped in the tent, shot short glances at those strewn about, and quickly left. There was no other action in the camp. The batches of those arriving at the camp must have been intermittent, and our arrival the day before was the last. Most around us were almost dead. Their bodies were limp and dry, and they were turning into the desert. I noticed Anahid staring at a woman who had a young child beside her. Both had their eyes open but were not alert. I believe that they were both dead. The woman lay on her back, with her legs bent so that her knees were in front of her and in the air. She was nothing but bones. Her child was nestled in the crimp of her arm and also lay on her back. Both were covered partially by the same soiled white sheet.

"Do you think they are in heaven right now?" Anahid asked, still staring at the woman.

"I don't know, Anahid. Doesn't it take forty days to reach heaven?" I replied.

"Forty days is such a long time. Why do they say it takes forty days? Wouldn't it make more sense that you just instantly go to heaven when you die?" Anahid asked.

"I think the soul takes some time to reach there. Maybe you go to heaven right when you die, but it takes time for your soul to find you there," I said.

Anahid looked at me and smiled. "Was that a try at a joke, Aran?"

The smile on Anahid's face remained as she awaited my answer. I hadn't meant it as a joke. I believe I was just repeating what I was told as a child by our mother, probably in answer to the same question, but perhaps the tone of my voice made my answer sound as a joke, and it seemed to please Anahid.

"Yes, Anahid, it was a joke."

"I like jokes," Anahid replied.

As Anahid continued to stare at the woman, her smile disappeared, and her face turned serious.

"When are we leaving, Aran?"

"We are leaving tomorrow early in the morning, before the sun comes up," I replied.

"Wake me up then, when you think it is time," Anahid said.

CHAPTER 27

It was early in the following morning, about five o'clock or so. I saw no sign of any soldiers. The night prior, I dug a depression in the sand by the edge of the tent wall where I slept. This depression allowed me enough room to slip beneath the wall of the tent and look to the outside. I placed my head in the depression and looked out and saw only the vast expanse of desert to the point where the desert disappeared into the darkness beyond. There was a stand of grasses approximately ten meters away. I saw no soldiers anywhere from this vantage. My stomach churned, and I was beginning to have second thoughts. I was beginning to sober, and I was consumed by doubt. I couldn't fight a soldier. I couldn't fight anybody. The caravan was just a notion put into my head by Bahir and Jemal, and they hadn't even known of it firsthand. It was only a rumor and probably sheer myth spread by the fat gendarme and others just to induce another form of torture, sent to wander in search of something that doesn't even exist. We would be left chasing salvation, only to learn after the pursuit that it was all a lie. I knew that there was no other choice, though. However uncertain I was about the existence of the caravan, if we stayed in the camp, we would die.

I nudged Anahid, and whispered to her, "Anahid, wake up. We must leave now." Anahid's eyes opened, and she seemed prepared to leave before she was awake. She didn't speak or resist in any way.

"Anahid, crawl under here," I said, pointing to the depression that I had dug. Anahid rolled under the wall of the tent. I pushed out our trunk and crawled beneath the wall behind her. We remained on our stomachs for several moments as we looked across the entire area. There were no soldiers visible, at least from this side of the camp. From the outside, the camp looked like a desolate place, the people within it abandoned and condemned. The authorities must have assumed that once in, the inhabitants were entombed, and there was no apparent effort to stand guards to prevent an escape. The tent was a coffin, and the desert around it was the vault to keep the dead things within from creeping beyond.

We stood to a stoop and stumbled to the stand of grasses. From this vantage, we confirmed that there were no soldiers in sight. There still remained enough cover from the partial darkness that we felt secure enough that we could run without being detected, even if soldiers were stationed on the far side of the camp. We made our way out of the grasses. We then began to walk toward the sun, which only hinted to its place by casting a modest glow.

CHAPTER 28

Anahid and I walked the entire day, and there was nobody within our sight. Each step was becoming more difficult. The sand grabbed each step, and we did all that we could to tear away. We were at the base of yet another hillside. There was a feeling of monotony in this area, where the topography lent itself to almost constant variations in grade, and where, within a single day, ascent of a hillside, descent into a valley, and the ascent of the next hillside would repetitively follow the traverse of the prior valley. In that way, the landscape assaulted the body and the mind. The mind could not deceive the body here. The base of a hillside offered no hope that the apex, once reached, would reveal some vantage to view an exit. This hill was particularly steep. From its base, there was little more to view than its upper crest, an almost unearthly view where the face of the hill almost entirely blocked the sky with a brown empty sheet of sand. Just as we did on the hills before, we dug our feet into the sand and pushed again through the diaspora.

There was no sign of a caravan, not even a single footprint in the sand that would have given us any assurance that we were drawing nearer to it. We had no choice in the matter, anyway. We were beginning to grow weary, and as the day began to wane, I had determined that we were lost. The pit in my stomach reached my throat, and I wanted to cry. I couldn't let Anahid see me cry, though, so I fought my tears back and decided to pretend what was becoming clear in my mind wasn't true. I needed to delude myself to believe that we were not lost and that the caravan was near. The delusion was as much necessary for me as it was for Anahid, and I needed to discipline my mind to suspend myself in the belief.

We had removed our boots in the late afternoon, as the weight of them seemed to be slowing our progress and making each step more arduous, but the sand was beginning to burn our feet, so we decided to stop and put our boots back on.

"Do you think that we are going in the correct direction, Aran?" Anahid asked.

"Yes, the sun is behind us now. In the morning it will be in front of us, and we will walk toward it, just as Jemal told us," I replied.

"What will the caravan look like, when we find it?" Anahid asked.

"I picture it in my mind to be like an army marching but without any soldiers. Just with regular people walking," I replied.

"Do you think that we will find people that we know there, people from home?" Anahid asked.

"I don't much know, but I guess we will. There should be people from home."

"I will be so much less scared then, Aran, when we reach the caravan."

Anahid had managed to put one of her boots back on her foot, but it remained untied. Her other foot remained bare, and Anahid stopped and leaned her back against the sand. I sensed that she had no more strength to walk or even put on her other boot. It was nearing night, anyway, and pushing further, even if we could have managed it, would have resulted in limited progress before dark. Anahid's body shook as she tried to rest. Her eyes were closing, and I hoped that she would fall asleep so that her shaking would stop. I was becoming aware that Anahid was growing too weak. I began to think in earnest that she would die before we reached the caravan. She was developing a cough like our mother's, and Anahid was wasting away to little more than skin and bones. Anahid lifted the flask of water that Bahir had given us. Her hand trembled as she tried to take a sip from it. I put my hand under the flask to help steady it, and she swallowed a little water. If there was a caravan, our time to reach it was limited. I was beginning to feel that there was nothing I could do to keep Anahid from slipping away. I couldn't bring myself to tell Anahid what I felt, but I think that she knew what was happening.

Anahid shifted uncomfortably on the sand, trying to find a position to allow some ability to induce sleep. After some time, I thought of an old Armenian lullaby our father sang often when he put Anahid and me to bed. Anahid and I simply referred to it as the "go to sleep song". When our father sang it, he knelt beside our beds and moved close enough to ensure that we knew that he was there, even after his singing trailed off into soft whispers, then silence.

"Do you wish for me to sing the 'go to sleep song', Anahid?" I asked.

Anahid's eyes were closed and she didn't respond, but I determined to sing her the song anyway hoping it would give her something.

"Go to sleep, my dear, close your eyes,
Let sleep rest upon your pretty eyes… ", I began.

When I finished, Anahid sighed deeply then we both fell asleep.

CHAPTER 29

When I awoke the next morning, Anahid lay on her side on the base of the hill with her knees pressed against her stomach and her pack still attached to her back.

"Aran, I hurt very badly, and I am tired. Can we stay here for a while?" Anahid asked in a soft, exhausted voice. Although I was feeling weak, I had not entered the phase that Anahid had. It was urgent that we try to find the caravan, and I had awoken resolved that we would find the caravan today, even if I had to carry Anahid on my back. I am uncertain of the reasons for my determination, but I believe the delusion had taken effect, and I had now convinced myself enough that there was a caravan and we would find it.

"Yes, Anahid," I replied. "We can stay here for a while, then we will walk."

"I can't walk," Anahid replied.

"You will, Anahid. We must. We won't survive unless we reach the caravan," I shouted. Anahid's eyes were only slightly open, and she had no immediate reply. I took the flask of water and placed it to her lips. "Here, Anahid, sip a little water. You just need a little water." Anahid lifted her head a bit and took a few drops from the flask before water began to trickle from her lips and onto the sand. I was beginning to feel desperate, and I reached for any device that I could.

"Anahid, how will we ever find Father, if you don't drink?" I asked.

Anahid's eyes opened, and she stared at me for a few moments, then she took a deep breath to force as much air into her lungs as she could and asked, "Aran, do you really believe that we will find Father?"

"Yes, Anahid, I believe we will find him." Anahid raised her head a bit higher and took a few small sips from the flask, then rested her head back on the sand.

There was still the matter of the truth and whether Anahid should know it. I weighed some considerations in my mind. If Anahid died before I told her, I would forever consider myself an interminable liar. It was too selfish a thought. Selfish because my only motivation then in not telling the truth to Anahid was to make myself feel better. It was selfish, too, because who was I to keep the truth from Anahid? It wasn't for me to keep it from her, but what of hope? If hope of finding him was all that could sustain her, then by learning what became of him, she would lose everything that she had left.

I felt uneasy about lying to Anahid, but she needed the hope, if for no other reason than to push her until we reached the caravan. I would try to wait to tell her until then, I thought, just until we reached the caravan. At least then there would be a new source of hope that could replace what would be lost when she heard the truth. There really wasn't anything more to it than that.

"Will you leave me here, Aran?" Anahid asked, after we sat silently for several minutes. I was startled by Anahid's question.

"What do you mean, Anahid?" Anahid was laboring to speak, and she was trying to gulp enough breath and summon enough energy to force out her words.

"If I can't walk any further, will you leave me to reach the caravan?" Anahid asked.

"No, Anahid, I am not leaving you here. We will reach the caravan."

"But, you shouldn't think that way, Aran. If I can't walk, you should try to reach the caravan yourself and get help, then you can come find me." Anahid paused for some time to catch her breath then she continued. "It may only take you a little longer to reach the caravan alone. With me, even if I can walk, we will probably never reach it."

"That's nonsense, Anahid. I won't leave without you. Even if I did, I wouldn't know how to find you, and you would be lost. I would be lost, too. Wouldn't you be scared, Anahid?"

"I think it is the only way that we are going to get help, Aran. Someone there may know Father and be able to tell us how to find him. I so want to find Father that I would rather be scared but know that we have a chance of finding Father."

Anahid's not knowing what happened to our father was affecting matters immediately now. I knew that if I left Anahid, I would never find her again. I also knew that if I did find my way back to her with help from someone in the caravan, she would be dead when I returned. Why was I keeping our father's death from Anahid? I thought. I didn't want to become separated from Anahid, and I was overwhelmed.

"Anahid, Father is dead," I blurted. When the words left my mouth, I regretted saying them, but I had no control of the impulse. Anahid sat stunned for a moment, then with an incredulous expression, responded, "You are lying, Aran. You said that Father is alive and that we would find him."

I had no adequate response for Anahid. What was I to tell her? That our mother told me to lie to give her hope? I couldn't bring myself anyway to blame our mother. Our mother wasn't the liar. I was, but I was too much of a coward to admit it to Anahid, or even to myself.

"I never told you that Father was alive. I only told you that we would find him," I replied. My attempt to parse words was insincere and hollow, and there was no use in attempting any further. I was laid bare as the liar that I was, and I resigned myself to it.

I had ample opportunity before to tell Anahid the truth, and it would have made all of the difference now, I thought.

Anahid began to cry, and as she did, she summoned the energy to shout, "You lied to me, Aran. Why would we be searching all this time for someone who is dead?"

We remained at this same spot in the desert for the entire day. Anahid was too sick to move. She went through episodes of being awake, during which her eyes opened for a time, but only enough so that I could see an empty gaze, and she would not talk or drink. I was wrought with guilt for having lied to Anahid and thought that the reason she would not talk to me was that she was angry and was punishing me. I grabbed Anahid's hand and pleaded, "Anahid, I am sorry for lying to you about Father. Mother did not want you to know. I was trying to do what Mother asked me to do, so I lied to you, and I am sorry." Anahid looked at me with her empty gaze and remained silent. I feared that I was losing Anahid forever, and I would never get her back.

I tried to shake Anahid awake the next morning. Her body was cold. I placed my ear to her mouth to listen for her breath, but I could detect nothing. She remained in the same position as the night before, curled, with her knees to her chest. I decided to take the bundle off of her back, thinking, perhaps absurdly, that the weight of its contents was making it difficult for her to breathe. I tried to move her arm, but it was rigid and immobile. I sat beside her for the next several hours, hoping that my gut feelings were wrong, but they weren't. Anahid was dead. I believe that I had determined then that Anahid died not so much from lack of food and water, but from lack of hope, and I was responsible.

I looked at her for the entire rest of the day. I knew then that I lost her utterly, even as she remained in front of me. Her body was an empty vessel, and she was lost to me in an instant. I asked Anahid many times throughout the day if she would please tell me where she went, so that I could come, too. I didn't want to be left alone. I thought that it must have been difficult for her to die, but I envied her for having left.

Anahid was my final tether to everything that I knew and that I had. Her death severed the tether, and I felt myself beginning to float away into the nothingness that I feared the most: a place where nothing was familiar, nothing was true, and nothing was recognizable, including me. I looked toward the horizon and wondered if there was a way out. All I could see was the nothingness, a fine place to hide things but the worst of places to find anything. It was all intended that way. This was the perfect place to make everything disappear. Who would know that anything ever really existed here?

As the sun began to wane in the evening, I began digging Anahid's grave with my hands, just beside where her body lay. I tried my best to make her grave deep enough that it would fully conceal her. After I reached an adequate depth, I lifted her body, and she felt as light as a dry gourd. I placed her body in the hole and covered her with the sand. I was struck at how the dry sand made the perimeter of her grave vanish as soon as it was fully covered. There would be no way that anyone would ever find her, I thought, not even me.

I remained where I buried Anahid until the middle of the following morning. I did not want to leave Anahid alone. Our mother told me not to allow Anahid to get away from me, and I worried that I would betray our mother by leaving her. I knew that if I walked even several meters, I would lose the place that I buried her, and it troubled me. My stomach had a deep hollow feeling that reached to my throat, until I could not hold it in any longer, and I wept. I cried for our mother, our father, and for Anahid, but most for Anahid, I think. I lost my sense of immortality here. There was no such thing, I determined. Death was inevitable, and it comes sooner and quicker than anyone could ever imagine. There is no escape from it, and when it comes, it makes you vanish so utterly that there is no evidence that you ever existed. Dead and forgotten by everyone, except those closest to you, until they die, too, then there is no trace. Death ensures a complete erasure of everything that was. I realized it then. There was no use in harboring any belief to the contrary. In fact, it was not helpful for survival. The sooner one was aware that death could come at any time, particularly in the desert, the better chance of making it at least for another day. It was best to keep the guard up against death. Better to know the enemy and be aware that it is everywhere ready to snatch you and reduce you to dust.

I knew that I had to start walking. I started to fear that I would probably die as quickly as Anahid if I didn't reach the caravan soon, but I felt the pull to stay with Anahid, if for no other reason than not to lose sight of where I left her. I decided to take Anahid's loose boot to mark where I buried her. At the least, I thought, when I looked back I could see where she was, if only until I reached the top of the hill. I placed her boot above her and pushed it into the sand enough that the sole of it was covered. As I did, I told Anahid that I was sorry to leave her all alone in the desert then I began walking up the hill. I looked back once to make certain that I could see where I left her, until her boot disappeared from sight.

CHAPTER 30

Forty days to travel seemed a long time, an almost impossibly long time, even if permitted to float on a cloud. Does the soul eat and drink while it floats to heaven, and does it know where it is going, and how long it will take to reach it? Does it know that it may never reach it and that maybe it is destined for someplace else, only to find out the truth at the end of the journey? Why forty days? Anahid was right. It would make more sense to know instantly. It was too much time. Would the soul even recognize the body? Perhaps the soul could use a picture to remind itself of how the body once looked, when it had the soul inside. A picture could be important. A perfect image frozen in time of everything just as it was, and as it should be, before being torn apart. What an arbitrary number, as if chosen because it was not so obvious as a month's time, or a week's time. It perhaps was thought to cheapen the journey if it was anything less than forty days, so forty days it was, and has always been since. Forty days for what, indeed? Could it be forty days for salvation, or something else? Why endure the journey? Couldn't we know the truth without having to search for it? Why the great secret? My mind raced through undeveloped fragments of these thoughts as I walked.

Images of the caravan began to take better shape in my mind. There were no human figures or faces, just blocks of stone, like columns driven into the sand from one end of the desert to the other. The only way to survive this was to become a block of stone. This was no place for a flesh-and-blood human. Flesh and blood dries up and dies in the desert, but sand makes stone. I needed to become stone.

Within a day's walk of where I buried Anahid, I found my first evidence in a deep valley that there were people somewhere in the vicinity of where I was headed. The evidence was a cauldron that sat upon a stack of partially burnt logs. I had first noticed it at some distance. It was made of a cast iron, which as I grabbed the outer rim of it, felt heavy with rust. I looked inside of it, hoping to find a scrap of food that may have been left behind. I reached inside of it and grabbed what appeared to be a piece of meat floating by the rim. It was white and appeared to be blanched by boiling. I noticed the bones of it, and I realized it almost instantly. It was a severed hand. Whether male or female, I didn't know, but I was repulsed by the sight of it, and it made me vomit. I had never seen the pieces of a dead person before, just a body in the whole.

Seeing a piece of a corpse was like a found piece of an elaborate puzzle that was beginning to take shape in my mind, however subconsciously. Piece by piece, we were all being killed, whether we were in the desert, in some prison death camp, or a garden in Constantinople. The Ottoman government was just hastening the process. Rather than a slow, imperceptible dismemberment, I was beginning to realize that I was being torn apart. I could feel it and see it. I ran as fast as I could from the cauldron. My fear carried me for several kilometers, where I collapsed in a patch of dry grass at the apex of another hill. It was there that I saw toward the horizon a thin, dark line that had no beginning and no end.

CHAPTER 31

The caravan wasn't comprised of columns made of stone. It was comprised of anything but stone. That was clear to me when I first saw their faces. They were no different than the people I saw in the prison, and in the camp, and on the train platform. These were simply the people who survived to reach the next gauntlet. The caravan was what I first imagined it to be. It had no ascertainable beginning or end. It stretched as far as I could see. There were breaks in the line, sometimes at significant distance, but not so great to permit those immediately in front or behind to be lost from sight. Ensuring a constant view of those behind and those in front was the only security from being lost or exposed. In that way, it was like a military column. The back flank was only protected if there were members of the caravan behind.

After first seeing the line of the caravan, I walked the entire day and night to reach it, making up ground as some in the caravan stopped for sleep. In the first day of reaching it, I didn't have the courage to approach anything but the caravan's outer flanks, keeping only close enough to guide my way. I was not so much a member of the caravan. I was simply taking from it what I needed. Simply being guided was enough. Within a few days, I approached closer to take a bit of bread or water from anyone willing to offer a crumb or a sip. I wove myself in and out of the line as I did, mindful not to stay within an area for too long. I didn't wish to become vested. Most would simply hand me a small piece of bread without saying anything, and that was how I wished to leave it. Any more communication than that prompted me to simply grab what I could and run away.

I spotted a group ahead that seemed as probable as any to throw me a scrap. A short man was walking with a sack of grain on his shoulders. A small amount of the grain was spilling out from a hole in the corner of the sack. I sped up my pace and moved behind him. I positioned myself just in front of him so that he could see me.

"Who are you looking for, boy?" a female voice called from behind me just as I was approaching the man. I quickly looked back, my eyes now directly fixed to hers as I realized she was speaking to me. I remained walking and redirected my gaze straight ahead of me. I quickened my pace. "Boy, do you hear me? Who are you looking for?" she asked again. She was look-ing directly toward me. She knew that I was aware that she was speaking to me, and I could avoid her no longer. I had rehearsed the answer in my mind, anyway, and had been pre-pared for it.

"My mother, sister, and father are ahead of me. I became separated from them a few nights ago, but we are headed to the border, and they will know to find me there," I replied. It was best that I lied. I determined that it was as necessary for survival in the desert as food and water. I did not want to be a conscript. I now knew what conscription meant, at least for a little Armenian boy with no parents. It was just another way to be exterminated, with an acceptable pretense, of course. I feared that if anyone knew that I was alone and that my parents were dead, I would be reported to the authorities or taken to a camp to die, and Bahir couldn't protect me now. I would appear certain of the direction I was going and who I would find when I reached there. This is what I would tell everyone, and I would make them believe it so that I wouldn't be sent to die.

"You are welcome to walk with us. We are going to the border, too, and my father tells me we are getting quite close to it," she said. I stopped, at first hesitant, but I believed I succumbed to being scared, alone, and hungry. She appeared to be better fed than I was, whether that was because she more recently came into the desert or had a stockpile of food, I did not know, but my instincts must have decided for me. I nodded my head and walked beside her.

"What is your name?" she asked.

"My name is Aran Pirian," I replied.

"And how old are you, Aran?" she asked.

"I am twelve years old," I replied.

"My name is Emma... Emma Kazarian, and that is my younger sister, Grace," she said, pointing approximately five meters ahead, where her sister was walking with her arms clutching a plain white linen that she had wrapped around her shoulders and that she appeared to be using for some cover from the burning desert sun. Emma appeared to be in her late teens. Grace was approximately my age. Emma, like her sister, had dark brown hair and skin of a moderate olive complexion. Emma had a gentle face, which expressed an interest and affability to which I had become unaccustomed. "That is my father, Keran," she said, pointing to the short, stocky man who was carrying the sack of grain. She then pointed to a woman who was walking beside her father and said, "And that is my mother, Sara."

"Mother," Emma called, as she cupped her hand by her mouth to project her voice. Emma's mother raised her head and looked toward Emma, her face expressionless. "This is Aran. He was separated from his family a few nights ago. He is going to cross the border, too, and intends to find them there." Emma's mother turned and motioned to Emma's father, who stopped abruptly and began to approach. As Emma's father approached, I felt uneasy and wished that Emma had left me alone. Emma's mother began to approach me as well. I now felt sick to my stomach.

"How are you, boy?" Emma's father asked. I could not offer any response. "Are you hungry?" he continued. I finally was able to muster enough to nod in reply.

Emma's mother pulled a piece of bread from a small cloth bag. She walked to me and put her arm around my shoulder. As she handed me the bread, Emma's mother said in a gentle, calming voice, "We are happy to have you walk with us, Aran."

I then began to walk with Emma and her family as we made the slow descent down the hillside where the day's light began to wash across those who were streaming into the vast valley below.

I assumed a place next to Grace. She looked straight ahead. Grace was a short girl, but she looked fearsome. She squinted her eyes and frowned in an angry manner, perhaps at no more than the prospect of the continued walk to seemingly nowhere, but I think I knew that there was more to it than that. She appeared the type to place her hand in a pot of scalding water and not flinch in the least. We walked for several minutes, and she didn't say a word to me, nor did I say a word to her. Finally Grace asked, "Where are you from?"

I felt nervous to speak and didn't believe myself capable of carrying much conversation, but from somewhere within me I summoned enough to sound human. "I am from Constantinople," I replied.

"I have never met anyone from Constantinople. My home is very far from Constantinople. We are from Sivas. It is a much different place, I am sure, than Constantinople. Do you like to live there, in Constantinople?" she asked.

"Oh yes, very much," I replied.

"And what do you like about Constantinople?" Grace asked.

"I suppose I like most the old buildings and other places," I replied.

"What kind of other places?" Grace asked.

"Well, there is a place called the Hippodrome. Have you ever heard of it?" I asked.

"What is the Hippodrome?" Grace asked.

"It is a place where in ancient times they raced chariots and horses. There are still monuments there, but they don't race chariots anymore," I said.

"I should think not," Grace replied. "There aren't any ancient Romans left in Constantinople, are there?" Grace said sarcastically. "Tell me something more about the Hippodrome." I thought for a moment, and my last visit to the Hippodrome with Anahid and my father came to mind.

"My father told me that long ago the people in Constantinople destroyed many of the monuments in the Hippodrome themselves. One was a statue of a goddess that the people believed was calling armies to invade the city, and the people eventually crushed the statue to bits themselves."

"The whole statue?" Grace asked.

"Yes, the whole thing. They just smashed it to bits," I replied.

I couldn't think of anything more to tell Grace.

"I overheard you tell my sister Emma that you have a sister, too. What is her name?" Grace asked after a short length of time of walking without speaking.

"Her name is Anahid," I replied.

"Does she like going to the Hippodrome, too?" Grace asked.

"Sometimes, yes, but not as much as I like to," I replied.

"What does she like to do?" Grace asked.

"She really just likes to play the violin mostly."

"Isn't the violin difficult to play?" Grace asked.

"Yes, I think so. My mother taught her how to play, though. My mother was a musician before I was born."

"And is your father a musician, too?" Grace asked.

"Oh, no," I replied. "My father is a professor." We walked a time further, and I felt a bit self-conscious about leading Grace on, but Grace didn't seem to have any suspicion, and I think I appeared to her as perhaps at least a useful distraction.

"Does Anahid have many friends in Constantinople?" Grace asked.

"She has some," I replied.

"Well, Aran, perhaps when you find your family, you can introduce me to Anahid, and I can be her friend," Grace said. I nodded my head, and we continued to walk until dark, and Grace and I talked most of the remainder of the day about inconsequential matters.

As most in the caravan near us began to stop for the night, I began to feel uneasy. Grace and her family began to set up their camp for the night, and I was beginning to feel that it was time to slip anonymously back into the caravan, if for no other reason than I assumed that the Kazarians probably thought that their duty was done. They gave me some food and water and some company. Now they would expect me to be on my way and take from somebody else. I stood outside their camp and lifted my trunk to my back. Grace's father saw me, and as he walked toward me, he said, "No, boy, you will stay with us."

CHAPTER 32

I had stayed with the Kazarians for approximately ten days. I was becoming accustomed to them, and they, I believe, were becoming accustomed to me. I was coming to learn that as much as the caravan was a line of people headed in the same direction, and with the same purpose, it was comprised of different threads, primarily differentiated by family and village. It was important to seek a place in one of these groups. Outliers were less likely to survive, as they frayed from the line and were easily plucked.

There was still no sign of the border. Grace cried almost every night. I hadn't let her know that I had heard her cry before, but this night I did.

"Grace, are you awake?" I asked as I looked at Grace, who lay curled on the ground on the opposite side of the fire made when we set up camp the prior evening. She didn't reply, perhaps not wanting to acknowledge that I heard her cry. "Grace," I called again, "Grace, are you all right?" Grace began to sit upright, the light from the fire just barely flickering enough that I could see her face. I sat up, too, and moved closer to her.

"I just can't bear this any longer," Grace said. She then lowered her voice to a whisper, conscious not to wake the others.

"Do you cry, Aran?" Grace was looking squarely at me, insisting upon an answer. I sat silently, unable to utter anything to her in response. My answer would have been too emotionless to be of any comfort, so I offered her nothing. I then lay back down, curled myself up, and tried to force myself back to sleep, but my eyes remained open, and I was fully alert. Grace turned toward me, hunched slightly, and asked, "Do you know where we are going?" I again offered nothing in response. I sensed that Grace was clearly becoming irritated by my silence. Grace pressed on, her whispered tones now becoming strained in her frustration.

"Aran, you seem to me to be a mystery. You don't seem to have come from anywhere. You seem to have always been in this desert." Grace, like her sister, Emma, let on to be very strong, without vulnerability. Now Grace clearly wanted to discard the contrivances, and I was not able, at least not now. The fire was waning, and I found my escape from the topic.

"The fire is getting low. I am going to collect some kindling," I said. As I stood, Grace almost immediately stood up to join me. We walked a few meters away, where Keran had stacked some dried material for the fire.

Grace clearly wanted to try again and asked, "Aran, aren't you scared?" Grace's question could be interpreted as rhetorical, but, even if so, seemed to suggest an answer that was inconsequential. Of course I was scared, but of what I wasn't at all sure anymore, and what use such an emotion would have to me now was not ascertainable. Before allowing my answer, she supplemented her question, which changed it from rhetorical to one that required a direct and substantive response. "Are you scared that you won't see your family again, Aran?"

I did not immediately reply to Grace. I turned toward the fire, and as I approached it, I threw the material that I gathered on what was left of it and sat. Grace sat beside me then asked again, "Are you, Aran?"

"They are ahead of me. I will find them," I replied in a terse and dismissive tone. Grace then stood and withdrew back to her place on the opposite side of the fire. She sat with her back hunched, her arms folded and resting on her knee, and her eyes fixed on the licks of flame that were consuming the thin pieces of twig and straw that I placed on the remains of the fire.

I did not wish to offend Grace by my terse reply and was sorry if I had. Grace sat for several minutes without saying anything then began to speak, the sound of her voice now coming at some degree of relief that she was not so offended as to completely disregard me. "We had a wonderful life. My father had a store in our town. He sold all types of goods, like colorful tapestries, linens, and beautiful rugs." She looked up from the fire and looked at me as if to confirm that I was interested before offering more. Sensing that I had no objections, she continued, "I had wonderful friends there, too. My best friend's name was Lucine. My mother and Lucine's mother were best friends, too. We had a beautiful church in our town." Grace asked, "Did you have a church in your town, Aran?" I nodded in reply as she continued. "Ours was a beautiful church. Even a little whisper in our church echoed. Lucine and I always laughed in church. It is almost impossible not to laugh in church. Isn't it, Aran?" She then said abruptly, "I fear that we have lost it all. My father and mother won't tell me that, but I fear that we have lost it all." Her eyes looked directly into mine. "Aran, do you feel the same, that you have lost everything, too?" Grace looked down for a few moments and waited for my reply, but I gave none.

CHAPTER 33

Night was the most terrible time. Every sound could be heard when the caravan stopped and camps were set up for the night. The sounds of screams were the most horrifying, and the reasons for them the most indescribable. Many in the caravan were killed in the night. The path of the caravan was purposely circuitous and wound through the most desolate areas in the desert. The Armenians in the desert were not exiled there and forgotten, however. Instead, the form of exile was the most hideous, as each of us was being pursued. There were a variety of pursuers. The formal Ottoman army, uniformed and officious, seemed intent on herding the masses and riding them out to oblivion. Some dispensed with any pretense of a deportation of Armenians and simply killed people on sight if they appeared too weak, too slow, or for a variety of other arbitrary reasons. The more informal militias were less organized and substantially more unpredictable, particularly given their lack of organization. Some appeared only to want to taunt and humiliate, while others were much more pernicious and approached the whole affair as sport, like a hunt in the wild. Whether man, woman, or child, it was critical to always stay within the path of the caravan. At night, it was often the militia that would commit heinously violent acts, and when they did, we heard the screams, most often at considerable distance to this point in our passage, and that only added to the terror as it was a sort of assault on the senses in the abstract.

We woke the following morning. I hoped that Grace would not be upset that I had not done more to respond to her the prior night. Even if Grace was upset, she had no time to dwell on it now. Keran woke early, as others who had stopped in our vicinity for the night, perhaps fifty or so people in total, appeared to be getting an early start of it. Keran wanted to stay near to them. I walked with Grace, while Emma, Sara, and Keran walked together, a few steps ahead of us.

"Did you hear the screams last night, Aran?" Grace asked.

"Yes, I did, Grace," I replied.

"I think it was a boy, Aran," Grace said.

"Yes, I think you are right. I think it was a boy," I replied.

"I think I heard his mother, too, Aran. I just can't imagine the horrible things that happened last night. It is just unbearable," Grace said.

"Yes, it is, Grace," I replied.

"How do you sleep in the night?" Grace asked.

"I try to imagine that I am in some other place, Grace," I replied.

"I can't do that, Aran. I can't trick myself into thinking I am somewhere that I am not. When there are screams or gunshots, I hear them. I know what is happening, and there is no way that I can sleep. I think that they are going to kill me next," Grace said.

"You must try not to think about that, Grace. You must try to think about anything but that," I said.

"Aran, more soldiers and militia are coming. If we don't reach the border soon, I fear that they will try to bother us and do something terrible to us," Grace said.

"Well, Grace, we can't be too far from the border," I said.

"I pray that you are right, Aran, because if we don't reach the border soon, I think I am going to lose my mind completely, if we don't starve to death first."

As Grace and I walked, Keran turned to us and, while pointing in the distance, said, "See there? Ahead several kilometers or so there are trees, which means there may be some food that we can find in the vegetation. We must reach there before darkness comes."

I looked in the distance where Keran was pointing. We were on the top of a hillside. There was what looked to be a green line on the horizon. Reaching there by dark seemed impossible, but Keran appeared intent on making it.

We pushed hard the entire day. By nightfall, we arrived at the area that Keran sought to reach. In relative terms, it was a rather vegetated area on a high hillside. The face of the hill was covered with grasses and stands of a variety of wild flowers. There were a substantial number of people who ended the day's passage here, and Keran thought it best to set up camp on the slope of the hill.

The day was extremely hot, and there was adequate light from the moon's reflection to illuminate the area where we were camped, so we had no particular need for a fire and determined not to make one. Sara and Keran sat outside the tent, which was pitched for the night. Emma was within it. She was ill for most of the day and was trying to recuperate. Grace and I were sitting approximately five meters or so from the tent.

"Aran, I am scared to fall asleep. Will you promise to stay awake, if I can't go to sleep?" Grace asked.

"Yes, Grace," I replied. "I will stay awake with you."

I thought the entire day about what Grace said, that she was unable to remove herself from the reality of what was happening in the desert. As we sat, I reached into my trunk, and I handed Grace a book that I had with me. "Here, Grace," I said, as I handed her the book. "This is a book that has Turkish poems in it." This was the book that Professor Daigneau gave me at Evren's house, and it had no apparent value to me now as I had exhausted its use and believed that I took from it all that I could.

"Perhaps you might like to read this book, Grace. You can probably understand it better than I can, and besides, it might help you forget about where we are for a little bit, anyway," I said.

Grace looked at the book and smiled as she took it from my hand. She turned the pages to survey the contents then said, "I will enjoy reading this book very much. I haven't read a book in a very long time, and I missed reading so. I do love books."

I stretched myself out on the sand and faced Grace, who was still sitting. She opened the book to its beginning and began to read. I tried to keep my eyes open, just as I promised Grace.

CHAPTER 34

It rained later that night. As the rain fell, the high-pitched sounds of the raindrops hitting an assortment of metal pans that were placed in our camp and in the close surrounding camps to catch the drops echoed. The presence of rain was extremely infrequent in the desert. When rain did come, it fell briefly and in such scattered drops that any water captured by a pan was in very small amounts. It was usually just enough to wet the bottom of the pan but not enough to form any pool of water in adequate quantities for drinking. Placing the pans to catch the rain was nevertheless done whenever it appeared that a bit of precipitation might fall, even if little or nothing of use could be obtained from the exercise. There was not so much as a single rain cloud visible for approximately one week prior to this night, so the rain came somewhat as a surprise and resulted in some scurrying to gather any type of object adequate to capture whatever drops fell. On this occasion, the rain was adequate enough to capture enough water to be swallowed, and this seemed to heighten the urgency of the efforts at collection.

The rain caused everyone in the camps to wake and capture what they could. In our camp, Keran woke me, while Emma,

Grace, and Sara raced to catch the rain in the few pans that the Kazarians had. When Keran woke me, I felt the drops hit my face. I lifted my chin skyward, opened my mouth, and tried to let as many drops of rain as possible wet my tongue and slip down my throat.

In the camp next to ours, I saw an elderly man standing with his arm outstretched and holding a little tin cup. As he collected the drops of rain in his cup, he bent and placed it to the mouth of a little boy, who was not more than three years of age or so and who sat at the man's foot. He repeated this action of collecting a bit of water in his cup and bending to place the cup to the boy's lips several times, until the rain stopped. When it did, the boy lay down in the sand, and the man sat next to him, looking up at the sky, waiting for a few more drops to fall.

By this time, I was sitting fully awake and not far from Grace, who had her back slightly turned to me.

"I am sorry that I fell asleep, Grace. I meant to stay awake, as you asked, but couldn't help myself," I said.

"There is no reason to be sorry, Aran. I was able to fall asleep, too. I woke a little time before the rain started, just by coincidence. I felt the rain hitting me, and I was able to wake my father and mother so that we could collect it. I am glad that I was awake when the rain came, Aran. I know I felt the first drops, so I don't think we wasted much, either. I do hope that it starts to rain again. Do you think it will, Aran?" Grace asked.

"I don't know, Grace. I think the only times it has rained before, it only rained for a short time. When the rain stops, it usually doesn't rain again," I replied.

"Well, perhaps this time will be different. I don't believe that a few more drops of rain would be too much to hope for, would it, Aran?" Grace asked. I didn't immediately reply to Grace, believing that her question did not require an answer. How could anyone believe that there was reason to hope for anything? I lost my sense of hope soon after my first few steps in the desert. Any good to come to anyone was utter chance, a random event. There was no good that could come from hope. Expect nothing, I came to learn, because nothing is what one will eventually get.

Grace was still awaiting my answer. "Would it, Aran? Would it be too much to hope for?" she repeated.

"No, Grace," I replied. "It wouldn't."

I was growing sleepy. Grace sensed that I wanted to sleep. She paused briefly then continued, "Fall asleep, Aran, if you wish. I will stay awake. If it starts raining again, I will wake you." As soon as Grace finished speaking, I must have almost immediately fallen asleep, with only the flicker of an old Armenian lullaby first intervening.

It didn't rain again.

CHAPTER 35

The sounds of people as they worked their way past where we camped for the night gave the impression of a bustling city. The area was vast but seemed fittingly populated for a city of thousands, however incongruous the thought of a city in this desolate landscape. The caravan was growing in size. There were many more people who were pushing from behind us. I could only assume that more people were trying to find an escape through the desert or were otherwise given no choice and were being forced into the caravan.

It was morning, and Grace and I were busy helping pack the items that were used in our camp. The morning routine was becoming ritual. Grace and I would fold the linen used for the tent, a plain white linen made of fine threads. She and I would take opposite ends, folding it once in half by its length, then in half at its center, she pulling tightly in the center at the fold, and I pulling at the ends, then once more again. Grace and I then took a cord reserved for the purpose and tied the linen tightly at the center.

"I will carry the grain," Emma announced, as she grabbed the leather strapping holding the bags that held the grain. The grain left was precious little and was of poor quality, given that it was foraged from the wild. As we began to walk, Emma said, "Father says we need to forage today."

I was growing to count on Emma's assertiveness, a quality that was becoming increasingly essential, as each day brought greater uncertainty and desperation. The hills and valleys in this stretch of landscape did have some vegetation from which could be extracted some edibles, as Keran suspected. This was evident by the numbers of people now bending in the patches of grasses and other plant material that were located just ahead. "Over there… that stand must have some grain that we can pull from those stalks," Emma said, pointing at a particular patch that seemed to have an adequate density of vegetation for the purpose.

As we approached, a young woman with a child bundled and strapped to her back was foraging from a stand of dry grasses that had some brownish dried leaf material at the head of the plant. She appeared to be severely malnourished, her teeth substantially protruding, with the skin on her face appearing just to barely cover her sharp cheekbones. She wore a long, torn dress, which was made of a cloth having brightly colored, circular embroidered patterns. Her dress was partially covered by a mustard yellow cloak made of silk. Her child was a little girl, perhaps two years of age or so, covered almost entirely in a blue checkered cloth that formed the woman's pack. The child appeared to be better nourished than her mother, with her cheeks still somewhat naturally full. On the child's head was a light blue scarf that covered her entire forehead past her eyebrows, leaving only the child's eyes exposed. The woman pulled hard at the stalks, stripping the dried material and placing it as she did in a small cloth satchel. Grace, Emma, and I walked further into the stand and likewise pulled hard on the head of the plants and took what we could.

When we finished, Emma began to walk ahead to where Keran and Sara were walking, and Grace and I followed. Grace then said to me, "I read most of the poems in the book that you gave me last night." Grace reached behind her as she spoke and pulled the book from her pack. "I must read you the first couple of stanzas of a poem that is in the book, Aran," she said as she quickly leafed through the pages to one in particular that had a bend pressed in the upper right corner of the page. Grace began to read from it:

Come, let's grant the joy to this heart of ours that founders in distress:
Let's go to the pleasure gardens, come, my sauntering cypress...
Look, at the quay, a six-oared boat is waiting in readiness—
Let's go to the pleasure gardens, come, my sauntering cypress...

Grace paused and looked at me to confirm that I was paying attention, then continued on to the poem's second stanza:

Let's laugh and play, let's enjoy the world to the hilt while we may,
Drink nectar at the fountain which was unveiled the other day,
And watch the gargoyle sputter the elixir of life away—
Let's go to the pleasure gardens, come, my sauntering cypress...

Grace finished reading the entire poem, and as she did, she closed the book and said, "Aran, I think that is the most wonderful poem. I want to be there, in the place that the poem describes. I think it must be a beautiful place." I was alarmed that Grace had chosen that poem, of all the poems in the book, but the binding was probably well worked, and the bend in the page undoubtedly drew her attention to it.

I didn't want to tell Grace what I believed, that the place described in the poem was not a beautiful place at all, not for the living anyway. I didn't want to tell her my conclusions about the poem's meaning, that the poem was about death and that it might have been a good source of instruction for the dying, but not the living. If Grace could only look beyond the veil, she would understand. She would understand what I had learned. There is no such thing as beauty. It is all an illusion meant to take one's eye off of the reality of it all. The reality would be too repulsive, and so the concoctions to mask it. The poem was an assortment of empty words, a mere contrivance meant to do little more than occupy the mind as it worked through contortions, less pain perhaps than simply sitting and staring at each other, aware all along of everything that we lost and could never get back.

"Do you think that I shall ever find a place like that, Aran?" Grace asked.

I looked at Grace's face, and she had an expression that I had not seen since meeting her. She had a broad smile, and her eyes were opened wide. The poem seemed to have infused her with something, and I didn't want to dash it. It was only a contrivance, after all, a way to allow the time to pass without knowing it and the cruel things that were happening while it did. Whether she mistook the meaning of the poem or not should mean nothing now anyway, I thought.

"Oh, yes, Grace," I replied. "I believe on the other side of this desert there are places like that."

Grace looked down at the book and pulled it close to her, where she kept hold of it the remainder of the day.

CHAPTER 36

Grace was paging through Professor Daigneau's book of poems while she and I sat by the fire late that evening. She somewhat abruptly closed the book, placed it down on the sand beside her, and asked, "Do you think sometimes that they are playing a joke on us, Aran?"

"What do you mean, Grace? Who is playing a joke on us?" I asked in reply.

"The soldiers in the desert. Do you think that when we approach the border, they just intend to send us in another direction, in a direction where the desert has no end? Could their joke be that there is no end to this, that there is no end to trying to find our way out of the desert, and they simply wish to have us die while trying?"

The soldiers were making sport of the whole affair. They clearly forced the caravan on a route at the soldiers' choosing, and the direction taken now by the caravan was changed. I knew that because we no longer walked toward the sun in the morning. Instead, we now began each day turning our backs to the sun and walking into the shadows. There was no promise offered by the shadows.

Determining whether there was a way out of the desert was meaningless, in any event. There was no use in letting Grace know my opinion. It could lead to other conclusions that I didn't wish to share.

"I don't think that's true, Grace. There must be an end. I think we will find the end of the desert and find our way out," I said.

"Why do you think that there is an end, Aran? Why does there have to be an end?" Grace asked.

"Because, Grace, there must be an end to everything. Even this desert can't go on forever," I said. I hoped Grace would take my response on its face and not inquire any further. In fact, what I sensed was that there was no end, and the truth of it was becoming clearer to me. It was nothing that Grace needed to know, not from me anyway, and it was better to lie. She would find out. It was inevitable that she would, because I believed it was predetermined. There was nothing that anyone could do to change it. Grace continued to push.

"Aran, not everything comes to an end. There are some things that never end. Some places don't have an end, like oceans, or the sky. I think the desert can be like one of those places that just go on forever," Grace said.

"Well, Grace, you just have to tell yourself that this isn't one of those places," I said.

"I can't tell myself anything, unless I think it's true. Do you really think it's true? Do you really think that we will find our way out of here?" Grace asked.

"Yes, I do, Grace. I believe we will," I said.

Grace sat quietly for a few moments, and the expression on her face brightened. She picked up Professor Daigneau's book of poems from where she had placed it, and as she opened the book to begin reading, she looked at me and said, "Then we just need to keep walking until we find the end of it, Aran."

"Yes, Grace," I replied.

CHAPTER 37

I was shaken awake by the sound of leather whips being smacked against the horses that were driving up the hill approximately one hundred meters away. I felt the concussion of the horses pounding hard on the earth, even from that distance, given the number of horsemen in the squad, perhaps twenty or so. We had traveled for another four days. Ottoman soldiers and militia, before seen only infrequently, were now visible on an almost-daily basis, and they were coming closer to the defined line of the caravan, not apparently content to menace from a distance.

We began the day staying in camp a little later than was typical, as Keran apparently wanted to wait the soldiers out as they passed through. Typically, their bands would appear, then move forward, not to be seen for at least the remainder of a given day, at least to this point in the passage. Keran and Sara were engaged in private conversation under the tent, as Emma, Grace, and I sat by the fire, which was almost completely reduced to a smoldering heap of white ashes.

We reached an area where larger encampments were visible in the distance, although it was unclear how organized these encampments were, or, if organized, who was responsible for them. I wondered if the encampments were death camps and wondered if the soldiers were trying to herd us there. Emma was staring at Grace, sensing perhaps that Grace was preoccupied by what appeared to be closing in around us.

"Grace," Emma asked in an obvious effort to distract, "do you think we should cut our hair to the new fashion, when we reach the border?" As she asked Grace, Emma bunched her long brown hair and lifted it closer to her shoulders while taking her other hand to tease her bent strands outward. Emma had an easy manner about her, even in these circumstances, but her best efforts could not move Grace to respond in kind. Grace appeared in a foul mood, which surprised me given that her mood seemed to be elevated somewhat in the immediate days prior, perhaps from the distraction provided by Professor Daigneau's book of poems.

Grace looked at Emma and, with a cutting tone, replied, "Whatever would make you believe that we shall make it to the border, Emma?" Emma looked stunned. Whether she was stunned by Grace's awareness of circumstances, which Emma knew but did not share, or just at Grace's frankness, I did not know, but the sting of Grace's reply lingered.

Emma rose to her feet and collected herself. She looked at Grace, then to me, and retorted, "Father told me that we are getting close to the border." Emma turned her back to us and walked toward the tent. She then stopped and looked back to complete her thought, "The least that you could do, Grace, is not make everyone else so upset that they wish to give up." Grace turned her gaze from Emma to the ground.

"I am sorry, Aran," Grace said a few moments later. As Grace spoke, she was pushing both of her hands into the sand, gripping handfuls, then letting the dry sand slowly trickle through the gap left between her small fingers and the palm of her hands. "I hope I did not upset you," she continued.

"You didn't," I replied. My response to Grace was truthful. Whatever I once had within me that would cause me some emotional upset was gone. That part of me, I believe, was lost somewhere further back in the desert. When I lost it, I was at that point unaware, but it was gone. I did want to find the end of the desert, but for no other reason than to have the physical pain stop, the pain of hunger, the pain from walking, the pain from the sores that were on my skin. Grace was unaware of the condition to which I had advanced.

As Grace and I sat, Keran called from the tent, "Grace, Aran, please come here." Emma had already entered the tent, and the others waited for us to join. As we entered, Keran said, "We will stay here today. We should not waste the time, though. We must try to continue to forage for some grain." I didn't question Keran's decision that we stay in camp, and we went about the day as Keran directed.

Later that day, I returned to camp from a failed attempt to forage from an area of grasses that was several hundred meters in the distance. When I returned, I noticed that Sara was standing alone by a small tree, "Where is your father?" I asked Grace, who had returned earlier with Emma to our camp, while I continued to forage.

"I don't know, Aran. He packed some items and told us that he would return in a couple of days," Grace replied. "Do you think that he will make it back, Aran? I am worried that he won't make it back," Grace said.

"Why wouldn't he?" I replied. "We are running low on food, and there may be an area to obtain food nearby. It can't be far, so I am sure he will be back within a couple days, just as he said."

In fact, I believed that Keran's leaving had little to do with finding provisions and more to do with something that everyone was beginning to realize. We were drawing closer to the death camps run by the Ottoman authorities. Although it was known to everyone in the caravan to avoid these areas entirely, the caravan was being forced nearer to them.

Grace, appearing not to have heard a single word of my reply, continued, "I am terribly afraid, Aran. There does not appear to be any way out of here." Grace's ability to discard pretense now gave one little room to breathe. By the same measure, however, Grace seemed to seek from me, and perhaps count on and accept, some of my extrapolations, but only if given in small doses and only after careful cross-examination.

"Grace," I replied, in a steady, assured tone, "your father would not have left us here if he didn't know where he was going and when he will be back. He must know that the border is near and is finding the way to it."

I had no basis for my belief, of course. There was no element of deduction or rationality, and I don't believe there was even an element of blind trust. I believed that Grace was correct, but I was not about to tell her.

"Perhaps you're right, Aran," Grace replied. Grace seemed placated for the moment.

Emma approached where Grace and I were seated. Emma kicked her foot across the sand in a sweeping motion and sat in the spot that she had cleared. "It is good that we did not have to walk today," Emma began. I looked at Emma as she spoke. Her face always said more than her words. She looked weary, and her demeanor led on to something more. "Father will be gone for a few days, and we mustn't move from here until he returns." Emma knew more about the reasons for his leaving than she offered, but it wasn't my place to ask, nor did I have much care. The only matter of importance was doing the necessary tasks for survival in that moment and that day. Staying in our camp seemed to me a perfectly acceptable plan for survival for the day. Emma then continued, "It may not be possible to reach the border by the route we are currently traveling."

Grace looked at Emma, Grace's eyes now wetting with tears, and she said, "I knew we would never make it to the border. Whatever could have made anybody think that we could have made it to the border?"

CHAPTER 38

Three days passed, and there was no sign of Keran. I struggled with thoughts of leaving the Kazarians and going back into the caravan alone. I think that on this day, I determined that another part of me had been lost. I had become a little less than fully human at some point. I viewed myself as a parasite. I required a host, and my methods of latching myself required deception and a degree of cunning to hide my intentions. I concluded that I remained with the Kazarians to that point only because my most base instinct led me to believe that my chances of survival would increase, even at the expense of Grace or Emma. My conclusion was drawn from my answers to questions I asked myself: Was my ability to survive dependent on other people dying? What was I in need of, and who was I to take it from? As a practical matter, did I simply need their food and water? Did I need them as a source of human camouflage? Whatever parts of me I had left led me to consider that if my survival now depended on being a parasite, it was better that I take from someone I did not know. It was better not to know whom I was devouring. It was difficult to determine if this sensibility came from a part of me that I still had, or from some phantom sensation which was tricking me into believing that a part of me that was gone was still there. Nevertheless, I had developed a feeling of affection for the Kazarians and especially for Grace. Only flesh and blood humans needed affection, though. Affection was not helpful for survival here and might even hasten death.

I was beginning to learn that death was a more complex matter than I thought. Even if one is aware that death is inevitable, even imminent, the body does not give up quite so easily. The body still demands sustenance, as if meant to go on forever, and it appears to become more voracious the closer one approaches death. Perhaps that is what is meant by death throes. The body and the mind grab for anything needed to survive. The grabbing can often be violent, and at the expense of everyone around. I could see that in the dead people strewn about. They looked to have died grabbing for their last scrap, their last step, their last breath, and their last moment. Each of them had it all in such abundance once.

Grace was sitting at a distance, her face obscured by her hands, which she was using to shield herself from the extremely bright sunlight. Emma was sitting outside of the tent pounding a rock into another, which she was using as a rudimentary tool for grinding the bits of wild stalks that we had gathered into a more edible form. Emma stood and walked toward me.

"Here, Aran," Emma said as she extended her arm and handed the mixture of wild grain, which she had finished grinding. "I don't know that this will have any taste, but you must eat."

"Thank you, Emma," I replied, as Emma poured the grain into my hand.

I put the mixture in my mouth and swallowed it as quickly as I could. It was dry and tasted like earth, and I felt like I was swallowing sand. I winced when I swallowed, not from the taste, but from the pain it caused my throat as I swallowed it down. Emma saw me wince and said, "I am sorry, Aran, but this is all the food we have at the moment. Hopefully we will get some real food soon." Emma sat beside me and continued, "I hope you are not upset. We are going to reach the border. Father knows many people, and he is very smart. He will know how to get us to the border. It is entirely possible that we are very close to the border. That is what my father estimates, anyway, and he said so when he left. We may just need to find a different way to reach it." I didn't reply to Emma, and she seemed content to just sit with me, leaving matters there.

After some moments, I became tempted to ask Emma whether the Kazarians wanted me with them. I was looking for any excuse to leave, and any indication that I was no longer wanted would have been more than a sufficient one to drop off and out of their sight. The Kazarians, though, for whatever reason, felt an obligation to me, I believe, and they seemed intent on saving me. I believe this purpose was sustaining them as much as it was sustaining me. I remained silent and said nothing. Emma, after some time sitting with me, returned to her place by the tent.

Whatever my feelings were about leaving the Kazarians earlier in the day, by the late afternoon I had decided against it. I simply didn't believe that I could survive without them, and that was the overriding factor in my decision to stay. The Kazarians were, I thought, trusting enough to believe everything that I told them about me. They were the perfect hosts. There was, I think, no more to it than that.

CHAPTER 39

The sun was down, and Grace was silent the entire day. I occupied much of the remainder of the day collecting wood with Emma. Our sources of firewood, like every other provision, were dwindling, and obtaining provisions from whatever scant sources could be found was essential.

While I was looking for firewood, I saw a dead woman. It was the woman with the little girl on her back whom I saw several days before, when Grace, Emma, and I were foraging for grain. She was lying face up, her eyes still open. She was a few steps from the main path used by the caravan, fallen, probably in mid-stride. I recognized her by the clothes she was wearing. Her colorful dress was still recognizable. There was almost nothing left of her. Her bones were left simply propping up her skin. Her little girl was gone, hopefully taken by somebody who would save her, but there was no way of knowing. Seeing dead people was common in the desert, and the sight of it did not shock me. It had become as common as one might see dead livestock, and I felt nothing upon seeing it. Every dead person looked the same to me. Any characteristic that may have been unique to them during life was lost at death. It had been many kilometers back in the desert that the sight of death made me realize that nobody was unique and that the notion that somehow each of us is recognized and known personally by God was false. I came to understand that anyone who was given to belief in such a notion had never seen herds of dead people, with wide-open vacant eyes and bloated bellies lying strewn about like discarded garbage. Why weren't they protected by God? At least I knew that I was on my own and whether I lived or died wasn't determined by God. I believed God didn't even know who I was, and even if he did, why would he care any more for me than he did for any of these dead people, or for my mother or father or Anahid?

I was sitting by the fire, which I had just lit. Grace walked out of the tent where she stayed with Sara for most of the day. Emma was also under the tent, and she remained there. Grace came and sat directly opposite of me, on the other side of the fire. She sat with her legs bent directly in front of her and balanced her chin on top of her kneecaps. The orange light from the fire flickered against Grace's face, and her eyes fixed directly on it. She sat quietly for what must have been about ten minutes then began to speak. "The day we left our home was a perfectly regular day. Emma and I were returning from school, and we were not more than fifty meters from our house. We were close enough to see my father in the small pasture that we shared with our neighbors. My father was detaching our horse from his carriage. It was a beautiful black horse that Emma helped my father care for. Emma and I used the horse for riding on occasion, although its main purpose was as a pulling horse for the carriage. As Emma and I walked, we passed two soldiers who stood in the middle of the road. There were other soldiers who stood at greater distance, and it surprised us because we hadn't seen soldiers near the residential areas of Sivas before that day. While we passed the pair of soldiers, one said to the other, 'The orders are to kill these Armenians, until none are left.' He was looking at Emma and me as he said it, and I believe he wanted us to hear him to scare us, because he sounded mean and cold. Emma and I ran home, and we called my father and mother and told them what we heard the soldier say. My father and mother already knew what was happening and had already made plans to leave. They heard that Armenians were already being killed elsewhere. They told us that we had to leave that night and that we needed to reach this desert to escape. There was no warning at all, and we had to leave most everything, including our horse."

Grace looked up at me then looked quickly down again at the fire and continued, "We left late in the night. We were not allowed to stop for a rest, not even for a little time. We walked for nearly three full days and had to hide along the way until we reached a train. There must have been over one thousand people trying to board the train when we reached it. The cars were just big, empty cars made for carrying things, not people, so we all climbed in and sat on the floor. We had to squeeze in tightly and sit with our legs crossed, so as not to take up too much room for the next person. We were in the train for over a day, and it stopped several times, probably, my father thought, because word was traveling along the way of the need to escape before it was too late. The train was almost entirely dark, except for a little light that came through the cracks of the door in the train car."

I was listening very intently to Grace. Grace seemed satisfied that I was sitting quietly and giving her all of my attention, and she continued, "When the train finally stopped, the huge doors of the train car were slid open, and the bright sun burned my eyes. The conductors yelled, 'There is no more track left. You must get out.' As soon as the last person was out, the train left and went back in the other direction. I remember looking out, and all I could see was this desert. There was nothing else, absolutely nothing else, and I asked myself, 'How are we going to find our way out?' Aran, I still ask myself that, and I so desperately want to know the answer."

It was now dark. I was too tired to say anything much in response to Grace, and I didn't have the capacity to comfort her. I wanted to tell Grace that my story was not much different, only that they took my father and killed him. I envied Grace, because she just went straight into the desert. The soldiers didn't bother with making certain the rest of her family was killed first. I had no answer to her question, either. I felt hopeless and lost, and I don't believe I cared much anymore. It was better that I said nothing.

CHAPTER 40

The next morning came. There was still no sign of Keran. Grace and I spent almost the entire morning helping Emma look for something to eat. Circumstances were growing increasingly desperate, and finding anything now that could be mashed into something edible was our almost complete preoccupation. We walked in the fields within a kilometer or so of our camp and gathered any piece of vegetation that appeared to have soft enough fibers that could be reduced to food of some sort. There were increased numbers of dead men, women, and children strewn throughout the area, their deaths resulting from multiple apparent causes.

The soldiers were becoming more indiscriminate. The dead bodies were coming even closer to the defined line of the caravan. Our reliance on staying within sight of those behind us and in front of us for security was becoming less certain as a strategy to avoid the soldiers. The killing still seemed to take place largely at night and in areas that were not directly in the line of the caravan.

Grace came to where I was sitting and sat beside me. Grace was becoming alarmingly thin, and I must have appeared the same to her. It struck me then how incredibly thin her wrists had become, and I could see the bones of her wrists through her skin. She was, though, like me, emaciated but enough nourished that we were not in any immediate danger of incapacity. Seeing the numbers of dead people that we encountered today was affecting Grace.

"What do you think happens when a person dies, Aran?" Grace asked.

"I am not certain Grace, but, I think, probably nothing?"

"What do you mean 'nothing'?" Grace replied.

"I don't really know what I mean, Grace."

"Don't you believe that the person goes to heaven, or some-place like that, Aran?"

"I really don't know," I replied.

"Well, what be the alternative?" Grace asked.

"Probably nothing," I replied.

"I still don't know what you mean by 'probably nothing.'"

"I mean that nothing happens. You just die and don't go any-where, then there is nothing after that," I said.

"That is a horrible thought. You shouldn't ever think that. I want to believe that when you die you go someplace," Grace replied.

"But if there is nothing, Grace, why would it even matter?"

"Because it matters when you are alive to think that there is simply nothing when you die."

"How would it, Grace?"

"You would feel trapped, Aran. That's how it would feel, and that would make everyone miserable."

Grace seemed agitated at my suggestion. I could have told her more, but she seemed agitated enough, and I needed to repair matters before I had revealed too much of what I thought, and there was no purpose in it.

"You are right, Grace. I didn't mean to say that we don't go to heaven when we die. I have always believed in heaven. I learned that in church. I just don't know what heaven would be like." Before Grace could respond, I decided to change the subject quickly, to throw Grace off any further discussion on the topic.

"You know, Grace, I have been thinking," I began.

"About what, Aran?"

"I have been thinking that, had we grown up together, you would have made great friends with Anahid instantly."

"Do you really think that, Aran?" Grace replied.

"Yes, I do, Grace, absolutely. You would have made great friends from the beginning," I said.

"Why do you think that, Aran?" Grace asked.

"Because I think you are much like Anahid. You are both honest," I replied.

Grace looked at me, and a small but perceptible smile came to her face. "I think I would like your sister, Anahid, very much. I think I know her already," Grace said.

My belief that Grace was like Anahid was sincere. What I saw in Anahid, I saw in Grace. Grace, like Anahid, was not given to engaging in any pretense. What Grace thought or believed, she expressed without reservation and with a frankness that did not permit any ambiguity. Just as with Anahid, this trait in Grace was a strength of character that I envied and believed that I didn't have. While honest with herself and others, I also believe that despite the circumstances and Grace's agony over our condition, she was an idealist, and her idealism contributed to the fear and anger that she expressed. Grace's idealism, I believe, was not centered on any yearning for some impractical or naive pursuit. To the contrary, I believe her idealism was built upon an ethic, and that what we were enduring in the desert was the most severe of injustices, and she would not accommodate the injustices by trying to cover their effects on her, or on anybody else. It was a simple matter for Grace. She was not able to conceal her fear and outrage over our circumstances and what was being taken from her, and her uncertainty over how she would get it back. She expressed her feelings accordingly without reservation. I was a liar. The more I lied, the more I became convinced that I could make others believe my lies were true. I just needed someone to believe me. I could fashion my own reality then, where Anahid, our mother and father were still alive, and finding home and finding Anahid and our mother and father was just a matter of finding the place that was just on the other side of the desert. It was a better place than the one I knew existed and the place that I knew we were all destined to find, if I was honest with myself.

CHAPTER 41

I only knew the caravan to travel forward. However circuitous the direction, it always moved forward. Later that day, it began to turn and come back. It first appeared as two parallel lines in the distance. One line, which was substantially more populated than the other, moved forward. The other, more sparsely populated, line walked back toward the area where we were camped. As the day passed, the line moving back became the substantially more populated line, and the first of those making their way back were reaching the area of our camp. I sat alone, watching an older man who was carrying a large pack stop several meters from our camp. He spoke loudly to another man, who was sitting in the sand by a small tent. "Don't leave your camp. They won't let anyone pass. They are killing a tremendous number of people about ten kilometers ahead, too many people to count. They are just chopping people down with their guns," he said.

When the man spoke, I looked into the tent where Emma, Sara, and Grace were to determine if they heard him, too. I stood and walked toward the tent. Emma saw me as I began to approach. She crawled out and walked toward me. "Did you hear that man?" I asked Emma. Emma looked down at first, and she seemed to wish not to respond. "Did you, Emma? Did you hear what that man said?" I repeated while pointing at the man.

"What did you hear him say?" Emma asked reluctantly.

"That they won't let the caravan pass. That they are killing people ahead," I replied.

"Yes, Aran, I heard him, but Grace is sleeping, and she doesn't know. My father received word of it the day he left. It is why he left, to find another way out. We must not let Grace know. Do you understand, Aran?" I nodded my head in reply to Emma then she continued trying to comfort me. "My father is very smart. He will find a way out. Don't be scared, Aran."

Emma had a sense about her that it was her obligation to look after me, almost as if her spotting me first in the desert made her primarily responsible. She never uttered anything of the sort to me, but I sensed it nonetheless by the way in which she always tried to smooth matters over, to try to protect me from the rough, hard edges of the truth. She couldn't be faulted for believing that I still needed the protection.

I sat down, and Emma sat next to me. I wanted to tell Emma that I didn't believe anything anymore and that she didn't need to protect me. Everything had already been taken from me, so there wasn't anything left worth protecting, and I already knew the truth. I wondered who Emma thought I was.

Emma looked at me for several moments and seemed to force a smile. She then covered her face in her hands and began to weep. I wondered what she saw. Did she see a scared little boy? Is that what was making her cry? "Don't cry, Emma," I said. "I'm not scared."

CHAPTER 42

I first saw him in the distance. He walked parallel to the caravan, and he appeared to be looking for us. Emma spotted him, too, and she began running down the crest of the hill.

"Father is back," I could hear Emma shouting in the distance. As he came closer, I saw that he was carrying a burlap sack and what appeared to be a bag made of animal skin. As Keran approached, he dropped the bag and sack, and as he walked to the tent, he said, "Open them and eat." Sara picked up the sack and opened it. The sack contained lentil beans, and the animal skin was filled with water. Keran had been gone for almost four full days.

Emma brought me some lentil beans that she mashed into a paste, and she scooped some in my hand. This was the first refined bit of food I had in some time, and I consumed it. The taste and texture absorbed all of my senses. These lentil beans could not have come from any of the outposts along the way, as the provisions found there were squalid, and any supply of water and grain seemed more a pretext than a means to provide nourishment, and anything of value obtained there could usually only be obtained in small handfuls, just enough to put in your mouth and in your pockets. Later in the morning, Emma came to speak to me.

"Aran, my father found some people who can help us reach the border. My father was at a camp. He found a couple of men that will help us. They gave my father the beans and the water. My father said it will take us over a full day's walk to get to that camp and that we must arrive there at night. You mustn't be afraid when we arrive. My father wants you to know that we won't be made to stay at the camp." As Emma was speaking, Grace was with her mother and father eating the same concoction that Emma had given me. As Emma finished speaking with me, Grace began walking toward me, her face now having a small hint of a smile.

"Aran, did you hear the news? Did Emma tell you what Father has arranged?" Grace asked.

"Yes, Grace," I responded, somewhat inaudibly, while nodding my head as I spoke.

"Are you happy, Aran? Are you happy that you will be seeing your family again soon? I asked my father, and he told me that where we are going there will be authorities who can look up papers and provide information about where someone's family can be found, if they were separated," Grace said. It was inevitable that the subject would come up.

"Yes, Grace, my parents and Anahid must have made it out of the desert by now. They will be waiting for me somewhere. I am sure that Anahid and my parents are worried that I may have lost them," I replied.

Grace smiled and nodded her head. What did it matter, anyway?

Whether Grace knew the truth now was of no significance. It was the least of my lies. Grace was finally able to see a way out. I saw nothing.

CHAPTER 43

We did not leave immediately. We remained where we were for another day. Keran watched the caravan line closely. The line working its way back had stopped by the end of the following day, and the caravan was moving forward again. The killing ahead must have ended, and the band of whoever was doing the murdering must have moved on. Keran told us that we would have to be prepared to leave the following morning. To the extent there was fear in moving forward after the killing on the route in the days prior, the randomness of attacks created a sense that no place was any safer than any other. It was simply a matter of moving forward, and the apparent opportunity arranged by Keran was enough to override any other consideration. It was also clear that simply staying in place was a greater danger. Death from starvation and dehydration was becoming the most imminent threat and was a more excruciating death than being shot.

We left the following morning and traveled for nearly two days toward the camp where Keran had apparently made arrangements. We were able to stay within the caravan route for only a short time. We broke off from the caravan route in the middle of the first night and, however dangerous to have broken off, we walked alone the entire second day. No soldiers were in sight. We arrived late the night of the second day, when it was dark, just as Keran had planned, our travel slowed to ensure the proper timing.

Keran stopped us approximately twenty meters from the camp. Grace, Emma, and I sat together, while Sara walked several meters ahead with Keran, until he headed on alone. Keran walked toward the boundary of the encampment, then stopped and stood for some time. He appeared to be speaking to a few men who were walking along the boundary of the camp, which was simply a large fenced area with almost no cover, except for a small tent, which was closed on all four sides and appeared for use not by the camp's inhabitants but for those guarding them. He reached and placed something in the hand of one of the men standing outside of the fence then the men disappeared with Keran beyond the fence and into the enclosed tent.

I sensed that Grace was growing increasingly nervous. She whispered to Sara, "Where are they taking Father?" Sara took Grace's hand and held it but didn't say anything to Grace in response. Emma appeared equally nervous and said nothing. Where we sat, the putrid smell of the camp was strong and sickening and seemed to come in waves. There was no use in telling anyone what I knew was inside.

Keran reappeared from the tent within approximately twenty minutes. Keran was being accompanied by one of the guards, and they were walking toward us. The guard was no more than sixteen years of age and was dressed in trousers and a waistcoat that looked too large for his thin frame. I could not discern by his clothing whether he was part of any formal military or militia, particularly because his clothes looked worn and not of any military issue that I was familiar with at the time. He slowed his walk as he approached and began counting our number, pointing to each of us as he did. "Five people!" he said in Turkish upon completing his count. "Five people!" he repeated, this time looking directly at Keran. "I was told that there were only four. I will need more lira."

Keran reached into his pocket and pulled out a cloth satchel. He opened the satchel. "How much more?" Keran asked. As he was pulling lira from the satchel, Keran fixed his gazed downward. The guard looked to the side and rubbed his forehead as he thought. The guard simply signaled with his hand the amount. I could not decipher the additional sum required. As he placed his hand out, waiting for Keran to comply, Keran pulled the lira from the satchel, counted it slowly, then placed it into the man's hand, while Keran's eyes were still fixed downward.

"Follow me," the guard said as he pivoted and began walking away from the camp, to a loosely delineated road. The road was approximately fifty meters or so from the camp fence. I was relieved that he was leading us away from the camp. We were led down a small hill, toward the bottom of which was an inconspicuous place, where we could not see the camp.

There, at the inclining base of the hillside, was a team of two old and unimpressive horses, their ribs clearly visible through their thin flanks, harnessed to a flat, uncovered cart. "Get in," the guard ordered, as he turned and walked up the hill in the direction of the camp. Sara, Emma, and Grace climbed into the cart first. Keran then grabbed me by the arm and helped me up. I was able to swing my leg over the sideboard of the cart and climb aboard. Keran climbed aboard next, sat beside Sara, and pushed in close.

An elderly man who was sitting in the front of the cart pulled the reins of the horse, and down the remaining incline of the hillside we went.

Keran placed his face in his hands, so that from his forehead to his chin, he completely covered himself. He looked up after some time and whispered something to Sara. He shook his head back and forth multiple times and looked as if he might be ill. His eyes were red and full of liquid, as if he had been stabbed right there. I could only surmise, but I believe Keran was sickened by what he saw, by what he did, and by what he was unable to do. To that point, Keran was inanimate to me. He appeared emotionally empty, and the only words he offered were words of direction. His surface was scratched now, and I could see the agony within him and felt tremendously uncomfortable because of it, perhaps because Keran seemed the least vulnerable among us. I now knew that he was like everyone else, scared and searching for some way out. As the cart picked up speed, Keran put his arm around Sara's shoulder and pulled her tight to him.

I could not determine the immediate direction that we were being taken. I sat in the rear of the cart with Grace. The road on which we were traveling was nothing more than a two-tracked desert road with deep ruts carved on its outer edges by carriage wheels and stamped smooth in the center by the tamping of pulling horses. There was no evidence of any human footsteps.

After some while, Grace whispered to me in a very soft voice, "Aran, do you have any idea of where we are going?"

"I don't know for sure, Grace, but I think we are headed out of the desert. It feels as though we are, anyway," I replied in an equally soft whisper.

"Do you really think so, Aran, or are you just guessing, because if you are guessing, and it turns out that we are only going deeper into it, I will be more distraught than if you just said nothing," Grace replied in an aggravated, but still whispered, tone.

"I told you, Grace, that I don't know for sure, but it seems that we are. Look, Grace, the caravan route must be some distance from here, because I can't see any footsteps in the sand," I said. Grace looked at me skeptically, sensing that I was, in fact, just guessing at matters, which I was plainly, but it seemed reasonable that the carriage path was a more direct route out of the desert than the path being taken by the caravan. The Armenians in the caravan did not have carts or carriages. It was reasonable to assume that anyone with access to carts or carriages would take the least circuitous routes through the desert, and that could mean that the path that we were taking was a shortcut of some sort, and I believed that this could be a source of encouragement for Grace.

Grace looked out from the rear of the cart at the road that was passing under and behind us, and she seemed to be focusing intently to find some evidence of something to justify her skepticism. A few minutes passed, and Grace and I sat silently, watching the road disappear behind us. Grace then whispered quietly, "I think I would feel better, Aran, if I saw footsteps."

The cart stopped once in the middle of the night so that we could get some relief. We stopped in a desolate area with no signs of any civilization. There were also no signs of the caravan, not even one or two Armenians who may have wandered off from the line. It began to make perfect sense to me that this was all a trick played on us by the soldiers that Keran had met. They would take his money then slaughter us without anyone knowing the better of it. There was no basis to believe anything to the contrary, because nothing made me believe that the entire ordeal was anything but an elaborate scheme to kill us, but to ensure first that we knew that we were dying before they finished us off. I wanted to tell Grace, so that she wouldn't be taken by surprise when the soldiers came to slaughter us. I wanted to scream to Grace the truth. I wanted to tell her that this is all about dying, and that it is all a lie, everything, even everything I told her. I thought I owed her that, and I think my need to tell her came from some part of me that remembered that I was once human.

We loaded ourselves back on the cart. Several hours later in the early morning and while still dark, I heard the sound of what had been denied us by God and the Ottomans, except in sips. We reached the Euphrates. I expected the driver to stop, but he continued, slowing just enough to ensure that he lined up the horses and wagon on a short wooden bridge. I wanted to tell Grace that there was water, as much as she could ever hope for, but she was asleep along with the others. She was resting on her side, with her back facing me. I tapped on her back and said, "Grace, look, a river. We are crossing a river." Grace stirred slightly but otherwise remained asleep. There was no use in trying a second time to wake her. We reached the end of the short span. The wagon picked up speed, and the river soon disappeared into the dark behind us.

CHAPTER 44

"Is that the border, Father?" Grace asked as the cart, after another full day of travel, neared what appeared to be the outskirts of a populated city a few kilometers or so away and situated at an elevation. Buildings stretched for a substantial distance to a point where the city appeared to end at the foot of a range of mountains.

"I can't be sure, Grace," Keran replied. Keran looked at the elderly man driving the cart and called to him in Turkish, "Sir, are we near the border?" The man said nothing in response and appeared not to hear Keran. Keran repeated, "Sir, are we near the border?" As Keran asked the second time, he knocked on the underside of the board on which the man sat.

The man turned and pointed to the city in the distance, and while nodding his head replied, "Aleppo."

Keran looked back to Grace and said, "Yes, Grace, we are almost there. We are going to Aleppo."

As we drew closer to the city, the detail of the city came into better view. There were numerous white buildings having large Byzantine domes, tower-shaped monuments, and the colonnades of fortress buildings. We pulled onto a road that ran into the

189

heart of the city and continued down this road past a large building that stood almost flush with the edge of the traveled portion of the road. The road was rutted and dusty and was occupied by pedestrians, horse-drawn carts, and livestock. It smelled of dirt and waste. This road led to a narrow side street that had very little room for maneuvering. The horses pulled the cart in a circle toward a building that appeared to be a residential apartment of some sort, as clothes were draped over balconies for drying. The elderly man stopped the cart and stepped down into the street, and as he did, he looked at Keran and said in Turkish, "Wait here."

Moments later, the man returned with a middle-aged woman. She wore a plain black frock that reached to her ankles, and a white scarf that covered her head, the ends of which were wrapped around her neck. She had a serious look, like one you would see on the face of a merchant bartering in a bazaar. She was stiff and mechanical and seemed to approach the whole matter as routine. We were just another throng of filthy Armenians falling out of the desert in need of rescue, and she was ready to oblige us for a price. A few days prior, we only hoped to swallow some dry stalks to trick our bellies into believing them full. Now, as if from thin air, we were dropped in the middle of a bustling, seemingly cosmopolitan city. In truth, though, we weren't dropped. We were smuggled. Those without the lira stayed in the desert, condemned. Those with enough lira could buy salvation. The prices were fixed. There was nothing to be gained by attempting to negotiate.

The woman looked at Keran directly and squinted her eyes as she did. "Do you have lira?" she asked. Keran nodded his head. Apparently annoyed that he didn't immediately reach into his pockets, she snapped, "Well, then, where is it?" Keran reached into the satchel in his pocket. She studied him closely as he did. Keran had some lira in his hand, and she must have been adept at a quick count of money, as she instructed, "Now five hundred more." Keran looked up at her, and he seemed at first poised to negotiate. He instead looked down again and pulled more lira from his satchel and handed it to the woman. She grabbed the lira and quickly stuffed it in a pocket beneath her frock. "Come and follow me," she said. "I will take you to a place where you can wash and have a change of clothes."

We followed her on foot to a small building immediately adjacent to the residential building and entered it. The floors were made of mosaic tile that surrounded multiple sunken stone baths. The baths were separated by half walls made of white marble. There was nobody in the building, and we were allowed to bathe in warm water. We were given fresh clothing. The clothes given to me, some wool trousers, a suit coat, and a full-sleeved shirt, were sized for a man, but wearing fresh clothes was a luxury and that the clothes were meant for a man, not a boy, was unimportant.

After we finished dressing, we climbed back onto the cart. The woman sat in front with the elderly man. The man turned the cart back on the main road, and we traveled several blocks more.

The cart slowed to a stop. The woman turned and motioned with her hand to Keran as she stepped down from the cart and said, "I will take you to the train station." In front of us was a large stone train station that fronted a swath of train track that extended as far as the eye could see. As we stepped down from the cart and walked through the threshold of the station, I was overwhelmed by the sight and sounds of people rushing from one place within the station to the next and their seeming apathy for what was happening in the desert, a short distance away. I could not grasp the enormity of our passage, or the stark change in my prospect for survival, from what appeared almost completely hopeless to what was now a deliverance of some sort.

After entering the train station, Grace and I sat next to each other on the stone floor of the station and rested our backs against the wall. Sara and Emma sat a few meters away on some chairs that were neatly arranged. Keran and the woman were at a bit of a distance.

Grace sat silently, and I am uncertain if we both fell asleep against the wall at some point, but our senses were so dulled that I believe we were both for a time at least in some state of reduced consciousness. Perhaps it was the body's method of restoring itself, whether or not we could coax ourselves to sleep.

"This is unimaginable that we are here, Aran. Isn't it?" Grace said, shaking me from a daze.

"Yes, Grace," I replied. "You can almost see the desert from here."

"Do you think that this means that we are safe, now?" Grace asked. Grace's question crossed my mind, too. The killing and deportations were happening not far from here, so I could only imagine that the soldiers could find us here, too, and perhaps send us back into the desert, but I was too exhausted to care. It was enough that for the moment we were not in any apparent imminent danger.

"We are safe enough now, I think, Grace," I replied.

I closed my eyes in an attempt to fall back to sleep, but Grace still wanted to talk.

"Aran, do you think that your family may have passed through this station, too?"

"No, I don't think that this is the border area that everyone spoke about," I replied.

Grace nodded and sat silent for a few moments. "You must be very anxious to see your family. Perhaps you should ask my father now to have the authorities help you find them." Grace seemed eager to push me along and was clearly dissatisfied that I was not beginning to plan these matters. "Aran, you should at least think about how you are going to find them, shouldn't you?" Grace continued.

"Yes, I have been thinking about that, Grace. I think maybe they will find me first." I said nothing in any further response, and we soon became distracted.

Keran was finishing a discussion with the woman who had brought us here. The woman was leaving the station through a corridor that led in the other direction from where we had entered and away from where we were now sitting, but not before taking more lira from Keran and passing some on to a couple of men who appeared to be working at the station. As soon as the money was exchanged, the woman disappeared.

"Where are we going, Father?" Grace asked, as she stood up and walked toward Keran as he approached.

Keran was carrying some cured meat and cheese, and he handed the food to Emma, Grace, and Sara. Keran walked over to me where I remained sitting, and while handing me some of the food, said, "Aran, you must eat." Grace's question to Keran still hung, and I was as eager for an answer now as was Grace. Keran looked at Grace, and then to Emma and Sara, and said, "We are going to Cairo, and, Aran, you are coming with us."

CHAPTER 45

We slept in the train station in Aleppo the entire night. It was early in the morning, perhaps 4:00 am or so. The station was still dark, and Keran, Emma, and Sara slept seated in the neat row of chairs where Emma and Sara had initially sat the day prior.

"Aran, are you awake?" Grace whispered.

"Yes, Grace, I am," I replied.

"It doesn't appear that we are ever going home, Aran," Grace said. "Father told me last night that we couldn't go home. That no Armenians can return home and that we will have to find a new place to live. We are going to Cairo, because my father knows some Armenians there that he thinks will help us. I hope that we will find a good place to live, Aran." I listened to Grace but was too tired to respond. Grace, after pausing momentarily to ensure that I was awake and listening, continued. "I won't see my friends again, Aran. Do you think that when you find your family, you and Anahid can be my friends? Do you think that we will all end up in the same place?" Grace now waited for my response, and as the moments passed, I hoped she thought I was dozing back off to sleep. But Grace looked directly into my eyes as she spoke, and she knew that I was alert.

"I don't know," I replied.

My answer was truthful, as I didn't know where I was going, or what I would do when I arrived, but my response hurt Grace.

"You don't know if you want to be my friend, Aran?" she said.

"No, Grace, that's not what I meant," I quickly replied, cutting off her words. "I just meant that I don't know where I am going," I said.

"Aran, you are coming to Cairo with us, aren't you? My father said last night that you are coming to Cairo," Grace said.

"Yes, Grace, I am coming to Cairo," I replied.

"Well, then, when we reach Cairo, I am sure that my father will help you find your family. After you find them, my father, I am sure, will make arrangements for them to come to Cairo. I can then meet Anahid, and we can all be friends, no matter where we all finally end up."

I nodded my head as Grace spoke, and her words seemed to take all the air from me. There was no need for any more contrivances. It was silent for a moment, and I couldn't take a breath, then I said, "No, Grace, I can't!"

"What do you mean, you can't?" Grace replied.

"I mean that I can't lie to you anymore," I said.

"What do you mean? How have you been lying to me, Aran?" Grace asked.

"I have been lying because my sister is dead, Grace. My father and mother are dead, too."

Grace sat for several moments with her hands clenched together and pressed against her lower lip and said nothing. She then began to speak, her hands still clenched together placed where they were. "Why did you lie to me?" Grace asked.

"I am sorry, Grace. I didn't want to lie, but I had to," I replied.

"Why, Aran? Why did you have to lie to me?" Grace asked.

"Because, Grace."

My mind was now racing through memories, images, and feelings that I had done my best to suppress, and I didn't know how to best describe these to Grace. I wanted to start from the beginning on the day they took my father from my house, and the time I spent with Anahid and our mother with Evren, and the visits by Professor Daigneau. I wanted to tell her about the night we tried to escape from Constantinople with Evren and Professor Daigneau. My mind paged through the images while Grace awaited my response.

"What happened, Aran? What happened to them?" Grace repeated, now demanding a response, and the clear narrative in my mind became jumbled as I tried to respond to Grace.

"My mother, Anahid, and I were put in a camp," I began. "It was a prison camp, with armed guards. They put us there because they found us trying to escape from Constantinople. We were there for over a month, and my mother died there. Anahid died in the desert before I reached the caravan. I didn't want anyone to know because I thought I would be turned over to the authorities and become a conscript and be killed."

Grace clearly wanted to know everything, and I wanted to tell her everything, the entire truth of what had happened.

"And my father," I continued, "they took him from my house. I thought they took him to help fight the war. I thought they needed my father, but they didn't. They just killed him."

Now I had given Grace a glimpse of all of the pieces. As broken and fragmented as they were, at least I had finally told Grace the truth—the essentials, anyway.

Grace sat silently. I knew that she felt betrayed, and I was too ashamed to say anything more. We just sat and waited until everyone woke and the train was ready to board.

CHAPTER 46

We boarded an ornate passenger train later that morning. The windows had curtains made of lace. The sunlight filtered through the lace, which transmitted the lace's patterns throughout the train car. The inner walls of the train car were made of light, honey-colored wood. The seats were made of a red silk. The seats were forward facing and permitted three people to occupy each. I sat next to Keran in one seat. Emma, Grace, and Sara sat in the seat immediately in front of us. To the other side of Keran in our seat was a man of approximately thirty years of age. He appeared to be Turkish and was dressed for travel in a brown suit, with black ankle-high boots. I noticed his boots because they appeared to have been just purchased new and shined like metal. They looked stiff and uncomfortable, and the leather groaned when he bent his feet. He looked at Keran and me intermittently. He studied us, and as I sat in my oversized suit of clothes, I felt like a spectacle. Keran kept his gaze forward and didn't appear to notice that the man was looking at us.

We had been underway for approximately one hour, and we had remained entirely silent. The man who sat next to Keran turned to Keran and whispered in Turkish, "Are you Armenian, sir?" Keran seemed to freeze and said nothing. The man sensed that Keran was made to feel uneasy by the question, and he sought to calm Keran. "Don't be afraid, sir. I know what has happened. You are on a safe train. There is no need to fear anything." Keran nodded politely. Keran fixed his gaze straight ahead again, and I sensed that he was trying his best to quell any further discussion. The man continued to look at Keran and seemed intent on further conversation.

"Is this your son?" the man asked, pointing to me. I felt uneasy. I hadn't had an opportunity or the courage to tell Keran, Sara, or Emma the truth, and Grace didn't speak a word to me or anybody else before we boarded the train. Keran looked at me, and I began to feel a cold sweat on my forehead. Would Keran tell the man that my parents were just up ahead and that we were on our way to find them? Would he repeat my lies? Keran turned his head toward me and looked at me for several moments then he turned back and whispered to the man, "No, sir, he is not my son. He is an orphan." Keran didn't intend for me to overhear him, but I did, and he realized that I had.

I was stunned that Keran already knew, as I'd never had the slightest sense that he suspected anything. The man's face became red, and he rubbed his forehead nervously, then he looked away and became silent.

I began to cry. I felt ashamed and wanted to explain myself to Keran, and at least explain the practical reason for my lies. Keran saw me begin to cry, and he whispered to me while patting me on the top of the head, "It is going to be fine, Aran. We knew what happened when we saw you for the first time. You are a brave boy, and when we saw you there in the desert, we knew that it was a miracle that such a brave boy like you made it all the way from Constantinople. You must think of it as a miracle, and continue to be brave."

The only person who believed my lies all along was Grace. She was the only one who didn't know enough to understand that it was all a lie. I was frozen in my seat and hoped that Grace didn't see me cry.

CHAPTER 47

The man who sat next to Keran disembarked at a train station near Hama later that afternoon. As he stood from his seat to leave the train, he handed me a handful of lira without saying anything, and I put the lira in my pocket.

The original train that we boarded in Aleppo was just the first stage of our trip to Cairo. There were a series of stagecoaches that led to junctions with other trains. The trains that we boarded, several in all, stopped frequently, sometimes at a station to allow passengers on or off, but more frequently stops seemed arbitrary, and in the middle of tracks without any civilization in sight. The trains and stagecoaches became less occupied as we went. Within two days out of Aleppo, we had become anonymous in areas that had no awareness of where we had been, who we were, or what we had been through. At the end of the second full day, we had boarded another train after a short stagecoach ride. Grace hadn't said anything to me since leaving the station in Aleppo. When we boarded, Keran sat next to Sara and Emma, and Grace came to sit next to me in the seat immediately behind them. I sat in the seat next to the window, and I looked out of the window as she sat down, pretending to be preoccupied by a man who stood outside the train selling rugs that were stacked on the edge of the street that fronted the tracks. Grace didn't say a word as she sat, and I sensed that she probably was counting the hours until we reached Cairo, so that she would never have to see me again. I took a quick glimpse at Grace. She closed her eyes and seemed to be trying to make me invisible to her. As I sat, I felt like a heavy stone was weighing on my chest, and I was unable to speak, especially to Grace. Now that we had left the desert, the fear that drove me was gone, and all that was left was an empty hollow where everything that I lost had been, and I couldn't feel anything other than that.

"My father thinks that you are very brave, Aran," Grace said as she opened her eyes and sat forward to grab the ends of a blanket that had been draped across her knees but had fallen to the floor as the train began to move. I was surprised that Grace was speaking to me, and I tried to smile at Grace in response but only mustered a small one.

"You mustn't feel badly, Aran, for not telling me what happened," Grace continued. "My father explained to me yesterday that it was best that you didn't tell anybody what happened, so I don't wish you to think that I am upset with you. Please don't feel badly, Aran." As Grace spoke, the heaviness in my chest began to alleviate, and as it did, I began to feel my throat clench, then I began to cry. I tried to hide it from Grace by putting my hands over my eyes, but she knew I was crying. Grace was entirely silent as I wept, and she looked away, I think trying to pretend that she didn't see me crying. I pressed my face against the window and felt the wet glass against my cheek.

"I am happy that I met you, Aran. We will always be friends," Grace offered in an attempt to console me, now making no effort to pretend that she didn't see me cry. I was trying to compose myself at least enough to utter something in response to Grace. I wiped my tears on the sleeve of my coat and looked at Grace.

"Yes, Grace, friends," I sputtered.

CHAPTER 48

We arrived in Cairo on a Sunday, eight days after we left Aleppo. It was night, and the train station was dark and cold, and the strange geometry of the motifs carved in the inner walls of the building made me feel like we had arrived in another world. We stood in the station's center while Keran took up conversation with a local to ask directions to the closest hotel.

We left the station within an hour and walked approximately three blocks to a small hotel. The front lobby of the hotel smelled of incense, and the walls were covered with dark tapestries. The portions of the walls that were not covered were shown to be made of brick, with a thin layer of plaster that had cracked and fallen off in several places. A short staircase led to the room that Keran arranged for us. It was small but had enough accommodation. I was given some linens, and Emma helped me make bedding from it on the floor, and I sat there.

"Tomorrow, I will look up my friend who lives not far from here in the middle of Cairo. We will determine then where we will go," Keran said.

"Will we be able to stay here, Father, at least for now?" Grace asked.

"I am not certain yet, Grace. I will know more tomorrow," Keran replied. Grace seemed satisfied enough for the moment, and she took a chair in the corner of the room and sat. Emma and Sara each sat on the edge of one of the two beds in the room, both looking at the floor.

"But what about Aran? Where will he go?" Grace asked, breaking a brief silence.

"Be quiet, Grace. There is no need to talk about that now," Emma shouted back at Grace with a stern and disapproving glare. Keran scratched his head nervously and didn't say anything in response to Grace.

I felt awkward and embarrassed, as Keran shuffled toward the bed where Emma and Grace were sitting and lowered himself next to Sara. I already had thought that perhaps the Kazarians were wondering when I would disappear, as mysteriously as I had appeared to them in the desert. I felt like a stray dog following the Kazarians and thought perhaps that they wanted me to stop following them now.

"We are going to see Aran through until he can find his way," Sara said. Sara then looked at me and said reassuringly, "Don't worry, Aran, we will see you through."

I wanted to ask Sara how I was to find my way. I wanted to tell her that I was entirely lost, and I didn't think that there was any place that I would ever find. I wanted to tell her that I felt that I was just being cast into nothingness, and I would be wandering in it forever. I couldn't say anything, though. I just sat awkwardly. They all knew that I was helpless, and I must have looked pathetic to them.

Within the hour, I began to fall asleep. I hadn't completely lost consciousness, although Grace apparently thought that I had, and I overheard a conversation that she was having with Emma.

"Where will Aran go, Emma?" Grace whispered.

"Father says there are agencies that help find people's families. Like relatives and such, who may be in America and other places," Emma replied.

"But he has no family, Emma. They are all dead. Will they put him in an orphanage? I heard Father say that there is an orphanage in Cairo where children without parents are made to stay," Grace replied.

"Be quiet, Grace," Emma said. "It is no business of yours. Father knows what to do."

"He's my friend, Emma, and I can say whatever I wish."

"Well, if you must talk, at least have the sense not to talk when he might overhear what you are saying."

"He can't hear me, Emma. He's asleep."

"You can't be sure. Just be quiet."

Grace didn't say anything more, but what she said was enough to keep me thinking and awake. The thought of being placed in an orphanage felt particularly strange. Why an orphanage? Orphanages were for children without memories.

CHAPTER 49

Within several days, Keran moved us to a flat in the center of Cairo. It was a depressing place, with no windows, and smelled of linseed oil. It was in a crowded part of the city, a poor area, where multiple families crammed into small flats. The building that housed our flat had several other flats, all of which appeared overcrowded. Long, dark hallways led to each apartment. Our apartment consisted of a small living room and two small bedrooms. Grace and Emma occupied one of the bedrooms, and Keran and Sara occupied the other. I slept on a sofa in the living room. The entire apartment had dark red carpeting that was worn in places to its backing. It was apparently the best that could be found on short notice, arranged by Keran's friend who had been located by Keran a few days after we arrived in Cairo. He was an Armenian man who Keran had met doing business, and they'd maintained their business relationship through the years. He had a business importing goods from throughout the Middle East, and he apparently had some influence, according to Keran. Keran introduced me to him the day we moved into the flat. I sat upon a box of assorted dry goods, fruit, and some rice that I carried into the living room of the flat at Keran's request, after we returned ahead of Emma, Sara, and Grace from the market. I heard a man's voice in the hallway outside of the flat.

"Keran, call out if you are there. I am in need of some help."

"Is that you, Garo?" Keran replied as he hurried into the hallway.

"Aran, can you come help us?" Keran called. When I reached the hallway, I saw a short man with gray hair standing with two large cloth bags at his feet. He had white cotton pants that had dirt worn in the front of the thighs and a straw safari hat that had a broken brim. He wore a white shirt, which was soaked with sweat, and his face was unshaven.

"Aran, I wish for you to meet my friend Garo. He is a good man, although he may not look it," Keran said jovially.

"I look like I feel, old and tired, so I am what I am," Garo said gruffly.

"Garo, this is Aran," Keran said.

As Keran spoke, Garo removed his hat and looked intensely at me.

"So you are the brave boy from the desert. I have been told about you." He spoke in short, driving phrases and bit off each word.

"Do you like cheese, boy?" he asked.

"Yes, I do very much," I replied.

"Good, then you can help me carry these bags in and have all the cheese you want. I just bought it fresh," he said. I tried to pick up one of the bags, but they were heavy, and I could hardly even budge it, and Garo laughed as I tried.

"Oh, you just need to put some fat on you, boy, and you will be able to pick them up just as I do," Garo said, as he hoisted both bags on each of his shoulders in a single simultaneous motion and walked into the flat. He placed the bags down and opened one of them.

"Please, boy, eat some of this. There is nothing better. It is the best goat cheese in Cairo," Garo said. The cheese was salty, and it burned my tongue.

"Garo will help us find your relatives, Aran," Keran said, as I continued to eat. "We plan to take you to the Armenian relief agency office to make some inquiries." Garo looked at me as Keran spoke, and I felt uneasy.

"Do you know of any relatives?" Garo asked.

"No, sir, I don't think I know of any," I replied.

"We plan to go to America, Aran. We are intending to try to determine if you have relatives in America. Many families have relatives in America. It is needed for you to travel there. We want to avoid having you stay here. There are certain rules that we must follow to be able to have you come. Do you understand, Aran?" Keran said.

"Yes, sir, I think I do," I replied.

Garo then looked at Keran, and while nodding his head, Garo said, "Good, then, I will have a visit arranged for tomorrow."

CHAPTER 50

The next morning, I dressed in the oversized suit that I was given upon our arrival in Aleppo. Sara told me to wear it in the event that a picture was to be taken of me for documentation purposes. She said that I should look my best because a relative in America might see it. After I dressed, I opened up my personal items and grabbed the handful of lira that I was given by the man on the train. I put it in my pocket. It made me feel grown up. I sat on the sofa to wait for Garo to arrive. He arrived in the middle of the morning. He and Keran took me to a building several blocks from the flat. It was a plain building. When we entered it, I felt like I was being taken to an infirmary. The room that we entered was large and sterile and had beds, approximately twenty or so, lined up against the walls. We walked to the far end of the room through a doorway that led to a series of offices. A sign on one of the offices read in Armenian "Refugee Relief." Garo knocked on the door and opened it. There was a woman sitting behind a small desk in the room. She had features like my mother, dark and diminutive. Before Garo or Keran said anything, the woman asked, "Are you refugees?"

"No, madam, I mean to say I am not, but they are," Garo replied, pointing to me and Keran.

"Please come and sit," the woman said, pointing to a long bench beside her desk. As we sat, the woman looked at Keran and asked, "How can I help you?"

Keran looked down at his hat, which he had removed and held in his hands. He appeared to be collecting his thoughts, and while he did, Garo answered, "You see, madam, this is my friend Keran. He was forced into the desert with his wife and children, and they found this little boy, this little orphan boy from Constantinople, wandering in the desert alone."

"We can help you here. We are equipped to house orphans. The room you walked through is for housing orphans. There are many of them finding their way out of the desert," the woman replied.

Keran lifted his head as the woman spoke and interrupted her. "Thank you, madam, but I want to find him a home, with some family of his own, if I could, madam. His name is Aran, Aran Pirian, and he is a brave boy who needs a home, a good home with family."

The woman looked at me as Keran finished speaking, then asked, "Do you know where you might have family, boy, like an aunt or an uncle?"

"No," I replied.

"You may have some and not even know it. If you do, I am certain we can help you find them," the woman said reassuringly. "There is a chance that we may even find them in America. Many have gone to America. That is why you may not know you have any family. We will see to it that we will do everything that we can to find them."

After taking some information, she took me to a room with black linen draped on the walls and photographic equipment placed in the center. It reminded me of the day that my mother and father took Anahid and me to a photographer in Constantinople to have a family photograph taken. My mother made me and Anahid dress impeccably. It was a special day, planned for some time, and my father could not contain his excitement of having arranged the photograph. It was new technology, he raved, so clear was the print that anyone who would see our picture would think that we were alive right before them, in flesh and blood. The photographer used the background of a painted olive grove framed by fluted columns, and my father laughed as we stood in front of it waiting for the photographer to ready his equipment for the shoot. "Who will believe that we stood in an olive grove for our picture?" my father joked. "Perhaps it would have been better if we would have come dressed as Romans. Think of that: Roman Armenians."

Keran and Garo watched as the woman placed me on a plain wooden stool. As I sat, the collar of my oversized jacket pushed above my ears. A man entered the room and placed himself behind the photographic equipment. "Remain very still, boy," the man said. "If you move, your image will look nothing more than a mess of ink on nice paper." When the powder was exploded, all I could see were the patterned images of the light bursting in the innards of my eyes.

CHAPTER 51

Keran and Garo dropped me off at the flat. They were joining Sara and Emma elsewhere to attend an appointment for Emma, who had been feeling ill the day prior. Grace was waiting for me when I returned. She sat on the sofa and watched me without saying a word as I entered. I wanted to change from my suit and sit in quiet, but Grace wouldn't let me. Her eyes pierced me as I walked toward the washroom, and she intercepted me before I could reach it.

"Did they tell you that you have family?" Grace asked.

"No, they didn't tell me anything. They just said that they would look," I replied.

"You probably wouldn't tell me even if you did, so it makes no difference," Grace snapped.

"What do you mean by that, Grace?" I asked.

"Just that you probably would keep it from me, if you did find out that you had family. That's all I meant," Grace replied.

"I would tell you, Grace, if I find out that I do," I said.

"Will you, Aran? You keep everything inside, so I would guess that you wouldn't," Grace said dismissively. Grace stood from the sofa and began to walk toward the door of the flat.

"Anyway, it really doesn't matter. Emma and my mother will be returning later, and when they do, we have a visit of our own to make. Father is arranging our travel to America, and we have people to see to receive all of our papers," Grace added.

I hadn't to this point been told when the Kazarians would be leaving for America. Grace, though, was now making it seem as if their departure was more imminent than I anticipated. Grace was acting cold and distant, leading on, at least, that she didn't care much what was to become of me.

"When are you leaving, Grace?" I asked.

"Father hasn't told me when, yet, but I think it is soon. I hope so, anyway. I am anxious to meet new friends in America," Grace replied.

"I hope to be able to come, too," I said.

"Yes, but if you can't, I am sure Father will find a place for you to live here in Cairo," Grace said tersely.

"Yes, Grace, but…"

"But what, Aran?" Grace replied as I stumbled to say more.

"I don't want to live here," I replied.

As the words left me, Grace shot back without pause, "Why not, Aran?"

"Why not what, Grace?" I replied absently while still in thought.

"Why don't you want to stay here?" Grace repeated.

"Because it feels like a prison," I replied.

As soon as I spoke, something immediately changed in Grace. I am uncertain if it was that she was simply waiting for me to exhibit vulnerability, but whatever it was, in an instant her tone changed.

"I don't want you to stay here, either, Aran. I want you to come with us to America and stay with us. You must ask my father, Aran. You must tell him that he must find a way to take you no matter what. You must tell him that, Aran."

"I don't think I can come with you, if I have no relatives there," I said.

"Why, that won't stop Father. You just need to tell him that you want to come to America with us whether you have relatives there or not."

"No, Grace," I replied. "There are rules. Don't you understand? There are rules."

"I don't think you should care about any rules. Whoever made the rules didn't bother to make a rule against killing your family and making you an orphan in the first place," Grace replied angrily. Grace looked at me immediately after she spoke, and her eyes became wide, then she dropped her head into her hands. "I'm sorry, Aran. Please forgive me. That sounded so hurtful. I shouldn't have said that."

"I don't feel hurt, Grace," I replied.

Grace remained looking at me, and I knew that she could sense that I was lying. She also knew, I think, that I couldn't admit what I felt to her or anybody else. I was overwhelmed by an overriding sense in me that everything and everybody that I knew was slipping away from me, and there wasn't much that I could do about it. My condition was becoming more clear to me as each day passed. My dismemberment was nearly complete, and all of the pieces were scattered here and there. They were dead little pieces of no matter to anyone. I needed to collect them wherever I could find them and put them in a box and close the lid tightly. It needed to be a box made of stone. I didn't want anybody to see the dead little pieces. Nobody should ever have to see the dead pieces.

CHAPTER 52

Approximately one month passed. The Kazarians continued their plans to leave for America. They planned to depart in another few months, their immigration expedited by sponsors in Detroit, Michigan, where they intended to eventually live. Despite Grace's telling me to ask her father to allow me to come with them, I didn't ask. I felt that the rules made it futile, and I didn't believe that Keran and Sara wanted me, anyway.

I was taken on another visit to the Armenian relief agency. Keran took me alone this time. The lady at the agency had processed my information, and she was able to report on the preliminary results of her search. It appeared that I might have had a great uncle in Kharaput. He may have been killed, though. "Most likely, anyway," she surmised, "given all of the killing there, if he hadn't died first of old age." It would take some time to determine where he may have gone and if he was still alive and in any position to take me, even if he wanted me. There was also the matter of returning to anywhere in the Empire. It was not possible, and anyone left, even if family, would not be suitable to take me. "Best to assume that he is dead," she said. "No sense in wasting much time searching anymore for his whereabouts. No relatives in America are known, and it is becoming less likely every day that any will be found there, or anywhere."

She read her findings from a sheet of paper written neatly in a beautiful Armenian script. When she finished speaking, she rose from her chair and folded the paper in half and handed it to Keran and said, "You may have this copy of my report, sir. I know it is not much, for now, but it may be all that will ever be found after the search is completed. Do you wish to have it?"

Keran took the paper from the lady's hand. He stared at it and said, "Yes, madam. Thank you."

"Is there anything more that I can do for you, sir, in the meantime?" she asked.

"No, madam, this boy just needs a family," Keran replied.

"Of course, but we must remain practical," she replied. "The boy will need a place to stay if we cannot find family."

"Yes, I know," Keran said while continuing to look down at the report.

"Can I show you our accommodations here?" the lady asked. "We have many children here. They are well cared for until we find them other homes."

Keran paused for several moments and looked at me. I believed that Keran and Sara had already made the decision to leave me here, if no other family could be found, but they probably just couldn't bring themselves to tell me, and the lady bringing the subject up now was apparently making Keran feel awkward, and he grew silent. Keran looked up from the paper, folded it, and, as he placed it in his breast pocket, said, "No, madam, there will be no need for that. This boy has a place to stay. He is staying with me."

"But, sir, if he has family who are able and willing to take him, he must stay with his family. Those are the rules, sir," she replied.

"Yes, but he has no family. Your report says that. So until you find otherwise, he will stay with me. Thank you again, madam," Keran said. He then grabbed me by the hand, and as we reached the street, he said, "Come, Aran, we have much to do. We need to prepare you to come to America. You will need special papers.

Garo will help us with the papers. He knows how to get special papers." I didn't know what Keran meant by special papers, but he seemed to already have planned this as a contingency.

Keran hurried us back to the flat. "I have news!" Keran exclaimed to Sara, Emma, and Grace upon entering into the flat.

"What is it, Father? What is the news?" Emma asked.

"It is news about Aran." I had a glimpse of Grace's face as Keran spoke, and she went blank.

"What about Aran?" Grace asked.

"He is coming with us to America," Keran replied.

Grace's blank expression left her as Keran spoke, then a broad smile came to her face. "That is good news, Aran!" Grace exclaimed.

"That is good news, Aran. Isn't it?" Emma repeated. I nodded my head in reply but said nothing. I believed it was good news only because it meant that I would be able to leave Cairo, but I had no real feelings of happiness, or any other feeling for that matter.

Sara walked toward me and placed her arm around my shoulder, "You see, Aran, I told you that we would see you through."

"Yes, ma'am," I replied.

That night I sat in the living room with Grace after Keran, Sara, and Emma retired to their rooms for the night. Grace said she was too anxious to sleep, so she stayed in the living room and tried to occupy her time reading a book. It appeared to be of no use in calming her. She looked up repeatedly and tried to engage me in conversation, while I occupied myself sketching the rough image of the Sphinx with an ink pen. I was sketching from a periodical written entirely in Arabic. The periodical contained photographs, and the photograph of the Sphinx was as clear and lifelike a photograph as I had ever seen. I thought that it was the closest to life that a photograph could ever be, so I sought to emulate the lines of it, just to determine if there was some secret to its creation that I could discover by simply copying it. It was the same technique that I learned as a young boy, but I was now attempting to adapt the technique for copying a photograph. This would be more difficult than simply copying the strokes of a penciled drawing, but I thought it challenging to try it and hoped that if it worked, there was no limit to what I could create. I hoped to create a person this way, a perfect image of a person.

"What are you drawing?" Grace asked.

"Nothing, Grace," I replied.

"You are most certainly drawing something, Aran," Grace said.

"It is nothing, Grace. I am just scribbling," I replied.

"Aran, why always must you hide something?" Grace asked.

"I am not hiding anything, Grace."

"Yes, you are, and I can tell when you are, because you keep your head down, and you can't so much as look at me."

"Here, Grace, you see, it is nothing more than scribbles," I said to Grace as I picked up the piece of paper.

"Those don't look like scribbles to me, Aran. It looks like you are drawing a person."

"Well, it's not a person, Grace. It is just a picture of a statue in this periodical, and I am just drawing it to pass the time. Are you satisfied that I am not hiding anything from you now?" I said tersely.

Grace at first withdrew to her book and was acting hurt. I became engrossed in my drawing and after a time hadn't even noticed that Grace was still in the room.

"Do you believe that they will hate us in America, too?" Grace asked, breaking me from my trance.

"What do you mean, Grace?" I asked.

"Will people in America hate us because we are Armenian, just like the Turks hate us?"

"I don't know, Grace. What do you think?"

"I think that they might," Grace replied.

"Perhaps they will not even know that we are Armenian. There are so many different types of people there. Maybe we will be anonymous," I said.

"The last thing I wish is to be anonymous. I think it is a great thing that we are Armenian," Grace replied.

"Why is it so great, Grace? I think I would rather be anything else but Armenian."

"You are not proud to be Armenian, Aran?"

"Maybe once I was, but not now," I replied. "I don't wish for anybody to know that I am Armenian. You said so yourself, Grace. They might hate us there, too, because we are Armenian."

"But that isn't a reason not to be proud, Aran."

"I think it is," I replied.

"Do you really feel that way?" Grace asked as she stood up from her chair. Grace was growing angry, and her voice was becoming louder, and I was afraid that she would draw attention to the others and tell them what I said.

"Grace, please, I don't wish to talk anymore about it. Just forget what I said."

"I can't forget it," Grace replied as she stomped from the room and slammed the bedroom door behind her.

I looked back at my drawing and recommenced my sketch. It was taking shape the way I saw it in the periodical. It at first appeared to be human, but upon closer look, it was clear that it was a beast, inanimate and without a soul.

CHAPTER 53

Within approximately two weeks, I received my papers that Garo had specially prepared. Keran said to pay the contents no particular attention, other than if asked by any authorities, in which case I should tell them that my great uncle lives in Detroit, just as my papers say. Keran assured me that they would not be the wiser. Keran didn't speak to me in particulars about where I would live once I arrived. The focus was simply on arriving in America. I didn't know whether I would live with the Kazarians or not. It was enough to be leaving Cairo. The rest, I assumed, would be determined when we arrived in America. Everything was nearing completion, I was told. Keran even had a picture of the ship on which we would be taking our passage. It was on a postcard that Keran gave me. It looked like a grand ship, with four large smokestacks that towered high above the shiny black gunnels of the ship's hull. It was depicted in watercolor slicing through turquoise swells topped with whitecaps.

Departure was scheduled to be on a Sunday in late November. Approximately one month prior to our departure, the lady from the relief agency arrived in mid-afternoon at our flat. I sat in the living room with Keran, Sara, and Grace. When she came to the door, I didn't recognize her initially. I had assumed that there would be no further need for the relief agency once I had received my papers from Garo. Keran answered the door, and he appeared not to have initially recognized her, either.

"May I help you?" Keran asked as he pulled the door open fully.

"Yes, hello, do you remember me? I am from the relief agency. We met, so that I may assist you in finding family for the little boy, Aran. Is he here?"

"Yes, he is here. Come in. Sit down," Keran said, pointing to the sofa where I was sitting.

"I won't trouble you for long," she said as she walked in. "I have news. It is news about Aran's family."

Keran remained standing as the lady sat beside me on the sofa.

"Aran, I have good news. Your mother, she has a cousin. She lives in New York City, in America. She sent a telegram back to me. She will sponsor you in America, and she wishes for you to live with her."

I became suspended—present, but suspended—as she began to provide the details. My mother had a cousin who had immigrated to New York City a few years prior to the outbreak of World War I, she said. Communication by telegram to her had been arranged by the relief agency, and there was a reply. My mother's cousin knew me. Saw me often as a young child, she said, and wanted me to live with her in America. I should be happy, the lady said. I was lucky, she said. It must have been my wish come true. She handed Keran the papers that would permit me my passage out on any ship that could be arranged. Keran was handed the papers, and he thanked the lady, while patting me on the head. After the lady from the relief agency left, Keran's face grew strained, and he didn't say a word as he handed me my papers. Keran just walked to his bedroom and shut the door. Keran stayed in his bedroom the rest of the day. Grace sat with me most of the day, but we didn't speak much until night.

"Do you want to live in New York with that person?" Grace asked.

"I don't know, Grace," I replied.

"What do you mean, Aran, that you don't know? You should know," Grace said.

"But I don't. I don't know that person. I don't know if she really wants me to come," I said.

"I can ask Father if you can stay with us, if you don't want to go," Grace offered.

"No, Grace, I think I have to go. There are rules about that."

"What rules, Aran?"

"Rules about who you have to stay with, if they want you."

"But you just said so yourself, maybe she doesn't want you to come. Then you wouldn't have to follow the rules."

"I don't think that it works like that, Grace."

"Well, it should, Aran. It would only make sense that you should be able to stay with who you want, and stay with people that want you."

"Who's to say that your parents want me?"

"Because they told me so, Aran," Grace replied.

"When did they tell you that, Grace?" I asked.

"When Father found out that you might have a relative in Kharaput. He said it to my mother that he didn't want to see you go to somebody else. I overheard them talk about it, Aran."

"Should I tell him, Aran? Should I tell him that you want to stay with us? He can send a telegram back and tell that lady that you want to live with us."

"You can't, Grace."

"Why, Aran? Why can't I?"

"Because it's against the rules."

Grace stared at me for a moment then an angry expression came to her face. "What rules, Aran? Who makes the rules?"

"Some government, I think, Grace," I replied.

CHAPTER 54

My papers had my picture, the one taken at the relief agency. I stared at it for a moment and didn't initially recognize myself. It might have been a mistake, I thought. Perhaps these were another boy's papers, the papers of a boy whose mother had a cousin in America. I looked at the picture for several moments, though, and I recognized the boy. He was me: a little scared boy with a man's suit of clothes, some lira in his pocket, and some dead little things in a box. There was nothing else. It was all empty, but for the dead little things. All the other pieces were scattered someplace else, where he couldn't find them. The empty part was where the pain was located, I surmised, like the hollow pain one feels with an empty stomach. A lack of sustenance causes that kind of pain. I learned that to be the case. The difficulty was finding the source of the pain, though. It was easy enough in the prison, or in the desert, to know that I could ease the pain with a crumb of bread or a little handful of grain. There was no sustenance that could avoid this pain, though. That was more than apparent to me. The picture was not perfect, to be sure. The powder must not have fully exploded, or there may have been some complications in the photograph's development as only my face was clearly shown. The rest of me was cast in blurred shadows. Perhaps I moved when the powder exploded, destroying the rest of me.

If only I could know what pieces I lost. It was worse having the hollow pain, and not knowing what was there before it emptied. I had some ideas, of course, and I spent a good deal of time thinking about my ideas and trying to formulate some determinations, but I was a good bit away from reaching any final conclusions. I was still determining if there was anything there to begin with, or if it was always empty, and I was simply not old enough to have been made aware of it yet. If I couldn't find the pieces, perhaps I could fill the empty parts with something else, I thought. Perhaps leaving for America would help. I would maybe find new pieces there to replace the ones that I lost. I wondered if it could be that easy, if it would all be made better by traveling to another place. I would have no choice now in finding out.

The final several days before our departure were approaching. It was the last ship making a departure to America for at least six months, I was told. We had to be prepared to leave so as not to miss it. However unexpected the news of my having family in America, I was still to make the passage with the Kazarians, and we would part ways at the point of arrival in New York City. I would stay there. The Kazarians would travel to Detroit at some time subsequent.

I wondered if Keran really was upset that I had family that was found. He didn't mention anything to me about it since the lady from the relief agency visited and provided the information. Regardless of what Grace told me, I wondered if perhaps he was relieved that he had no further obligation to me once in America, and I wouldn't be underfoot complicating matters. I would no longer be a parasite on them, and I should have felt relief from that because it was growing as much a burden on me as it probably was on them.

It was best anyway that I be alone, left to fend for myself. I could finally determine then if anything was left of me or, if once removed from the host, I would just dry up and fall off, like a dry grape off of a reticular vine. What was sustaining me, if anything?

I hadn't any answer for it. I wanted the answer, though, and the sooner the better, so that I could get on with matters or allow myself to die completely. I needed an escape from this trap, a perpetual suspension of not being who I was and not knowing what I would be, or if I would even be at all. I was familiar with death, and it didn't scare me. It was a final outcome, and that was all that I believe I was searching for, just an end to all of it, and a final resting place. I was through with the slow march toward it. I just wanted to be finished off quickly, if that were to be my lot. It was a process less painful, and I wouldn't feel trifled with anymore, not by a government, not by a history, and not by fate. I was beginning to see that now, at least.

CHAPTER 55

Keran and Sara were becoming preoccupied with Emma's
health. I only understood the issue to be constant fever.
They were taking her almost daily to visits with a doctor
who was some distance away in the center of Cairo.

Keran, Sara, and Emma had been gone for most of the day on
a visit to the doctor. Grace and I remained in the flat, and I spent
almost the entire day quiet, churning through thoughts that
raced in and out of my mind. I must have appeared detached
to Grace. Grace was becoming frustrated with me, perplexed by
what she perceived as my passivity, and she was beginning to boil
over.

"Tell my father and mother that you wish to live with us, Aran!
Tell them, before it's too late and we go on that ship to America,"
Grace demanded, as we sat alone in the flat. "Tell them, before
it is too late."

I just sat as Grace spoke, and I must have appeared obstinate,
and Grace grew even more frustrated and continued to press.

"Don't you want to stay with us, Aran? Is it that simple? Do you
want to go live with a perfect stranger and never see us again?"

"No, that's not it, Grace," I replied.

"Then what is it, Aran?" Grace demanded. I didn't know all that I felt, or why, but I did know that I couldn't be part of any other family. I knew that I simply couldn't replace Anahid with Grace, and my parents with Keran and Sara. I wasn't searching for a surrogate, as a means of putting all the pieces back together. I was beginning to accept that I had been damned to my circumstances and that I wouldn't be permitted escape from the hell of it. It was against the rules. Whatever the force was that created the rules, I was becoming to understand that it was pernicious and it had me in its sights, just as it had Anahid and my parents. It was against the rules.

Grace looked at me and wanted an answer.

"What is it, Aran, then? Is it that you don't want to stay with us? Is that it? Just say it, Aran, because that is obviously what you think. Just say it."

"No, Grace, it's not that," I replied.

"Then what is it?" Grace asked one last time.

"It's just that it's against the rules, Grace," I replied.

Keran, Sara, and Emma returned to the flat later that afternoon. Emma had a patch on her eye, and she appeared distraught.

"We can't leave Cairo because of me," Emma said as she walked into the room and sat in a chair that was in the corner of the room and across from the sofa on which Grace was sitting.

"What do you mean?" Grace asked.

"The doctor said that I have a bad eye infection, and we can't leave the country."

"We can't leave the country? Then we must stay in Cairo?" Grace asked.

"Only us," Emma said. "Father said that Aran is going on the ship without us."

"Is that true, Father? Aran is to leave alone without us?" Grace asked.

"Yes, Grace, Aran must go. His family will be waiting for him, and the next ship out will not be for another several months. So he must make it on the ship," Keran replied.

"That means we will never see him again. That is what that means. Father, how could you just let him go like that, without us?" Grace asked angrily.

"We must, Grace," Keran replied.

"Who says, we must, Father?" Grace asked.

"Those are the rules, Grace, and there is nothing that can be done about it," Keran replied.

Grace walked into the bedroom and slammed the door shut. Keran looked at me and said, "You will be fine, won't you, Aran? You want to go to America, don't you?" Keran asked in a manner that suggested that he was as much trying to assure himself as he was me.

"Yes, sir," I replied. I was self-conscious as I answered. It was a lie, and I was certain that Keran sensed it.

Keran sat on the couch and looked straight ahead for several moments before he began to speak. "I want you to know, Aran, that if you hadn't found family, we wanted very much for you to come live with us. Will you promise me that you will remember that?" Keran asked.

"Yes," I replied.

CHAPTER 56

G race seemed upset with Keran and me over the ensuing few days. She avoided as much as she could any conversation. I felt that I had disappointed her. I sensed that she expected that I would beg Keran to stay or that Keran would fix matters to permit me to do so. I was simply resigned to my having to leave, and I believe Keran was as much resigned to perhaps the natural order of matters.

The evening prior to my leaving for America, after we had finished eating supper, I sat with Grace alone on the sofa in the living room of the flat, while Keran, Sara, and Emma retired to their rooms for the evening. I sat silently, without the courage, or the words, to say anything, as I feared that Grace was still angry with me. Grace looked at me and smiled as I sat, and it appeared that she wanted to mend matters.

"I am happy that at least you will be able to leave for America. Father tells me that when we arrive in America, we can perhaps make arrangements for you to visit us."

"That would be fine, Grace, really fine," I replied.

"Aran, please be happy that you are going to America."

I was becoming terrified to leave. I could not shake the fear that my leaving Cairo for America made me feel that I was abandoning my mother, father, and Anahid. In fact, I feared that, even though they were gone, I was leaving them behind, and that they would be finally lost to me forever, and that I wouldn't know where to search for them, along with everything else that I had lost. It was an incoherent thought, perhaps, but it was what I felt, and there would be no way of telling Grace, so I just smiled and I obliged her. "Yes, Grace, I think I am very happy to be going to America. It is a wonderful place, I hear," I replied.

Grace sat silently for a few moments then said, "Well, perhaps if you decide that you don't like it there, you will find a place someday that you will love and be able to live there instead." Grace looked at me as she spoke, then fixed her gaze directly to the floor and continued, "That is what I hope for myself anyway… that I will find it…that I will find that place where everything is as it should be, and as it was before, at least as near as possible. Do you think there is such a place, Aran?" Grace asked.

The instant that Grace finished her question, I believed that I knew the answer, and I believed that my answer would have been so dark that it would have shattered Grace. I couldn't tell Grace, because I couldn't bring myself to tell her the truth.

Grace was still waiting for my response and again asked, "Do you think so, Aran? Do you think there is such a place, because I do?"

"Yes, Grace, sure there is."

It was in the end better that I lied to Grace than to tell her what she would probably learn soon enough herself, and it wasn't the time anyway to speak of such things. She still had some hope, and there was no reason to dash it with the truth.

"I am very excited for you, Aran. I really am. I might not have seemed it, when Father told us you were leaving before us, but I know that it is good that you are leaving and that you will be staying with family. We can still be friends no matter what. We can write between visits. Will you promise me that you will write, Aran?"

"Yes, Grace, I promise," I replied.

CHAPTER 57

The ship on which I was to depart was berthed in Alexandria, a few hours by train from Cairo. Keran, Sara, Emma, and Grace would accompany me on the train. Before we boarded the train, Sara pinned my papers to the inner lining of my suit coat so I wouldn't be separated from them. Of everything I carried with me, Sara insisted that the most important were my papers. Without them I would be lost, she said, so I kept feeling for them every few minutes to make sure that they were still where she had pinned them.

I sat next to Grace on the train. Keran, Sara, and Emma sat in the seat behind us. Although quiet initially, within thirty minutes, Grace nudged me with her elbow and whispered, "Isn't it strange, Aran, that we may never see each other again, and we haven't spoken a word to each other since being on the train?"

"Yes, I suppose so, Grace," I replied.

"Well, then, perhaps we should speak about something, if for no other reason than we might never again have the chance," Grace said.

"What would you like to speak about, Grace?" I asked.

Grace paused for a few moments, then replied, "I would like to know what it feels like to be going to America, I think."

"What do you mean? How is it supposed to feel?" I asked.

"I think it should feel like you are going to an exciting and beautiful place, like a beautiful park, with games, like a carnival," Grace replied.

"Well, I don't feel like that, Grace," I replied.

"What do you feel, then, Aran?"

"I don't know. I suppose I don't feel much of anything right now, Grace."

"You must feel something, Aran."

"Well, I can tell you that I don't feel like I am going to a carnival."

I was growing angry and didn't wish to talk any longer, and I feared that my anger would cause me to snap at Grace, but I was able to hold everything in and let the anger shred my innards without Grace suspecting anything. I looked at Grace, who was awaiting my reply, and I sensed that perhaps she wanted some assurance from me that everything was as it should be.

"Yes, Grace, I suppose I really do feel excited," I replied. A small smile came to Grace's face, and she nodded slightly and turned her head to look out the window of the train. I then closed my eyes and tried to sleep for the remainder of the trip.

The train stopped in Alexandria several blocks from the port. Keran arranged a carriage to take us the remainder of the distance. The carriage left us by large rusted iron gates, which marked the port's entry point. There were authorities there manning the gates and a large line already forming. Keran pulled my trunk from the back of the carriage, and I stood there for several moments while the Kazarians looked at me. No one appeared to be able to gather any words to say. There was a chill coming from the water, so Sara placed her hands on the collar of my coat to cinch it tight and pass the button through the top buttonhole. Keran put his arm around my shoulder and pulled me close. Grace and Emma smiled slightly and waved their hands at me. Sara, Emma, and Grace each hugged me, then stepped back. Keran walked with me several meters to the line and carried my trunk. He placed the trunk beside me where the line ended and placed his arm around me again and held me tight for a few moments. "You are a brave boy," he whispered. I looked at Keran, and his eyes were red and full of liquid like he had been stabbed right there, just as they had looked when we were on the cart headed out of the desert. I knew what he saw, and I had no faculty to assuage him or anybody else, including myself. I was just a little boy: a scared little boy, not brave at all, with a box.

CHAPTER 58

There was a line of people on the other side of the gates, and as I stood in it, I looked up and saw the enormous ship that we were preparing to board. It wasn't anything like the picture on the postcard. The hull of the ship was rusty, and its stacks were gray from smoke. The water of the harbor was brown and stagnant, and it smelled of rotten fish and fuel. I walked up the incline of the gangway slowly behind the line and dragged my trunk along with me. When I reached the top, a man dressed in a shipmate's uniform grabbed my trunk and helped me place it on the deck. I walked several meters down the deck, where others were standing to wait for the ship to depart, and put my chin on the ship's rail. I stood there for about an hour then felt the ship begin to vibrate as the propellers began to turn, and the ship began to back away from the dock. I looked along the ship's rails to its stem and felt the land separate from the ship. The ship then made a quarter turn, which left me on the port side facing the sea and blocked from any view of the land. The ship was pushed to forward and made its way to the port's opening. It was just as well that I couldn't see the land. I had left everything there, but I wouldn't have known where to look to wave any final good-byes. The smoke for the ship's stacks blew in plumes then settled on the ship's deck. I would be suffocated by the smoke if I stayed on deck any longer, so I picked up the front end of my trunk and followed the line through the cabin door.

It was a dark ship, with no source of light in the main salon other than trickles of light from a stairway leading up from the salon to the ship's bridge. The ship may have had a glorious past, but whatever it had was now lost. It appeared old, tattered, and hollow, with steel floors, which may have once been covered with wood or rugs, and bare riveted steel walls, probably once paneled like a proper ship's salon should.

The ship's officers were stationed in the cabin way to process the passengers. I unbuttoned my suit coat and opened it so that they could see my papers. An officer held my coat open as I did and nodded his head. He called to a man who was dressed in a plain deckhand's uniform. The deckhand lifted my trunk on his shoulder and steadied it there in the curl of his arm. With the other hand, he motioned to me to follow him. We took a hallway to a flight of stairs lit with portholes and with a view through them of the sea. The stairs were made of black metal grate that permitted a view down the stairwell shaft. We took several flights, almost to the ship's bilges, well past where the portholes ended, and exited the stairwell through a heavy iron door painted thick with black paint. The door opened to a narrow hall, so narrow that a man's shoulders could touch each wall while passing through it. The deckhand placed my trunk on the floor, and he picked up the front end and dragged it while I followed him. He led me to a cabin and opened the door. The cabin was no more than three meters in length and width, dimly lit by a small lamp with two empty berths aside it. I chose one and sat upon it. The deckhand pulled my trunk to the foot of the berth and left the cabin without saying anything. As I sat, I heard others walk down the hallway, and I waited for someone to enter the cabin and take the other berth, but no one did. It was an empty berth meant for nobody else, and it seemed a waste. When the ship was well underway, it became quiet, and the ship became cold from the seawater that encapsulated the ship all around and above me.

I placed my hands around the glass shade of the lamp to warm them. The cabin would suit me well enough. It was a dark little cold place without anything in it.

I took the photograph of me that was pinned to my suit coat and placed it on my berth. I decided to pass my time by attempting a self-portrait. I took some paper and a pencil from my trunk and began to copy the outer lines of my face as it appeared in the photograph. It was a crude attempt, and it looked nothing more than a child's drawing. I drew my head round with no dimensions. It looked nothing like me. In fact, it looked nothing like anybody. It wasn't even identifiable as human. I ripped the paper up and threw the pieces in my trunk. I stared at my photograph and wondered if it was an accurate depiction of me. I still thought not. I looked scared and weak, buried in my oversized suit. I put my hand over the photograph so that all I could see were my eyes. I recognized my eyes. They were the same as my father's. They were round and large, and everyone always told me how they looked like my father's. Perhaps I should try to draw my father's portrait, I thought. I believed I had the old photograph of my family somewhere in my trunk, taken from my mother's things before we left the prison. I looked in my trunk, and I found it, buried among the other things. I pulled it out. It was the picture of my family taken with the olive grove backdrop.

I decided to put it back in the trunk. I took my photograph and pinned it back with the rest of my papers in my suit coat. No sense in wasting time trying to make a new picture. The photograph was as close to real as could be made, anyway, even with a painted olive grove. There was no use in it, and there was no way in which my mind would permit me even some small escape in such trite diversion. I knew it wouldn't. It had me trapped, and it wouldn't permit me out. "Oh God, get me out of here," I whispered. It was a futile request, and I knew it. I lost God back in the desert, at about the same place that I lost hope and everything else.

CHAPTER 59

I arrived in New York City on December 17, 1915. I stood on the ship's deck for a few hours and was able to see the first sight of land. It was a strange sight to see the edges of the horizon transform from a thin imperceptible line to shadowy bumps, then to a city. It was like the makings of a drawing. The outline appeared first then the details were shaded in stroke by stroke. When the city came into full view I had first determined that it was not real. It had no beginning and no end. I had never seen a place with no beginning and no end. I once believed that everything must have a beginning and end, and so there was nothing about it that could be real. It was the most accurate perspective of the place. Whoever inhabited such a place couldn't be real, either. Nobody real could ever live in any such place.

I was dressed in my suit when I disembarked the ship. I kept my papers pinned to the inner lining of my suit. It was good that I had, because I needed all of the strength in my hands and arms to keep ahold of my trunk as the crush of people disembarking the ship pushed me along. I couldn't see anything for a few hours, except for the backs of people in front of me. When I reached the point where the authorities were stationed, I heard them speak in English, and I couldn't understand a word of anything. I just placed my trunk in front of me and unbuttoned my suit coat so that they could see my papers. An officer grabbed me by the shoulder when I did and put me in a different line. When he did, I wanted to tell him that I thought I might be lost, but I didn't know the words in English, so I just stayed silent and followed the line. It was long, and it led to a large building. They put me on a ferryboat there, and I thought that I might be sent back out to sea, rejected for entry for whatever reason.

I was taken to an island just a short distance away, and when I disembarked, I stood in another line. When it was my turn, a lady grabbed my chin and looked in my mouth. I held out my suit coat as she did so that she could see my papers. She looked at them carefully. Included in my papers was the telegram from my mother's cousin, which stated that she would take me. The telegram included a translation that the woman read. The woman pinned a small tag on my coat. I was then placed back on the ferry, which took me to where I originally disembarked from the ship. An officer led me to a building, where I sat on a long bench and waited for some direction. There were others sitting there as well. One by one, they were taken by an officer and led to a large gate where people holding papers waited for them. The officer would take the paper and walk back to the bench. The officers would call out a name, and people would rise and walk to the officer, who then led them to the gate to be taken. Most were families waiting, so they rose together, and they walked together. When each person reached the gate and was led out, they hugged and smiled and laughed. They must have been their relatives, and in each case it appeared to be a happy reunion, there right at the outside of the gates. It had been almost three hours that I waited there. I hadn't any idea who was coming to claim me, or really if anyone would. The bench was almost empty, and I assumed that I would be unclaimed. I began to wonder if they would put me on the ship back. The tips of my fingers were cold, and my stomach fluttered.

"Aran Pirian," an officer who walked toward the bench called. He spoke my name with an accent that I had never heard, and my name sounded unrecognizable. I didn't respond at first. The officer looked down the bench then looked directly at me. He walked toward me, and I opened my coat so that he could see my papers. After looking at my papers, he said, "Aran Pirian," now looking directly in my eyes and nodding. He took me by the hand and walked me to the gates. A woman unfamiliar to me stood by the gates. She was a short, heavy woman. She looked me directly in the eye with a stern expression at first, giving the impression that she was unhappy with what she saw. The officer walked me directly to her. The officer opened my coat so the woman could see my papers. She nodded as he did. She introduced herself to me as Marie. We then walked to a carriage that waited on the side of the road.

CHAPTER 60

Marie was my mother's cousin, an older woman already into her sixties when I arrived, the daughter of my mother's great aunt, childless and untouched. She was pleasant but seemed disconnected and anonymous. It was clear to me that I would be cared for, but not loved: enough to keep me preserved in my existing state, but not to be nurtured into anything more. It was of no bother to me and was rather a relief, really. I would not wither any more than I already had, and nothing more would be taken from me. I was placed in a preserving suspension: not embalmed but, rather, encased. It allowed people to look at me without revulsion or pity so as not to make it unpleasant for them. A standard-issue immigrant from the outside; a little dead boy buried within. I didn't want anything more than I was given and felt ashamed for even having that. Who was I to complain for anything more? There may also have been some comfort in knowing that I owed nobody anything in return. Nothing was expected by me or from me, and that was best. I was not capable of sustaining any other arrangement.

I lived in an apartment building on the lower end of Manhattan, where the city's edges became rough and the inhabitants dissident. The city suffocated me, especially here where the buildings formed impregnable barriers to streets with an indeterminate end and no apparent escape from the strange, gray canyons. People walked to and from one place or the other. They were faceless, inanimate people with no understanding that rushing about from one place to another was simply a waste. I thought then that they should have known that what they were searching for didn't exist, and they should have known the futility of the pursuit.

I decided early on to remain detached. There would be no purpose in commingling the dead among the living. This was best for everyone. There was no need to divulge the truth to anyone else. They would all learn soon enough, and I did not wish to be the one that they learned it from. I remained in my room mostly. I had it to myself. I was safest there, where I wasn't questioned about my past or laughed at for having pants too short or a nose too big. Everyone was safe, if I simply remained there.

My arrangement permitted me the solitude necessary. I was looked after, and that was enough. I lived in the apartment only with Marie. My bedroom had a window, but there was no use in having it. All that was visible from it was the light-brown brick of the high rise building a distance of approximately five meters from our building. Our apartment was on the sixth floor, and the view to the ground was of an alleyway, which was empty mostly, and so even when the window was lifted open, there was nothing to see or hear. The space between the buildings formed nothing but an empty vault. I left the curtains drawn over the window most of the time. They were white sheer curtains that smelled of mothballs, and when I looked outside the window, I would often press my forehead into them and allow the sheen of the curtain's fabric to create a kaleidoscope of abstract images with the limited sources of light that penetrated the room. My room was otherwise plain, with two steel bed frames and my trunk placed directly beside my bed. I kept all my important things inside my trunk, where only I could see them, and only when I permitted myself to look.

CHAPTER 61

On January 15, 1918, a week after I turned fifteen years of age, I received a postcard from the Kazarians, who I hadn't seen since leaving Cairo, and the only correspondence since our time in Cairo was an occasional letter or telegram from them. I never wrote them back, and I thought that they should have long since determined that I was dead.

It was a plain card with a single white birthday candle embossed on the front, with "Happy Birthday" written below it. Marie placed it on my bed, and it was waiting there for me when I returned to the apartment from school. I stared at the card for a time and envied its plainness and simplicity. The picture of the candle was embossed with a glossy oil paint and was depicted with melted wax collecting on a candleholder painted in gold. A yellow flame was painted in varying shades of yellow paint, and the application made the flame appear to glow. If only it were real. I had reached my final conclusions and knew that matters were not so plain and simple.

Didn't the Kazarians know that I had died? It was a cruel fact, I suppose, but it was the truth. I also knew the answer to Grace's question, and the question that I asked myself since as to whether there was a place where everything is as it should be. There was no such place, and I believed that Grace would waste her time looking for it, and even if there was such a place, I didn't believe Grace, or me, or anybody else that lived through what we lived through could ever find it. It was all taken from us. Everything that we had was lost, and we could never get it back. In fact, I believed that such a place never existed in the first place. This I had concluded after believing to have come to this fundamental realization: It wasn't the lie that killed Anahid. It was the truth: the truth that I came to believe that there is nothing beautiful on the other side of the desert. That what we are instilled with in our youth, an appreciation for beauty, and a sense of joy, hope, and faith are based on an intricately created mythology, which we adopt and delude ourselves with so that we may perpetuate them for as long as we can, until the truth disabuses us of the luxury of harboring them any further. When we become disabused of them, we die, and we die the most hideous and lingering of deaths, at first spiritual, then physical, and when we die, we just disappear and are lost forever. That is what I believed. I just learned it earlier than most, prematurely to be sure, but I learned it nevertheless. It was all a lie. Nothing of it was real. My body just hadn't caught up with my soul. Time would take care of that, though. As for others, I would continue to deceive them because I resolved to keep the truth inside. In this way, I considered it only human to spare others from it. I may have appeared to be a fifteen-year-old boy, but, in fact, that boy was smashed into bits and scattered around the desert, lost forever and never to be found again. I was resigned to the belief that everything had been irretrievably taken from me.

The birthday card made me think about Grace and the last time that I saw her just before leaving Cairo. I wondered if she learned that it was all a lie, too, that it was all just an intricate mythology. I wondered if she had died, too. I determined not to inquire and, in any event, determined not to divulge the truth to Grace. I would not take anything more from the Kazarians or from Grace. It would require my remaining distant from them, no matter how much I wished to see them, or to correspond with them.

I took the Kazarians' card and placed it in my trunk so that I could pull it out from time to time to provide myself some light from the candle.

CHAPTER 62

Ireceived a letter from Grace dated July 15, 1918. It was her first letter to me. The letter was written on buff-colored stationary with a gold border. I could tell that the fountain pen that she wrote with must have flowed with a bit too much ink, because her hand smudged some of her writing as it passed over her words, and she apologized for it at the end of her letter. It was the beginning of her letter, though, to which I paid the closest attention. She wrote,

> *Dear Aran:*
> *You haven't written to me as you promised, and I am afraid that I haven't held up my end either, so I have decided to make amends and begin writing to you as a general habit. I hope that you will do the same. I need to know that you are doing well and that you are making do in New York. I have been thinking that it would be a shame if you are not. I hear it is a wonderful place. I am making do here. It is nothing like home, but it is a beautiful place to live, with all types of interesting places to visit. Is New York anything like home? Perhaps it really makes no difference. Father tells me that it is better sometimes to look forward and not back.*

I began writing Grace a letter in reply in an attempt to say something to her without divulging anything. I wrote that I agreed with her, because memories were dangerous. Nothing good could ever come from memories, and, in fact, I believed that they could only cause trouble. I wrote that I tried my best to erase my memories and that she should probably do the same. There was no point to them, and for those memories that remained, it was best to recast them into some form that they could be tolerated, like rolling something bitter tasting into a bit of sugar to mask it the best one could. If anyone would understand, it would be Grace, because she saw what I saw, and nothing of it should be remembered by anyone who still wished to be human. And with regard to her question whether I was making do, I wrote that I didn't think about it much one way or the other and wondered how I would know whether I was or not. Was there some way of knowing if I was, and what would it mean, anyway?

I finished the letter there and began thinking about a man that I saw earlier in the day while walking on Thirty-Second Street. He was an interesting-looking man, like one that you might have coffee with and talk about poetry. I decided to draw a sketch of him. I started with his tufts of hair then drew his eyes and the outline of his face. I engaged him in conversation as I drew him and asked if he would like to talk about poetry, fine poetry, where the meaning is so well hidden that you can't decipher it from reading: the type of poetry that can only be written after it is lived. As I shaded the outlines of the creases in the man's face, I told him that I had a good friend once. I told him how much he reminded me of him. I told him about how my friend was first a friend of my father's, then a friend to me. He was a good man who was very brave. He tried to teach me about things, but I was too young to understand. I hadn't lived enough. After a short time, though, I understood what he was trying to teach me, I told the man. It was about dying. As I drew the man's eyes, I told him to hold very still, because this was the hardest part. I explained to the man that what I needed most as a child was to learn about what was real, not about myths that made me comfortable as a child but had no use in helping me survive. I remembered a poem he once gave me to read; I recounted for the man: a complicated poem about dying. I read it before I heard that my father had died. Good preparation, of course, for what I found to be the truth later. "Be prepared to die at any moment. You could even be dead now and not even know it. It comes that quickly. Even if you aren't dead yet, you are dying anyway, day by day, piece by piece," I told the man. I caught myself before saying too much more. Who was I to give advice to this man, this perfect stranger? I apologized to the man for speaking in such a way. "Just forget about what I just said. This is why I shouldn't be around people," I told the man. Who was I to be the one to tell anybody the truth?

I finished shading in his eyes and stepped back for a moment to look at my drawing. It was a good start, and his expression appeared friendly enough, the way he seemed when I saw him on the street. I had adequately captured the deep crevices of his face and the character of his eyes to make him seem real. "Sorry to have been of any trouble, sir. You just remind me of a friend, a good friend," I said to the man, as I tossed him into my trunk along with my unfinished letter to Grace.

CHAPTER 63

I received a letter from Grace dated October 9, 1918. She wrote:

Dear Aran:
You did not respond to my last letter. You have me wor-ried. If you failed to write because you are not well, or worse, then you have an acceptable excuse. I suspect, though, that you have failed to write for none of those reasons, and because of it I am now more determined to write you more frequently, at least until I receive a response from you telling me that you are fine. Do you remember that we are friends? I shouldn't think that you have forgotten such a thing. Whether you have, or not, I still believe we are friends, and I will not think any differently. I visited my favorite place today. It is a beau-tiful place, called Belle Isle. It has a park and places to see interesting things, like beautiful flowers and colorful birds. The autumn colors are so beautiful there. If you should ever visit, I will take you there, so that you may see it for yourself.

I didn't even attempt writing a letter in response to Grace. I did wish to tell her that she was my friend, the only one that I had and the best that could ever be asked for, and because of that I didn't want her to know the truth. Nothing that I could say to her would make any sense to her, and there was no use in trying. Birds and flowers? Those were preoccupations for those still believing in something that I had long since recognized as myth. Grace was in a place that wasn't real. I really wished she would understand that I was dead, if for no other reason than she would know that she should walk past me as quickly as she could and not look at the dead things strewn about. It was best that she stay in whatever place she found, however distant she was from what was real. It was what any good friend would wish for her. It was nothing that I could say to her in a letter. I thought that perhaps it was best that I draw Grace a sketch of me and send it to her. It was best that I communicate to her in this way. Words were too difficult for me.

I grabbed my sketchpad from my trunk and gave another try at drawing myself. It was another in many attempts at it, all unsuccessful. The problem was the same on each attempt. None of the drawings looked anything like me. Like in every prior attempt, I began with the outer edges of my face, then began to shade in the features. It was the same result. This is a child's drawing, I thought. No different than any of the others, not even human. "Who are you?" I said as I pushed the point of the pencil into the paper, shredding the drawing as I did. "You are not me! Not even a small resemblance. You look like a little boy, pretending to be someone. But you're not anything. You're not even human," I shouted. I dug the pencil in and shredded the paper to bits. Perhaps I should just send Grace this, I thought, as I threw the torn pieces into my trunk. Perhaps she would understand then, that she should just walk past. Beautiful flowers and colorful birds? Where was she that she was able to see beautiful flowers and colorful birds?

Another several months passed without any word from Grace, and I assumed that she must have realized that I had no wish to write, and I hoped that she had determined that there was no further reason left to try. My assumption was wrong, though. It was there on my bed, when I returned from school, a postcard from Grace. It was a colorful picture of Belle Isle, which appeared to have been painted in its original form in watercolors, with blurred hues of green for the trees and an unnatural flag blue used for the water around the island. I hesitated to flip the card to read the message, because I knew that Grace was angered for my failure to write.

Dear Aran:
I thought you might like to know that the birds returned to Belle Isle, the same ones I wrote to you about last in the fall. I don't know how they found their way back, but they did. I can only assume that once they find a place that they love so much, they are determined to find their way back. They seemed very happy about it when they arrived, too. The little ones jump in the fountain and frolic about. They don't seem to pay any mind to their splashing about and the ruckus they are causing the other, more sensible, birds who seem to keep their distance and stand upon the edge of the fountain in a disapproving sort of way, as if unable to suffer the nonsense. I prefer the approach of the little ones, who don't seem to pay the others any attention in the least. I hope you are well, and will write to me.

Love, Grace

It was the final letter that I received from Grace. She had other matters of importance to attend to, I supposed. I think her letters were like searchlights. After a few passes, she probably determined that there wasn't anything there, simply nothing left to find. I did my part in hiding from the light so that I couldn't be found.

As much as I had thought it was best that she realized I was dead, I felt abandoned. Grace was my last tie to whatever I had before, and I let it go, unable to determine how to bear it. The truth was I couldn't bear it, and it was easier to just let go of everything and fall out of sight and just disappear. I would erase it all that way. I needed to reach oblivion and urgently, and the only way there was to erase everything as quickly as I could. I threw Grace's final letter in my trunk without response. I closed the trunk and latched it tight. I determined then that I would never open it again. After all, you never open a coffin once the lid is shut tight for good. I then determined to set out for oblivion, a place where I could forget, and be forgotten.

CHAPTER 64

I wanted to forget as much as I wanted to be forgotten. I was coming to realize that being forgotten was a relatively simple task achieved most easily by not giving anything to anybody and not taking anything more than needed to remain in suspension. As to forgetting, matters were more complex. A memory can be useful in most cases when it functions as intended. The mind is meant to function in a way that emphasizes the good memories and casts away the bad. It is meant to be pliable in that way to ensure that it maintains the body in a functional state without breaking, no matter the expense to the truth of the natural state of matters. My mind was not so pliable. It cast away the good memories and only permitted me to recall the bad. My mind was full of the bad. The dead carcasses stacked in a heap, the parched earth, the squalid death camps, the tormenting gendarmes. My mind was proficient at collecting all the dead little things. Without the dead little things, my mind was just an empty box.

By the age of eighteen, I had succeeded in pushing most everyone away from me. At home, I took Marie's shelter and her food, but that was all I took from her and all that she gave me. In school, my classmates treated me as an outcast. They knew me as the Armenian immigrant boy, and that was all. They knew nothing of my past, where I was from, or whether I had a mother, or father, or sister. My teachers thought I was slow. I didn't speak in class and performed only at a level not to be categorized as worse. I stayed to myself and constructed an elaborate wall, false mostly, so that nobody could enter. I resolved to complete my high school education and receive my diploma if for no other reason than the diploma could be used as an effective disguise to continue to hide the dead little boy within. Only grown men had high school diplomas. They were salesmen and headed factories. A little boy couldn't do that. So receiving a diploma was, in that way, a means to enable me to continue the charade and to allow the dead little boy to wander outside the prison gates without being found.

Only a couple of months remained until summer recess, which would conclude my senior year and my graduation from public school in New York City. I was anticipating my release, or, more accurately, my escape. A smug-looking boy entered my math classroom and walked to the teacher with a note. Everyone recognized the boy as the messenger who would deliver a note now and then that summoned the recipient to the principal, typically for causing some type of trouble. He was well dressed and pudgy. The sight of the boy made everyone cringe, as the principal was a cantankerous man who was best to avoid. I believe he knew the effect that he had, and it undoubtedly gave him a certain sense of power and importance. He pranced on the tips of his toes like a show pony, in a manner that reminded me very much of the fat gendarme. The teacher looked at the note and handed it back to the boy and, with the nod of her head, the boy turned to face the class, and as he did, he announced, "Aran Pirian." I could feel the blood rush to my head and face, and my eyes began to blur. The boy approached me, and as if to heighten the effect, instead of handing me the note, he slammed it with the palm of his hand on my desk and turned abruptly and walked out of the room. The note contained a simple instruction: "See the principal immediately." As I rose from my desk and gathered my books, the other students gazed at me then began to snicker. I felt sweat begin to run down my face, and my ears burned as I began to make my way. I heard a female student sitting directly behind me whisper loudly, "Look at the poor, dumb boy with the big nose. I think he is going to cry." Her joke elicited more audible snickering, and it accompanied me out of the room.

It was a hot day, and the inner corridors of the school baked all of the odors of the school into an acrid stew. My hands shook, my stomach turned more, and I could taste acid. The principal's office was located in the middle of a long corridor on the upper floor of the school, apart from any classrooms. The principal's secretary sat at a desk immediately in front of the door that led into the principal's office. She was an older woman with gray hair pulled back tightly in a bun. As I approached her, she looked up briefly, then quickly fixed her gaze down again toward the desk. "Your note, please," she instructed while holding out her hand.

"You are Aran Pirian?" she asked.

"Yes, that is me, ma'am," I replied.

"Please sit. I will tell Mr. Cornwall that you are here," she said, pointing to a wooden chair placed against the wall, immediately in front of the secretary's desk.

"Thank you, ma'am," I replied.

The secretary returned to her desk without saying any further word and began shuffling papers. She then stood and walked back to the principal's office with a stack of papers, and I waited.

The seat of the chair was very small and shaped in a manner that required an almost perfect upright posture to avoiding falling off the front edge of it. It seemed to be almost purposeful in design as a means to heighten the anxiety of anyone occupying it. After several minutes, though, of sitting, the sweat that had soaked the back of my shirt and the legs of my pants was causing me to be stuck to the worn open pores of the chair's wood, and I had to shift myself slightly from time to time to peel my clothing from it.

"He will see you now," the secretary announced as she walked from the office.

"Yes, ma'am," I replied.

I walked toward the door, which was only a quarter opened, and felt awkward. I wondered if I should knock first, so I stopped.

"Go on, boy. He is waiting in there for you," the secretary instructed.

The principal sat at a narrow desk, looking down at the stack of papers that the secretary apparently brought to him. He was a thin, short man, with almost no hair in the middle of his head, but enough on the sides to curl beneath his ears. He had very light skin, and what hair he did have was blond. He looked up at me in a disapproving manner.

"Didn't you learn to knock where you are from?" he said as he shook his head, furled his brow, then looked down again at the papers.

"Yes, sir, I am sorry, sir," I replied.

"Sit," he said tersely as he pointed to a chair that was in front of his desk. It was the same type of chair that was in front of the secretary's desk, and as I sat, I could feel myself becoming glued to it.

"Do you know why you were sent here, Mr. Pirian?" he asked.

"No, sir, I don't," I replied.

"You don't?" he replied in a sarcastic tone, and in a manner that suggested I wasn't being truthful.

"You haven't any idea?" he continued in the same sarcastic tone.

"No, sir," I replied.

"Then I will tell you," he said as he sat back in his chair. "Your teachers think that you are not capable of doing the work required to obtain a diploma this year. What's more, you are too quiet. They have no confidence that you understand English well enough to speak it. I have found many times, with students like you, immigrant students... I mean, of course, that you may be from a part of the world that never required that you learn even how to read and write. Where are you from, boy?" I didn't want to tell him anything about my past, so I froze and looked down at the floor.

"Did you hear me, boy? Where are you from?" he asked, now demanding a response.

268

I continued to feel frozen and unable to speak.

"From the looks of your clothes, and your face, and your heavy accent, I would guess that you are from a part of the world that is barbaric when it comes to valuing pursuits of the mind. Am I right, boy? Were you raised a barbarian, which makes learning a difficult task for you? It says here that you are Armenian. Are there barbarians where you are from? It won't do to simply grunt, boy. You must speak!" His tone was plainly mean, and he was simply taunting. He appeared to be enjoying the sport of it. I turned into myself fully now and did not provide any response. I had no ability to fight. I just sat and looked down at the floor.

"Nothing to say for yourself, boy? Very well, then, I shall decide that your teachers are correct. You will come back next year to repeat the grade and learn to be less Armenian, and more American, if you wish to pass. If you don't like it, go back from wherever you came from."

I wanted to tell him that I couldn't go back and that even if I could, there was nothing left for me to go back to, but I said nothing and walked out of his office.

I sat upon a bench in the courtyard that formed the common area within the school's quadrangle. I cursed the principal under my breath. I cursed his cruelty and his ignorance. I cursed that I was trapped, and I couldn't find my way out, and I cursed that I had given up trying, not able to summon even a bit of a fight.

I spent a good portion of that night awake, excoriating myself for not defending myself, or my mother and father. "You should have told him that he was an ignorant ass," I kept repeating to myself. "You should have told him that where I came from we are carved in stone. You should have told him that your father was a professor, and your mother was a musician, and you should have told him about Anahid." I knew that I couldn't, though, because then he would have asked. It would have been inevitable for anyone to ask, and then I would have been forced to tell him that they were dead. I could never tell anyone that they were dead. It was better left that way.

CHAPTER 65

"You can't stay here much longer," Marie said as she picked up a dish from the table and walked to the sink. Her back was turned to me, and she began washing the dish in the sink. "You are a grown man now. You must find a place for yourself," she continued.

Approximately one month remained before the end of my senior year of high school. I didn't tell Marie that I wouldn't be graduating. I rarely spoke to her about anything of substance, and there was no opportunity to discuss it, nor would I have provided her with the information even if the topic arose. Her back remained turned to me, and she seemed embarrassed as she rubbed the front of her wrist against her forehead. I knew that she must have been thinking about matters for some time, as she was particularly reticent more recently, perhaps burdened by it. She was mistaken, of course. I wasn't a grown man in the least. I was a little boy, a dead little boy shattered and lost. It was understandable that she was mistaken. I hid the little boy in me and didn't allow her to see him, not even once, no matter how badly he wanted to come out to show himself.

Since I had arrived in New York, I'd had the uneasy feeling that Marie took me in out of obligation, and she was marking the time when the obligation would cease. She tried to hide it from me, I think, and perhaps she believed that she had done an ample job of it, but I knew how she felt all along. There was nothing she needed to explain to me now. The dishes rattled as she placed them one by one in the dishpan. She was hunched over the sink, and the silence must have been excruciating for her in the aftermath of laying the truth bare.

"Yes, Marie, I was thinking the same," I began. "I was hoping that you wouldn't be upset if I told you that I planned to leave. I plan to rent an apartment soon. The apartment is in the Bowery, and I plan to rent it with some friends of mine from school. One of my friends has an uncle who has a shop. He makes clothes. He agreed to give each of us jobs when we graduate. They seem to be good factory jobs, where I can make some good money."

It was a total fabrication. I hadn't thought at all about leaving and taking an apartment in the Bowery or anywhere else, and there wasn't any job awaiting me upon my graduation, even if I were to graduate, and there weren't any friends. Marie turned as I spoke, and the expression on her face lightened, relieved of the burden now.

"When will you be taking the job?" Marie asked.

"I plan to take it by the end of the summer."

"At the end of the summer, then. You can stay here until the end of the summer," Marie said as she nodded. She then turned back toward the dishpan and resumed cleaning the dishes.

I walked to my room and closed the door. I sat on my bed and looked at the trunk, which I had since shoved to the corner of my room. I was enticed to open the latch and dig within it to find something of use, perhaps for no other reason than to find some bearings. I resisted it and reminded myself that there was nothing there of value that could help me now. It was just an empty box with dead little things. I told myself that everything was gone, and there was no sense in trying to look for what I had lost. I told myself that there was nothing left of me, so no need to grab for bearings. Any journey from where I was now to where I would go would be determined by others. I was simply being cast adrift again: this time by Marie, and before that by the Turks. My mind was efficient at exorcising any thought that would lead me out of where I was and to some better place, where everything is as it should be. I thought that this time would be no different. After nearly seven years, I had become accustomed to the exercise, even proficient at it. I snuffed out the light before it had any oxygen to breathe. There was no use in trying to find anything living among the dead little things.

I stayed awake most of that night. I sensed that this may have been my last opportunity to find my escape, to find a little bit of light, and to allow it a little glow so that I could find my way. I began to allow the thought to creep in. Perhaps I wasn't dead after all. Perhaps I just needed to collect the rest of the bits of me.

I stared at my trunk. It sat there closed tight. Three years prior, I had vowed to never open it again, and I hadn't for that entire time. I had spent most of the night staring at it, wondering if there was any value in looking through the contents again. There were just shattered pieces of this and that. I determined to open the latch and lift the lid slightly to at least smell the trunk's familiar scent. As I did, I hesitated only slightly before I opened it fully and began to rummage through it to dig for the pieces. I began to make an inventory in my mind of what I lost and where I last saw it. I began to remember where I last saw beauty, and when I last felt hope and joy, and faith. I searched my mind for when I last felt human, and not like just another among a dead herd. I needed to determine what was real. Were faith, hope, joy, and beauty just part of the illusion, or were they real, an essential part of who I was, and who I was supposed to be? Was it all taken from me, or did I simply relinquish it? What was real?

Anahid returned late in the afternoon within the month. She hadn't returned earlier because she remained upset with me, I think, for my having not told her the truth about what happened to our father, and she punished me for it with her silence. I tried to explain to her many times since that I didn't tell her the truth because I didn't want her to lose hope. She stayed silent despite my pleading with her to speak to me.

I heard her voice first. It was at first faint and imperceptible, then strong and unmistakable. She was as I remembered her. She was plain and beautiful, her eyes were closed, and her voice was seamless and melodic. As she spoke, she made it clear to me that I needed to rethink matters and to begin to search again for what I thought I had irretrievably lost.

I was walking several blocks from the apartment when she returned. I ran home, and once inside hurried into my room and shut the door closed to hold tight to her, scared that if I didn't she would leave again. I checked in from time to time on her that first day to ensure that she wouldn't leave, and she assured me that she wouldn't. She was still there, and it appeared that her return would be permanent. I spoke to her about Mother, and Father, and if she remembered them. She helped me search my memory and what they taught me and Anahid about the way in which we must live. She reminded me about what was essential. Anahid spent most of that first day upon her return sitting on the edge of the spare bed in my room with the tips of her shoes barely reaching the floor. She appeared to me mostly in silhouette, but I knew she was there because I heard her. She spoke softly, just to me, so that only I could hear her. She was trying to make it clear to me about what was essential; about what was real; about faith, hope, joy, and beauty; about living.

CHAPTER 66

I wrote a letter to the principal in my most precise English. My letter described the life that I lived in Constantinople. It described how I lived among temples, and churches, and mosques that were centuries old. I described for him the monuments there that had reliefs made of stone carved with scenes depicting fanciful monsters, ancient warriors, and the omnipotence of the pagan gods. I told him that many of these monuments are still there, but some are not, because they were destroyed by the people of Constantinople themselves, because they didn't know what they had. I told him what a strong military the Ottoman Empire had when I was a boy and how it destroyed everything else. I told him that there was nothing that I could go back to and that all that I had left was me and of that fact I was now certain. I told him that I didn't wish to be trapped any longer and needed my diploma to get on with my life. In August of 1921, I received my diploma in the mail. Over the months that ensued, I began to walk further down the path beyond the prison gates, and piece by piece find and reclaim parts of myself.

I first found faith. I did not find it in a book, or in a ritual, or in a belief in the abstract or unseen. Rather, I came to simply believe that there is a place where everything is as it should be, even if only for a short moment, and I witnessed that fact first-hand. The evidence that I had was captured from time to time in a photograph, a measure, and a memory. Each contained evidence of the existence of life's essentials. Anahid helped me find it, to where it was all lost and scattered, and so did Grace. I owed Grace an acknowledgment that her searchlights helped me find my way. I worried that Grace mistakenly thought that I was lost, that I turned my back on her light and disappeared into the darkness forever. I also owed Grace and the Kazarians some gesture, however small, that they sustained me, and that I kept an account of what they gave me. Perhaps a part of me was also hoping that I gave them something too.

I decided to visit the Kazarians. They lived in Royal Oak, Michigan, a suburb of Detroit, only several miles from the city proper. I decided to arrive on a Sunday, to ensure that they would be home. I would stay for a brief overnight stop on my way to Chicago, where I intended to look for permanent work. I wished to arrive unannounced. I did not wish any fuss. I simply intended to stop in briefly, to see that they were well, and to perhaps have a bit of time to speak to Grace. I would then be on my way. I made the arrangements for my arrival in Royal Oak in late May in 1922.

The train pulled into downtown Royal Oak, after several stops and junctions, in the late afternoon. The station was a simple wooden structure with a small wooden platform that led directly from the train tracks. I stepped from the train with my trunk and walked directly through the station, which consisted of a single room having a short ticket counter and a bench in the center of the station for waiting passengers.

After passing through the station, I jumped from a platform on the opposite side of the station onto the public street that it fronted. Royal Oak was a beautiful little American town, with an assortment of wood clapboard and red brick buildings lining its downtown streets. I walked from the main road that led through the center of the town onto a cobblestone sidewalk, adjacent to which were several small stores. One store that I passed was a traditional general store with a soda fountain and a line of children waiting their turn to be served. I was told by a man in the train station that this street, three blocks' distance in total, if taken to its end, led to a residential street, where the Kazarians home was located. I reached the residential street and made my turn. As I did, I felt my heart begin to pound, and a feeling of nervousness overtook me, an emotion that I didn't fully expect. I pulled from my coat pocket an old postcard from the Kazarians, the birthday card with the embossed candle. I looked at the return address on the card as I looked at each posted address on the homes. I picked the Kazarians' house out. It was a wood-shingled American bungalow-style house, with a neatly trimmed lawn bisected by a narrow concrete sidewalk that led to an elevated covered porch.

The entry to the Kazarians' sidewalk was flanked by two square, freshly painted white wooden fenceposts. The posts were an American design with simple wood trim on the outer edges, and atop each post was a round wooden ball cap. I stopped in front of the house and began to have doubts as to whether I should have come unannounced and then wondered if anyone would be home or even whether the Kazarians still lived in the house. As I turned onto the sidewalk, I reset my course by grabbing the ball cap of the fencepost and swinging myself around until I squarely faced the front facade of the Kazarians' residence. I walked up the front porch and could feel my heart pounding in my chest. I knocked on the door, then stood and waited. The door opened, and a woman who was unfamiliar answered.

"Hello, my name is Aran Pirian. Do the Kazarians still live here?" I asked. The woman looked at me as anyone would look at a total stranger, and I prepared to apologize to her for the disruption.

"I am sorry, ma'am..." I began.

Before I could finish, the woman's expression began to change, and a smile came to her face, and she said, "Is that you, Aran? Aran, it's me... It's me, Grace." As Grace spoke, I searched for traces of the girl that I last saw in Egypt. Her hair was cut to shoulder length, and it was in a current style. Her face was adult and mature, and she looked utterly transformed from how I remembered her. Grace walked onto the porch and wrapped her arms around me and held me tight. "It is so good to see you, Aran," she said. She then just stood and stared at me, and neither one of us said anything for several moments.

Grace then broke the silence. "Come, Aran. My parents and Emma will be so glad to see you." As we walked into the house, Grace called excitedly, "Mother, Father, Emma, Aran is here to visit us from New York!"

Keran and Sara and Emma then came into the main room. They looked almost exactly as I remembered them when I last saw them in Egypt. We all stood there for a moment silently. Keran then embraced me; he simply said softly, "I waited so long to see you." Sara and Emma stood with smiles and shook their heads as if in disbelief that I had come.

As we walked into the house, I was struck by how modern everything looked. There was a large sofa in the middle of the room, which was placed opposite the fireplace. The fireplace had a wooden mantel, atop which were several pictures of apparently succeeding years in which the Kazarians had posed. In front of the sofa was a coffee table, upon which sat an assortment of neatly displayed periodicals.

"Come sit, Aran," Grace said, pointing to the sofa.

Emma said, "I will help Mother bring you out a drink," and she and Sara rushed into the kitchen. Grace sat next to me on the sofa, while Keran took a seat in an armchair placed at the opposite end and off center of the coffee table. There were a few moments of silence, and I was searching for something to say but couldn't come up with anything, as my nerves were leaving me in tangles. A few moments more passed, and I began to feel somewhat self-conscious. Grace seemed to be feeling the same. She looked down at the floor and nervously smoothed the front of her dress with her hands.

"How on earth did you find the house, Aran?" Keran mercifully asked.

"Oh, I had your address from the letters and postcards. I had no trouble at all," I replied.

Sara and Emma then came back into the room. Emma carried a tray of glasses, and Sara followed closely behind with a pitcher of lemonade. Emma placed a glass down in front of me, and Sara quickly poured from the pitcher. "Please, Aran, drink. Don't let Grace make you talk until you drink," Sara joked. Grace and I both laughed, and I think that made us feel a little more at ease. I drank, and the room was silent as I did. I placed the glass on the table and looked down at the glass, still trying to come up with something to say. I was unable, and I felt awkward. I had so much to tell them, and I was too paralyzed to provide so much as a polite passing comment, and I was embarrassed.

Emma seemed to sense my embarrassment and came to sit beside me on the sofa to my other side. "Aran, tell us all about New York. Do you like to live there?" Emma asked.

"Yes, I do like it very much," I said.

"And what do you like most about it, Aran?" Emma continued.

I thought a moment, and then I said, "I love the buildings. New buildings, and taller ones, are being built every day, you know. And there are now many lights that stay on the entire night," I said.

"Did you bring any pictures of New York?" Grace asked.

"No, I didn't, Grace, but I did bring a few other items to show you, items from my family that we had when we lived in Constantinople. They are in my trunk." As I spoke, I pulled my trunk close to me. I opened it and pulled out a photograph. As I placed the photograph on the table, Keran, Sara, Emma, and Grace hunched over the table.

"This is a photograph of my family, which was taken when we lived in Constantinople," I said, pointing to the photograph. "This is my mother and father, and this is Anahid standing next to me." Grace moved the picture a bit closer to her and looked carefully at it.

"This is how I remember you, Aran, when I first met you in the desert," Grace said.

"Oh yes, Grace, this picture must have been taken only a couple of years before I met you," I replied. Grace pushed the picture back toward Keran, Sara, and Emma, and they each took a closer look. As they did, I reached into my trunk, and I looked at Grace.

"I know how much you love to read books, Grace, so I brought you this bookmark. Anahid made it. She made it by pressing tulips," I said. Grace looked at the bookmark as I handed it to her, the white parchment paper that it was made from backing a perfectly and crisply pressed red tulip. "Anahid worked hard to get this tulip pressed without having the red pigment bleed onto the paper. It was a real living tulip. It took her several attempts, and she had to give the tulip time, but she eventually got it right, and she was very proud of it. It is probably best to put it in a book, so the petals of the tulip don't fall off," I said.

"Thank you, Aran. It is the most beautiful bookmark that I have ever seen," Grace said as I handed her the bookmark. After Grace spoke, she paused a moment and then said, "I have just the place to put it." Grace stood as she spoke and walked from the room. The room became silent while everyone's attention shifted to Grace as she left the room, then reentered it. Grace carried a book in her hand and came and sat back down beside me. She placed the book in front of me and said, "This is the book that you gave me in the desert. Do you recognize it?" I looked at the book, and I recognized it instantly. It was the book of Turkish poems given to me by Professor Daigneau.

"Yes, Grace... Yes, I recognize it," I replied. Grace opened the book and leafed to a page that had a bend in the upper right corner of it. "Do you remember this poem?" Grace asked. She then began to read from it: "*Come, let's grant the joy to this heart of ours that founders in distress...*" I nodded my head to Grace in acknowledgment as she read. Grace then took the bookmark that I gave her and placed it in the book at that page and placed the open book on her lap. Grace stared at the open page of the book for a few moments, then said, "Aran, I think this is the perfect place for Anahid's bookmark. Don't you think so?"

"Yes, Grace, I believe it is," I replied mechanically. As I finished speaking, my words bounced back to me, and they sounded hollow and reflexive. It was the perfect invitation to tell Grace what I came to tell her. Fragments of what I wished to say raced through my mind. I wanted to tell her that she was right; it was about living, not dying. I wanted to tell her that it was all about living. I took a deep breath to push out a response, but I couldn't manage any words. I just exhaled nervously and shifted awkwardly in my seat.

Grace smiled, and the room became silent, and as the silence continued, I began to feel uncomfortable again. Emma then picked up the pitcher of lemonade and poured more into my glass, and while she did, Emma said, "Here, Aran, you must be thirsty. Have more." I lifted the glass and drank almost the full glass, and as I did, the room again fell silent. I placed the glass back down on the table and began to search for some words. My mind was now racing through several thoughts, but none that I had any confidence in that I could communicate cogently, and I hesitated with the fear that if I tried to articulate my feelings I would fail, so I just sat and stared into my lap. I sat a bit longer and began to gather some courage, and as I did, I reached for my trunk.

"Here is also something I wanted to show everyone, something of Anahid's," I said. Keran, Sara, Emma, and Grace watched as I struggled to open my trunk fully to pull the item out. "This is Anahid's," I said, now having the object firmly in my hands in front of them. "This is Anahid's violin." The violin's chin rest still had the paint worn off where Anahid's chin had rubbed against it, and the patina of the wood at the neck of her violin still remained as evidence that Anahid's hand held it as she played.

Grace paused and looked at the violin carefully, and as she did, she rubbed her fingers gently over the neck of the violin where Anahid's hand had created the patina on the violin's finish. Grace then asked in a somewhat confused manner, "Aran, where did you find Anahid's violin?"

"I had it with me the entire time, Grace. I carried it through the desert in my trunk. I carried it the whole way," I replied.

Grace was silent for a moment, and I feared that she would be upset and that telling her that I hid Anahid's violin for the entire time we were in the desert together would remind Grace of everything else that I concealed from her. Grace, though, to my relief, simply gazed at the violin and smiled, then said, "Aran, I am so grateful that you brought the violin to show us."

"Well, yes, of course, Grace. I just wanted to show you that I still have her violin. I remember how it sounded when she played it," I replied nervously and clumsily. I now felt as if I were sinking into the sofa. There was so much more that I wanted to say, but I was helpless, left without the faculty to express myself. Emma sensed, I believe, that I had more to say, and that I was embarrassed to speak freely in front of Keran and Sara. Emma stood and said, "Come, Mother and Father. Let's go into the kitchen to prepare some food for Aran." As Emma spoke, she, Keran, and Sara stood and walked into the kitchen and left Grace and me alone.

After several moments, Grace sensed that I wanted to say more, and she looked at me and asked, "Aran, what is it? What is it that you wish to tell me?" I was frozen, unable to say anything to Grace, and I just stared at her awkwardly.

I wanted to tell her the reason I brought Anahid's violin. I wanted to tell her that I couldn't remember the sound of Anahid's voice for a very long time. That it faded from me. No matter how hard I tried to search my mind for the sound of Anahid's voice, I couldn't find it, and I was angry because I thought it was taken from me forever. I thought that everything was taken from me, and lost forever. The sound of Anahid playing her violin came back to me, though, and then I realized that I had found it. I had found what I thought was lost. It wasn't lost at all. It was within my grasp all along. I wanted to tell Grace that the sound of Anahid's violin made me remember the life that we lived. That when she played, everything that life is intended to be filled with, beauty, hope, joy, and faith, were present, that these feelings were real, that they were an integral part of me, and they weren't in any place that I needed to travel to. I wanted to tell Grace that I found me. I knew that I was certain of it because I had looked in all of the other places to find a different answer, and one that would provide proof that I had died, too, and that each part of me was cast away and entombed in the desert forever.

"What is it, Aran? What do you wish to tell me?" Grace repeated. Before I could reply to Grace, Emma swung the kitchen door open and reentered the room to take some plates from a china cabinet, which was placed adjacent to the kitchen door. As Emma walked back into the kitchen, Emma said, "Grace, bring Aran to the kitchen." Rushed by Emma, Grace began to sit forward in the sofa, and as she did, Grace said, "Can you tell me, Aran, what do you remember Anahid playing on her violin?"

It was an easy question to answer. It was what I heard when Anahid came back to me and remained with me every day since.

"I remember her playing 'Soorp,' Grace. I remember when Anahid played 'Soorp'."

Grace looked closely at the violin, then she looked down at the open book in her hands, and while standing to walk to the kitchen, she positioned Anahid's bookmark snugly in the binding of the open page of Professor Daigneau's book, then closed the book gently over the bookmark.

Keran, Sara, Emma, Grace, and I spoke until late into the evening, until only Grace and I were left awake and still wishing to talk. We spoke about beauty, hope, joy, and faith until the sun hinted to its place by casting a modest glow. It was the mark of the journey's end.

NOTES

*(p. 50-51) From an 18th century Turkish poem attributed to the Ottoman Turkish poet Ahmet Nedim Efendi.